"You have no right to think or assume for me, Aaron. You don't know me, and even if you did, I haven't given you that permission."

"Point well taken."

He exhaled evenly, and she literally felt his exhalation, along with a tremor-inducing hot flash that definitely was not caused by the tropical breeze, but rather by the sensation of his hands gripping her, his eyes piercing into hers, and the way the corners of his mouth curved into a scintillating slow burn of a smile, the same smile that had mesmerized her two years ago.

The Sea of Aaron

Kymberly Hunt

Genesis Press, Inc.

INDIGO LOVE STORIES

An imprint of Genesis Press, Inc.
Publishing Company

Genesis Press, Inc.
P.O. Box 101
Columbus, MS 39703

Copyright © 2011 Kymberly Hunt

ISBN-13: 978-1-58571-440-7
ISBN-10: 1-58571-440-2
Manufactured in the United States of America

First Edition

Visit us at www.genesis-press.com
or call at 1-888-Indigo-1-4-0

Dedication

This book is dedicated to the readers who requested Valerie and Aaron's story and to the real life heroes who always come to the rescue when there is need, whether that be here in the United States or in the most distant regions of the land.

Acknowledgements

I wish to thank my sister who shares the dream, as well as the friends and family whose encouragement prevented me from locking the story in the file cabinet. As always, I acknowledge the Divine Creator of the universe and look forward to the day when there will be no more foreign lands and everyone will speak the pure language of love.

PROLOGUE

Gordon J. Allard lay dying in the bedroom of the home he had once shared with his beautiful wife, Julia. The lung cancer he'd battled for over two years had spread throughout his body and he had resigned himself to no more chemotherapy, radiation, or hospitals. What difference did it make? He was ninety years old and had long since outlived most of his family and all the friends of his generation.

There wasn't much time left at all. Hours, maybe minutes, to make peace with his one major regret in life: his inability to convince his granddaughter Carolyn to change her ways. Because of the gulf between them, his will would have to remain as he'd written it a year ago. She would inherit nothing. There was no point in leaving his earthly possessions to the destructive whims of a senseless young woman who meandered pointlessly through life, hooked on illegal substances and sordid relationships. She hadn't married or left a great grandchild. Julia would be as upset as he was, but she would understand.

Most of the money, multi-millions earned from a patented invention and carefully invested in stocks and bonds, would go to his favorite charity, and the house that had been so special to Julia—special to both of them—would now temporarily pass to his nephew. The other person of significance in his will was Valerie Redmond, his young African-American nurse, who for the last few years had been the only real friend he possessed.

He gazed feebly around the dim room. Two people shifted about like sentries changing guard—the attending physician and the black-clothed priest. Yes, Valerie was there, too, a constant presence sitting quietly by his bedside with her hand resting warmly on his cold one. He could not speak to her anymore, but she seemed to channel his thoughts and anticipate his needs. She was no blood relative, but he was convinced that in the imminence of death, ethnicities and cultural differences cease to matter as everyone confronts the same eventuality—a return to dust. Because of this knowledge he was confident that he'd selected the right one for his posthumous gift, and he almost smiled at the thought of her reaction. Valerie would be the keeper now.

As the priest spoke his final words, the lights in the room seemed to dim and the steady buzz of the now-disconnected respirator faded. A shimmering aura of peace and light filled him. It's all right, he murmured soundlessly. *Julia's waiting and I must go.*

Chapter 1

Pathetic. That's what she was—truly pathetic. There was no other way Valerie Redmond could describe why she, a mature thirty-something woman, should be standing in a Manhattan subway station on a frigid January day, amorously visualizing an enigmatic man with whom she had absolutely nothing in common. And if that wasn't bad enough, there was no reason why the man, Aaron Weiss, would even possibly be thinking of her. Shuddering at the realization, she tried to refocus her attention on the present moment.

"Are you *really* going back to that dead guy's place to get those books?" her cousin Denise asked.

Valerie stiffened. "I have the key to his house, don't I?"

"Whatever, but when you do, don't expect me to come along with you."

"Wouldn't dream of it." Valerie glanced at her watch. Denise had definitely driven reality home.

The books were gifts willed to Valerie by Gordon J. Allard, her recently departed patient and good friend. Through the years she'd grown extremely fond of the eccentric inventor/philanthropist, and the void left by his passing still resonated deep within her.

Her unexpected inclusion in his will explained why she and Denise were in the city. But as they stood on the platform with the evening rush hour crowd waiting for the train to pull in, Valerie couldn't help acknowledging that the end result of the visit to Mr. Allard's lawyer had turned out to be more burden than gift. She definitely did want something to remember him by—a small memento of sorts—but just what was she going to do with an international collection of over sixty Bibles, as well as all the books from his vast library?

Valerie had been shocked beyond words when she'd received a copy of the will in the mail because it had never entered her mind that she would be bequeathed anything. She had coerced Denise into accompanying her from her home in New Jersey to the Manhattan office of Mr. Allard's lawyers, Stein & Brenner, in order to ask questions.

Mr. Stein had informed her that one of his associates would go with her next Tuesday to open the decedent's house so she could collect the books, a mission that he explained had to be acted on before the house and everything in it was turned over to Mr. Allard's nephew from England. Because there was no place for countless books in her tiny apartment, she had already decided out of necessity to decline most of them, but she did want the Bibles.

The lawyer didn't know that Mr. Allard had given her his duplicate house key the year after she'd started working for him and that she'd never had the opportunity to return it. Because Tuesday was not a good day for her to go out to Long Island, she assumed it would be less complicated if she just drove down to the Allard estate over the weekend and picked up the books herself. After all, she knew better than anyone else where the Bibles were located.

As far as Denise was concerned, the trip to the city was a total waste of time. Valerie knew that her cousin had hoped that she had been willed something of significant monetary value—material prosperity that might possibly trickle down to her as well. Upon realizing that was not the case, she'd complained constantly on their trek back from the lawyer's office, saying that she should have kept her hairdresser's appointment instead of ruining the day.

Valerie felt no sympathy for her. The chatterbox actually had nothing better to do. She'd been fired from her job and wasn't even looking for another.

Denise nudged her. "Unlike you, I've got some real plans for the weekend."

Valerie shrugged apathetically and attempted to tune her out, but the alternative to ignoring her was even worse. Ignoring Denise would mean that she would return to envisioning the seductive Aaron, whom she'd first encountered two years ago at her best

5

friend's wedding, a man with whom she'd shared one slow dance, very little conversation, and enough heart-pounding chemistry to ruin her for life.

"Tony's oldest brother is coming up from Arizona," Denise continued. "He's single, about your age and…"

"Stop right there." Valerie held up a hand and, with a wave, dispensed with her cousin's unfinished suggestion. "I don't do blind hook-ups, and right now meeting some guy is the last thing on my mind…even if he is your fiancé's brother."

"He's a dentist and he's nice-looking," Denise insisted, well aware that she was being annoying. "You're being totally ridiculous, you know. Even Jasmine told you to forget *him*, and she's your best friend."

"Denise, we are not having this conversation." Valerie drew herself up haughtily, casting a sudden icy glare at a nefarious-looking leather-clad male who had migrated into her space and was ogling her shamelessly, obviously thinking himself the epitome of cool.

Oblivious to anything else, Denise rambled on. "Yes, we are having this conversation. Unless you intend to stay single forever, it's about time you stop hanging on to that…that fantasy."

Single forever? Valerie glowered, watching from the corner of her eye as leatherman retreated into the shadows. She had, in fact, been married once before—a long time ago—and it hadn't worked. "Are you finished?"

"No. I haven't even start—"

"I don't do fantasies," Valerie interrupted. "That's more my mother's territory." A faint throb prodded her temple. The headache had been threatening since morning, fanned by Denise's badgering and the realization that, once she got back home, she'd have to make her nightly visit to the local nursing home to see her Alzheimer's-stricken mother, who most of the time couldn't remember that she even had a daughter.

Denise was annoying even on a perfect day. Valerie had asked her to come along only because she didn't feel safe going into the city and using public transportation alone—of the millions of fears her mother had attempted to impose on her as a child, that one had actually stuck. Now she was sorry she had listened to the childhood voice of impending doom.

"Once upon a time you didn't do fantasies," Denise continued mercilessly, "but you've been like totally out of reality about men since Jasmine's wedding. You're losing every opportunity that comes by because you keep comparing every guy you meet to that one, and in your mind none of the others measure up."

"For the last time, I'm not discussing this."

Undaunted, Denise tugged her bright fuchsia scarf tighter around her neck "And what's really insane is I don't get what you see in him." She hesitated for a second, frowning. "Wait. I take that back. He *was* kind of handsome in an exotic, evil Rambo sort of way…but he's not the marrying type. He's too old. And…well, let's face it, he's pretty darn scary."

Valerie clenched her hands in the pockets of her thick down coat, her fingers connecting with the keys to Mr. Allard's house. "Scary? Maybe he is to someone like you, since you prefer those boring, docile mama's-boy types like Tony." She drew in a sharp intake of breath. "And for your information, forty is not that old."

Denise shot her a mildly scathing look, but this time she actually had sense enough to remain silent. The look, however, reminded Valerie of how much she disliked being goaded into verbal retaliation by her younger cousin.

Unfortunately, the overreaction confirmed that Denise was right—at least the rant about comparing other men unfavorably to the fantasy one and shutting out all possibilities. In fact, in the last year alone, she had ruined at least three potential relationships with hardworking, seemingly decent men, and at this point she was almost convinced that she would remain single for the rest of her life. There just seemed no point in being with someone who wasn't able to stir the same passionate emotions in her that he had with just one steely-eyed gaze.

She was a lost cause, and it certainly hadn't helped that she had briefly encountered him again only a month ago and realized she hadn't lost one iota of her infatuation. Even after two years, she could feel the strength of his arms as he held her, guiding her effortlessly into the slow waltz step of the dance. The music still played in her head—the romance and its potential for being right up there on the same level with that of Jasmine and Noah, the charmed bride and groom. And then there was the awful dream-defying reality that her chance of ever sharing one starlit night with the object of her affection was about as likely to happen as the moon colliding with the sun.

The masses of humanity jockeying for position on the platform had increased, their voices like a cacophony of angry bees. Deflecting tension, Denise fiddled impatiently with her watch. "Where is that train? I can't wait to get home and forget that we came all the way down here just to find out about some books."

Valerie smiled wanly. "Not just books, Denise, Bibles…God's word."

"Yeah. Whatever. Oh, that's Tony." She whipped her cell phone from her bag and stepped back from the crowd, looking for a good spot to talk. If such a spot really existed below street level, Denise would find it, Valerie thought, smirking. Amazing how her obnoxious cousin had heard the phone ring amidst the noise and echoes.

The train was at least ten minutes overdue. Impatiently, restlessly, Valerie moved closer to the edge of the platform and peered into the yawning abyss of the tunnel. A faint rumbling sound ensued, assuring her that the train was about to make its appearance. Instinctively, people gathered closely behind her clutching newspapers, briefcases—commuters eager to get home from work.

As she spotted the distant glimmer of light penetrating the darkness she started to step back, but suddenly before she was completely aware of what was happening, a violent jolt catapulted her forward, knocking the wind and the scream right out of her—launching her into space with her arms flailing out wildly as though demonstrating an ability to fly. In reality she was plummeting like a stone, vaguely aware that in a few seconds her life would be over, crushed by tons of hot, shrieking steel. The scream that had eluded her a fractured second ago now pierced through the station. But the ear-splitting shriek came from Denise's mouth. Was this for real? Was a human even capable of making such a sound?

Someone very familiar was speaking, and Valerie tried to rouse herself out of what had to be a partially sedated daze. Why had she been given a sedative? She didn't need one. If anyone required such treatment it should have been Denise.

"How are you feeling?"

The familiar voice again. Valerie brushed a hand against what was obviously a bandage on her forehead and looked up at her best friend, Jasmine, who was bending over her with concern etched on her face. Immediately, her sense of awareness returned. "How am I feeling? I guess not bad for a woman who almost left her body parts scattered in the bowels of Manhattan."

"Really, Val." Jasmine feigned irritation. "Haven't you been told never to stand on the edge of the platform?"

"I guess one can always use a little reminder." Using her elbows, Valerie pulled herself up further in the bed. "Seriously, I can't imagine how that happened. One minute I was standing and the next I was flying through the air."

It felt odd being the patient instead of the caregiver, and it was a most unwelcome experience that made her realize why so many patients complained about the discomfort of hospital beds. The undeniable oddity, however, was that she was even thinking about such trivia, considering that her life had nearly ended.

She barely remembered taking the tumble onto the tracks, let alone scrambling to her feet just in time to be hauled up by onlookers. The whole incident had been so absurdly atypical of her that a strange, nagging speculation persisted that she hadn't merely lost her balance and fallen but had been pushed. In the trauma of the moments following, she hadn't been able to verbalize the possibility to the police, and maybe it was just as well. Why mention something she wasn't sure of?

The overnight stay in the hospital meant she wouldn't get to visit her mother—not that Ruth Ann Redmond would even notice. In fact, Ruth Ann probably wouldn't even notice if her daughter had died. The overnighter was simply because of a minor laceration on her forehead, which normally would have been stitched up and she would have been sent home. But, no, in her case things weren't so simple. Born with a defective blood-clotting factor, Valerie was prone to unexpected hemorrhaging when traumatic injuries occurred.

The only comfort was having Jasmine Arias at her bedside instead of Denise, whose boyfriend had finally hauled her hysterical carcass home. Her childhood friend looked stunning with her long, rippled hair held back by a jeweled band—stunning even though she was dressed for business in a conservative gray pantsuit. Jasmine had always been pretty, but in the last few years she had truly blossomed. Valerie attributed this to her being happily married with a family and a challenging job.

"So when did you get back from Africa?" Valerie asked. She had known that Jasmine would be returning home a week before the rest of the family to oversee an architectural project in Trenton. The others would continue vacationing in her husband's native country, Cielo Vista.

"Actually, I'm just off the plane. I got Denise's garbled message on my cell, and since I was at JFK, I came straight here."

"Sorry about Denise," Valerie replied. "How are Noah and the kids? How's— " She bit her tongue, repressing the urge to ask about Aaron.

Jasmine didn't notice the slip, or pretended not to. "Noah and the kids are great, and don't apologize for Denise. Considering the circumstances, it's understandable."

She exhaled deeply and then pulled up a chair and sat beside the bed. "Thank God you're okay. Now, do you mind telling me what you're doing in Manhattan anyway? You hate cities."

Valerie smiled wanly and blinked. The fluorescent lighting in the tiny hospital room was way too bright. "Good question. Now you know exactly why I hate cities."

"Val, tell me."

"Okay. Okay. I had to talk to Mr. Allard's lawyer about that will…I think I mentioned this whole thing to you a while back."

Jasmine nodded. "And did…"

"Wait a sec." Valerie interrupted, starting to get up as she suddenly remembered that her handbag had been the one casualty of the subway.

Jasmine attempted to hold her back. "What are you doing? Maybe you shouldn't get up right now."

"You're probably right," Valerie said as a wave of dizziness swept over her. "Could you look in that closet and get my coat?"

"Sure." Jasmine opened the tacky but functional metallic wardrobe and retrieved the coat, handing it to her.

With bated breath, Valerie reached into the pocket and pulled out two keys. "I still have them, thank God." She nearly laughed at the irony and at Jasmine's exasperated questioning expression. "My bag was lost." she rambled. "Not much money, but I'll have to replace my license, credit card, and my own keys, but the keys to Mr. Allard's house were in my pocket, so I still have them. I can't believe this, Jas. It's so odd. I never keep valuable things in my pockets."

Jasmine sat back down abruptly. "Obviously you're losing it, Val. Mind telling me what you're doing with Mr. Allard's keys in the first place?"

"Sorry." She shook her head as if to clear it. Her unusual behavior probably had everything to do with the obsessive fantasizing about Aaron she'd been indulging in before the incident. She went on to explain to Jasmine the details of the will. When she was finished, Jasmine remained silent.

"Well, aren't you going to say it?"

"Say what?"

"That I went through this horrible nightmare all on account of some books."

"No, I'm not." Jasmine ended her silence. "You always said that Mr. Allard was special, and the books are Bibles…I would assume you'd like something to remember him by."

Valerie smiled. "There you go. And that's why you're my best friend."

Jasmine stood up for the last time that night. "And the reason for that is, we're both insane. Okay, it's settled, I'm coming back for you in the morning, and if you want to pick up those books I'll be free to help you out on Saturday."

With anyone else, Valerie would have argued or protested that she could take care of everything fine by herself, but this was Jasmine she was talking to and Jasmine would never take no for an answer.

Chapter 2

The towering masts from the numerous sailing vessels that dotted the harbor were thwarted in their vain attempt to touch the sky. Anchored and devoid of their billowing sails, the ships appeared naked and fragile. Aaron considered this a metaphor for his temporary vulnerability as he slouched in a deck chair with his feet propped up on the railing of his own tall-masted forty-five-foot schooner. Staring out at the sea around him, he heard and felt the rise and creaking inhalations of the boat on the gentle swells.

Her name was *Saniyah II*, and for him she was close to human—maybe even more so. She had sailed the Caribbean numerous times, but somehow she always ended up here off the coast of Belize, not far from the tiny island of Caye Caulker. It was here that both man and boat found respite.

As at home in the air as on the sea, Aaron, who co-owned Avian International, a rapidly expanding air freight company, was recovering from a nearly fatal injury he'd received a few weeks before on a clandestine mission. A former government intelligence operative, these days he also headed his own security group, Global Defense Force, known only to a few. Aaron realized that it was probably time to stop rolling the dice and get out of the game. The GDF no longer needed him as a special agent anyway since their ranks had swelled to form an elite army, all of its members being highly skilled former ex-U.S. Navy Seals, U.S. Army, FBI, and CIA operatives.

His associate, Ben Cassidy, a decorated ex-marine and co-founder of Global Defenses, had long since retired from active and managerial duty, handing over the reins to his equally skilled oldest son. Aaron was more than twenty years younger than Ben and he definitely wasn't ready for fishing all day and watching the sunset over Bora Bora, but he had to admit that the thrill of saving the world—a world that half the time didn't even realize it was in trouble—was gone. The savannas of Africa and the narrow twisting alleyways of Cairo no longer intrigued him, nor did the echoes in the mosques or the sun setting over the vast Persian Gulf.

The long years of espionage had left him a steely cold man who feared little and felt even less, an attitude that was surprisingly more of a flaw than an asset in the espionage business. Fear was the thing that kept one alive—kept one from being careless—but lately he did not care. If he remained active, his stellar record was in jeopardy. Aaron had never bungled an assignment, even if he'd been physically damaged in the fallout, and the most amazing thing was that his numerous aliases had never been compromised—not even once.

After many years, only a handful of trustworthy individuals knew that Aaron Weiss was more than just the private citizen co-owner of a billion-dollar air-courier service.

What bothered him as he stared restlessly at the waves, the smoke from his cigarette curling into the atmosphere, was the fear he instilled in others. Most children trembled in his presence, men gave him a wide berth, and despite some intimate dalliances with women, only three had ever looked him directly in the eye. And two of those three were long dead.

The third was named Valerie Redmond. And who would ever imagine that a nurse, a Christian no less, from Englewood, New Jersey, whom he'd first met at his business partner and friend Noah's wedding reception, would be among those exceptional women who dared to have a conversation with him, and did so without showing any sign of apprehension. She hadn't even trembled during their brief dance together. Well, that wasn't quite true. She had trembled. But it definitely wasn't the kind of trembling that came from fear.

He'd coincidentally come in contact with her again, shortly before embarking on his last nearly disastrous mission. She'd been at Noah and Jasmine's home, temporarily babysitting the couple's two children, when he'd stopped by to drop off an important package. They had exchanged very few words beyond the usual civilities people express while in a hurry, but the brief meeting had confirmed what he'd felt about her initially.

Taller than the average woman and stunningly curvaceous, Valerie had smooth coppery-colored skin—a complexion one might concoct from a mixture of cinnamon and orange cayenne pepper—thick, black, shoulder-length hair, and the assertive posturing of a Nubian queen. She was not an outrageous stop-dead-in-your-tracks beauty; he'd encountered those types—usually femme fatales—in all locales of the world, but she was the sort of woman whose attractiveness grew the longer he looked at her and the more time he spent with her.

So what was he planning to do about the mutual attraction? And he was positive it was mutual. Nothing. In the event he decided not to retire, it was best that way. Lovers and close family ties were a liability, an Achilles' heel.

On Saturday afternoon, when Valerie and Jasmine pulled up in the circular driveway of the Allard estate, the temperature was hovering in the low teens with clouds threatening snow. A dirt-streaked white van was parked to the side of the house a few feet away from them.

"Looks like someone's here," Jasmine said.

Valerie frowned. "Probably just a caretaker. I hope I can talk my way in."

The Long Island home, a modest brick mansion with withered brown ivy snaking up its foundations like arteries, greeted them half-heartedly. The house boasted a pillar-supported entrance portico with weathered, peeling paint. Icicles fringed the edges of the roof.

"A typical Colonial Georgian, very nice but badly in need of restoration," Jasmine said, looking around, noting the two chimneys on opposite sides of the house. "Looks as if it were originally built in the early 1800s."

Valerie smiled, bemused. Her friend was seeing the once stately home from an architect's perspective. "You're right. This place is not only old, but it's got history. Mr. Allard told me that the original owners were rumored to have used it as part of the underground slave railroad."

"For real? If that's true, maybe it could be recognized by the historical society. Too bad the place has gotten so run down."

"Unfortunately, Mr. Allard didn't have much in the way of family to help him out," Valerie said. "He did have a granddaughter, one he raised, but she turned out to be a wild one. So wild that he disowned her."

Jasmine shook her head. "What a shame. Who's getting the house? Even in the state it's in, it's still worth a lot of money."

"Nephew from England. He's supposed to be coming up this week."

"England, huh? He'll sell it, no doubt. Probably take a while in this economy, though."

Valerie banged at the door using a brass knocker that could have awakened the dead. No one answered. She repeated the performance. The van, which they'd both assumed to be unoccupied, suddenly rumbled to life and moved out of the driveway.

"Weird," Jasmine said. "Whoever it was could have acknowledged us."

Valerie frowned again. "Let's just get what we came for."

She unlocked the door and they entered the dark, musty-smelling foyer. "Is anyone here!" she yelled loudly. No response. She automatically reached for the light switch, which of course yielded no illumination because the electricity had been turned off. Heading into the frigid living room, she drew the curtains, bringing in some gray mid-winter light.

Being in the house without Mr. Allard was eerie. Any moment she expected him to come rolling up in his creaky wheelchair to greet her with a British-tinged "Good afternoon, Valerie, my dear." For a brief second, as she vividly remembered the hours they'd spent debating politics, discussing novels, reading passages from the Bible, and playing chess, she almost forgot why she was there.

"The books," Jasmine reminded her. "I'm not too crazy about hanging around here long."

Valerie didn't comment because she was feeling a bit unsettled as well, and it had nothing to do with the injury she'd received from the subway platform fall. She led the way up a flight of long, winding stairs where an abandoned chairlift waited for a rider.

When Valerie parted the heavy drapes and feeble light poured in, Jasmine gasped to see that the entire second story had no individual rooms at all. Instead it was a private library boasting aisles of shelves loaded with books. In the center square of the room was an open area that was dominated by a long oaken table and several matching chairs. The hardwood floor was partially covered by a heavy Persian rug.

"Here we go," Valerie said, getting down on her knees and peeling back part of the rug.

"What *are* you doing?" Jasmine asked.

"You'll see." She removed several loose planks and stuck a key into a locked panel in the floor. At this point, Jasmine tried not to laugh.

"Hidden floor panels? Get outa here."

"Mr. Allard told me that I'm the only one who knows about this space."

"Okaaaay…so why would he hide Bibles? Other than being God's word, are you sure they're not worth money?"

"Well, they *are* worth something, but nothing to get excited about. He had the oldest one appraised by a collector and was told that the most he'd get for it was two thousand dollars, and that would be pushing it." Valerie wiped her hands off on her jeans. "Plus, I did warn you that Mr. Allard was eccentric. He was obsessed with the prophecies in the book of Revelation, and he believed that soon the world's political systems would turn totally against Christianity and it would become a crime to own a Bible. He said that Bibles would be burned and no one would be allowed to own any." She hesitated, coughing from the dust that had been released into the air. "It became his mission to preserve as many as he could."

"That's quite a theory," Jasmine said with a touch of awe. "Imagine the world actually getting to that point."

Valerie chuckled nervously. "I'm sure if it does, you and I won't have to worry about it. We'll be long dead."

The two large cartons full of dusty books were impossible to lift from the concealed space, so they had to remove a few books at a time and take them out to the SUV. The process was awkward and took longer than either of them desired, but after several trips up and down the stairs, the mission was accomplished.

"Wait. What about this?" Jasmine pointed to an attaché case that was also hidden in the panel.

"Leave it," Valerie said, stifling another cough. "I don't know what's in there."

"Probably more books. It's kind of heavy," Jasmine said.

Shrugging, Valerie hauled the briefcase up to the surface and, since it wasn't locked, opened it and glanced quickly inside. Jasmine was right, it contained more Bibles, smaller, more modern copies. They added them to the collection already in the car.

Mission completed, Valerie locked the compartment, replaced the planks and pulled the rug back into its original position. Her unsettled feelings lingered even after they'd secured the house, double-checked everything and were in the SUV, pulling back onto the road.

"Think we'll make it home before the storm?" Jasmine asked idly.

"Doesn't matter to me. You know I love driving in snow."

"You love driving, period. Wish I felt that way."

Valerie relaxed and pulled onto the expressway. The sky had gotten gloomier and the air was cold and slightly moist. She kept her eyes on the traffic ahead, but took note of Jasmine in her peripheral vision. "Jas, is Aaron in Cielo Vista, too?"

Jasmine, who had been fiddling with the radio, looked up, exasperated. "I knew it. I just knew you were going to ask about him."

"C'mon. Humor me."

"No. He's not there."

"Does Noah know where he is?"

"Probably."

"And that's all you have to say?"

"Yes."

"You twit."

"Bite me."

Valerie mimicked a snarl and they both laughed like high school kids.

The car filled with the emotive sounds of the legendary Miles Davis, and the traffic sailed at a good clip around them. Valerie eyed the rearview mirror and noticed with sudden irritation that a weaving box truck was practically on her bumper, and she wasn't creeping. Annoyed, she checked the side mirror and swung into the center lane. She accelerated, passed a string of cars until she gained a good distance, and then pulled back into the right lane.

"I've got something to tell you," Jasmine said.

"Something good, I hope."

"Oh, it's definitely good. The timings a little off, but that's not a problem." Jasmine leaned back in the seat and studied the first drops of snow starting to hit the windshield. "Just last week I found out that I'm pregnant."

Valerie felt her own heart lilt. "Wow! That's great and…" She stopped. "You idiot! Why didn't you tell me that before? You had no business carrying those books."

Jasmine laughed. "No problem. You did most of the lifting."

"Is Noah pleased?"

"Ecstatic."

Valerie was happy for her friend. The new baby would be a biological first for Noah and Jasmine. He had a young son from a previous marriage and they had an adopted daughter.

Unfortunately, having a baby was something she'd never experience. During the fiasco of her short-lived marriage, Valerie had learned that, due to health issues, she'd probably never conceive. Although she loved children, the dire pronouncement from a doctor had long since stopped bothering her. She knew she could be tested again because there were medical advances in fertility treatments, but she'd had enough of being prodded, poked, and subjected to false hope, and she accepted her fate. After all, she was the favorite aunt to Jasmine's kids and since there was no hint of marriage on the horizon, she might one day consider adopting as a single parent.

The box truck had caught up with them again. "Darn!"

"What?" Jasmine asked.

"That truck is following me."

Jasmine glanced back. "You're imagining it. Get in the other lane."

She sped up, passed two more cars and a tractor-trailer, and moved back into the right lane, aiming for the next exit.

"You're being a wacko, Val," Jasmine said. "This isn't our exit. That truck is…"

"Don't believe me, do you? Look behind us."

The box truck had slammed on its brakes, nearly rear-ending a Fiat, and jumped into their exit lane. Jasmine gave a gasp of alarm as she saw the truck roaring up behind them like a raging demon.

With her heart pounding and her brain calculating rapidly, Valerie prayed for clearance and plummeted the car down the ramp toward the merge, but what she saw was a huge tractor-trailer approaching. At that moment the box truck slammed into their bumper, forcing them into the path of disaster. Valerie clenched her teeth and refused to brake or relent.

"Hang on!" she shouted to Jasmine, who had covered her eyes. Jamming the accelerator to the floor and steering hard right, she rocketed the SUV forward, scraping a guardrail and causing the vehicle to shoot barely a yard ahead of the alarmed tractor-trailer driver whose horn blasts and screaming brakes filled the air. She waited for a sickening crash; there was a faint one, but it didn't involve them. Luckily, the tractor-trailer had not jack-knifed but had sideswiped the box truck, pinning it against the shoulder.

Valerie kept driving, her hands clenched to the wheel. "JZL555. JZL555," she recited. "Write that license down."

"Umm…" Jasmine stared at her, eyes glazed in shock. "Shouldn't we stop…call the police?"

"Are you kidding? This car's still drivable, and the only time I'm stopping is when we're back home. Now write that number down."

"Someone is trying to kill me," Valerie stated emphatically.

"What happened was an incident involving a maniac with a truck," Jasmine said. "We were just random targets. No point in trying to rationalize why we were, either."

Valerie took a long, slow, deliberate pause. "I suppose it was also just random…a coincidence that someone tried to push me in front of a train?"

Jasmine blanched. "Push you? You never said anything about being pushed."

"I wasn't sure then. Now I am, and I'm almost certain it's got something to do with Mr. Allard's will. I mean, really. This weirdness started happening right after I saw the lawyer."

Well into evening, they were sitting in the sumptuous living room of Jasmine's spacious home in the secluded Ramapo Hills, flanked by the cartons of Bibles they'd taken from Mr. Allard's house. A muscular teenage neighbor of Jasmine's had helped them bring the cartons inside.

Valerie slid one of the books out and inspected its well-preserved, gold-lettered spine. The Bible was written in a foreign text, possibly Italian. The copyright was 1935.

"I don't want to believe that," Jasmine said. "But suppose…just suppose it's true. Do you think we were followed here?"

Valerie shook her head. "No way. That fool in the box truck was thrown off when he sideswiped the tractor-trailer. And if I really were still being trailed, he would expect me to go to my place, not yours. Plus, I deliberately made all those zigzags to throw off any tail. Make sense?"

"Of course it doesn't make sense. None of this does." Jasmine looked flustered. "I also must say you never cease to amaze me. Where did you learn those evasive driving maneuvers?"

"They're a combination of paranoia and defensive driving. A retired FBI agent gave a night course at the community college."

Jasmine shook her head incredulously. "You said the driver was a he...did you actually get a good look at him?"

"No. Just in the rearview mirror I couldn't make out much, only that it was a man—a white or Hispanic man. I was kind of hoping that you might have gotten a better look."

"Oh, please. At that moment all I saw was a truck bearing down on us. We did get the license plate, though...for all the good it'll do. The truck could have been stolen." Jasmine stood up and paced around. "And you're absolutely positive that those Bibles are not overly valuable?"

"Absolutely. The oldest one was printed in the early 1800s. Mr. Allard told me that Bibles printed in that time period were plentiful. Generally, the ones that would be worth a lot would be Gutenberg's or ones from the fourteenth century, and most of those are in museums or private collections."

Jasmine looked at her directly. "Maybe someone *thinks* they're valuable."

"That could be true," Valerie admitted. The thought had already occurred to her. She randomly flipped a page of the Italian Bible and a dollar bill fluttered out, landing on the floor. Distracted, she picked it up and realized it was not a dollar but a hundred-dollar bill.

Jasmine was still pacing and muttering to herself while Valerie, overcome by an eerie realization, placed the bill on the coffee table and flipped some more pages. Sure enough, there were more hundred-dollar bills. Lots of them.

By the time they had gone through each and every Bible in the cartons, the money that was stacked on the table amounted to nearly a million dollars. The modern Bibles in the attaché case contained no money, but they had been placed on the surface to conceal additional stacks of hundred dollar bills, along with an envelope addressed to Valerie in Mr. Allard's spidery handwriting. Her hands shook as she opened it. The note read:

My dearest Valerie,

The treasures of the heavens and of the earth have opened up to you. Thank you so much for being there when I needed you. My deepest apologies for blending the monetary with the spiritual, but I assure you there were reasons for this blasphemy and I'm positive it will all work out. Please accept my gifts, as they can only go to one who is worthy. I have implicit trust that you will use the mammon wisely and, more importantly, that you will always treasure and preserve the spiritual.

❧❦

"Two million dollars! I can't keep this. No way can I keep this," Valerie repeated in dazed delirium. "This money belongs to the Allard family. It's got to be a mistake."

"Don't be absurd," Jasmine said. "Sounds to me like he definitely wanted you to have it. And you did say that his family was cruel and never visited him."

"His granddaughter did visit…once that I knew of."

"You told me that she visited only because she needed money."

"True, but she's still his blood."

"At the time of his death was Mr. Allard senile?" Jasmine asked.

"No."

"Well, like I said before, he meant for you to have it." Jasmine began checking the security system. "Boy, am I glad Noah had this security system installed. You're staying here tonight. We have a safe where the money can be kept temporarily until you de…"

Valerie stood up. "I'm not keeping it. And I'm going to the police."

"Oh, please. Not tonight. It's too risky."

Valerie sat back down, feeling more confused than ever. "You're right. I can't do anything about it now. I mean, I could call the police and…"

"I've got a better idea," Jasmine said. "How about if I give Noah a buzz right now. He'll probably have a worthwhile scheme…and he knows people."

"Great idea. Call him."

❧❧

Hours later, when Valerie awakened in the guest suite of Jasmine's home, she had no clue where she was. At first she thought she was at Mr. Allard's house, reading aloud passages from Ecclesiastes. In his final months, Mr. Allard had enjoyed listening to what he proclaimed to be her theatrical voice. It finally dawned on her that she was at Jasmine's place and that she was in trouble.

Because of the time difference with Africa, Jasmine had been unable to reach her husband last night, but she had left him a message. What time was it now? Valerie stared at the clock and shook her head in disbelief. It was almost 9 a.m. Dressing quickly, she hurried to the bathroom, washed up, and rushed down the exquisitely designed staircase, not even bothering to gawk out the windows at the panoramic views of the snow-blanketed forest and hills.

Jasmine had a light breakfast ready in the nook just off the rustic kitchen. She could afford a cook but she preferred to do things herself.

"It's about time," she said mockingly. "I heard from Noah."

"Why didn't you wake me?" Valerie sat down and gulped a glass of orange juice.

Jasmine ignored the question. "It's a good plan, but…" She gazed at the ceiling. "I'm afraid it's also a double-edged sword."

Valerie looked hard at her friend. Jasmine didn't usually play games when she had something to say. "Can't be that bad. Does it involve police protection or something?"

"It involves you leaving the country temporarily."

Valerie nearly choked on her orange juice. "Leave the country! If you're talking about me going to Cielo Vista, I can't do that. My agency is about to set me up on another job and…"

"You haven't officially accepted the job yet," Jasmine interrupted. "So hold on, I'm not finished. You won't be going to Cielo Vista. The country is in Central America, Belize to be specific."

"That's even worse. I don't know a soul in Belize."

Jasmine took a deep breath and suppressed an eye roll. "Oh, yes you do. Aaron's in Belize."

Aaron. Valerie's head, already spinning, would have fallen off her neck had it not been attached. Her heart surged and nearly jumped out of her throat. She said nothing.

"My thoughts exactly," Jasmine said, noting her reaction. "Anyway, keeping you safe is the highest priority, but if you cooperate you'll also be doing Noah a favor. He's worried about Aaron."

"Why is he worried about him?"

Jasmine inhaled deeply for the second time. "A couple of weeks ago, Aaron was injured on some…er, mission. He checked out of the hospital in Saudi Arabia way before any sane person would have. He calls himself recovering in Belize."

"How seriously injured was he?"

"A gunshot wound. He had surgery and everything. Collapsed lung…something like that…I don't know all the details. But trust me, the man has supernatural recuperative powers."

Valerie shook her head. "You knew all about this, didn't you? And you couldn't tell me?"

"You know exactly why I didn't. And I'm telling the truth when I say I don't have details. Noah doesn't talk much about Aaron's life aside from Avian International, but we both know he's ex-military and somehow tangled up in espionage."

"And I'm sure Aaron is going to be thrilled about Noah's scheme to get me down there to nurse him."

"Surprise! Noah presented your case to him, but the actual plan was Aaron's idea." Jasmine hesitated, giving her a chance for the information to sink in. "True, though, he doesn't know about the nursing part. That's not going to be easy."

Valerie barely heard the rest of what Jasmine said. So Aaron was concerned about her welfare—so concerned that he wanted her to be with him. Her worries about her own dilemma nearly dissolved. Even before she gave Jasmine her final answer, she knew what her decision was going to be. "What about my mother?" she asked lamely. "Aunt Marilyn would normally check up on her, but she's away."

"While I'm here, I can do it," Jasmine said. "I'm sure Denise will, too."

"Denise? For a price, no doubt."

Jasmine smirked. "You have two million dollars at your disposal."

"Very funny."

"Who's laughing? Sounds like you're moving from the devil to the deep blue sea."

"Don't worry. I'm a good swimmer, definitely a lot better than you are."

Chapter 3

From the office window of a small hub that Avian International had at Philip Goldson airport in Belize, Aaron scanned the not-too-distant airstrip, awaiting the landing of a specific cargo jet carrying consumer electronic goods and, of far greater significance, a certain woman. Her arrival was going to cause a few complications as well as aggravations for him, but not as much as the thought of her floating around ripe for picking off by some low-life whose identity he already suspected.

Two FBI agents from the New York branch were on the case. Normally the FBI did not investigate domestic affairs that could be handled by the local police departments, but Aaron knew the director of the branch and the man owed him big time.

He had already arranged Valerie Redmond's accommodations at a small family-run inn on Caye Caulker. From what little he did know about her, he was sure she'd prefer it there, as opposed to a touristy hotel in Belize City, even though the latter would have been better for him because she would be farther away from his territory. His decision to keep her close was saying a lot about what boredom and convalescence could do to a man's mind.

The jet was approaching now. He watched the huge bird touch ground and taxi down the runway, the mighty roar from its engines deafening to most, but music to his ears. He'd once flown fighter jets in the Israeli Air Force and had been in the aviation business as a whole for a long time, but the exhilaration of flight still gripped him.

As he stood well off the tarmac, waiting for the small crew to disembark from the modified 727, freight handlers were already milling around. When the first person emerged, the pilot, he acknowledged the man with a nod.

His first glimpse of Valerie consisted of feet in sensible flat sandals and a pair of legs—long, shapely Tina Turner legs—descending the ramp stairs. He watched, actually pleased that he was not completely immune to the sight of a striking woman. The legs were topped by white capri-length pants paired with a coral-colored V-necked T-shirt. She was looking downward as she maneuvered her way carefully to ground level, her thick hair falling against her oval face, shadowing it. Behind her, an Avian freight handler carried her luggage. One suitcase. This surprised him. From what he knew about women, they rarely traveled light.

"Good morning, Valerie. Welcome to Belize," he said.

Surprised, she looked up, squinting slightly in the bright sunlight as she recognized him and smiled. "Hello, Aaron. Thank you."

She sounded somewhat tentative, quite unlike the self-confident woman he remembered. Perhaps her reticence was triggered by stress and jet lag. He hoped it had nothing to do with what he assumed to be his less than healthy appearance.

Valerie's pulse quickened at the sound of Aaron's sensually deep, Israeli-accented voice. She had not been prepared to encounter him the instant she stepped off the plane. For some reason, she had assumed he would send a lackey to pick her up.

"I'm sorry that we are not meeting under different circumstances," he said.

Under different circumstances, you wouldn't want me near you, she thought. "My life seems to have gotten rather bizarre lately."

He was thinner than the last time she'd seen him, but the loss of weight didn't suggest poor health or diminish his presence in the least. In fact, it looked good on him. Possessing an exotic blend of Semitic and African blood, Aaron was tall, lean, and sharp angled, with close-cropped black hair that was mottled with a few streaks of premature silver. He wore dark sunglasses, a navy blue T-shirt that displayed well-defined muscles, and a pair of worn jeans bleached nearly white.

They strolled in silence to a Jeep parked near a warehouse. The young freight handler tossed her suitcase in the backseat, then headed off to join the rest of his crew. Aaron opened the passenger-side door of the Jeep for her and she got in.

Once they were on a hot bumpy road leading to who knows where, he spoke without taking his eyes off the road. "We're going to a small offshore island called Caye Caulker, where I've arranged your room and board. I hope you won't find it too remote."

Valerie shrugged. "I certainly won't complain. After all, I realize I'm not here on vacation."

"Tell me about Gordon Allard, the man you worked for."

The question jarred her. It didn't seem like something a person would typically ask at that moment. But why be surprised? The person asking was Aaron. She didn't let her reaction show.

"I worked three years as his nurse. In the beginning, he was a bit difficult to deal with...you know... very British, cantankerous—"

"How did Mr. Allard acquire his material assets?" he interrupted.

"Money? Oh...um. He was an inventor. A mechanical engineer, actually. He told me he designed a specific type of helicopter engine that ended up being used in helicopters during the latter part of the Korean War and in Vietnam. He—" She stopped abruptly, frowning, feeling exasperated. "You know all of this already, don't you?"

"Yes."

Darn him. He was playing with her. She did not bother to state the obvious, *Why did you ask?* Instead, she remained silent.

"Tell me something you think I don't already know," he said.

She bit her lip, took a deep breath and stared ahead at the tropical greenery around them. "His wife, son, and daughter-in-law were killed in a car accident on the Long Island Expressway years ago. His granddaughter, who was only two at the time, survived." She paused for a second, not caring anymore whether he knew this detail already or not. "His granddaughter suffered serious head trauma and spent months in the hospital. When she was well, he took her in and raised her as his own."

"Did Mr. Allard talk much about his relationship with her?"

"Some. He said he loved her and did the best he could, but he was already in his sixties when he was raising her, and Carolyn became difficult when she hit her teen years."

"In what way?"

"Like a lot of teenagers, I guess. She started hanging out with the wrong people. Wouldn't listen to him. He refused to let her drop out of high school, but she did drop out of college. She moved away from home, and for a few years he didn't even know where she was. Later she resurfaced and came back, but it wasn't because she was concerned about him. He said she was always borrowing money. He had established a trust for her, but she'd get it only if she straightened her life out. She never did."

Aaron's expression was impassive. They had arrived at a grassy field with a primitive dirt runway. Off to the left of the field, a small two-seater plane awaited, white with two black and yellow stripes on each side.

"Your chariot awaits," Aaron said.

Chariot? They were flying in that toy? She had never been in a single-engine plane before. "Why didn't you just fly out from the main airport?" she asked.

"Too much air traffic to contend with. The island's smaller regional airlines use this one. Don't worry. It's a very short flight. Only a few minutes. By boat it would take almost an hour."

Get over it, she told herself, not wanting him to see her nervousness. Although she was certain the man could smell fear like a bloodhound, to his credit, Aaron gave no such indication. He seized her suitcase and tossed it in the back of the plane before she could even protest. His easy handling of the luggage did not in any way suggest that he'd been injured.

"You do realize that what you and Jasmine did was darn foolish," Aaron said.

Startled by the statement and his bluntness, Valerie almost forgot where she was and glared at him. "What *we* did? What are you talking about?"

"Going to Allard's house without benefit of a reliable witness. You should have turned that key over to the lawyer and taken him with you. I have complete trust that all you took were those books, but you left yourself wide open for an accusation of theft by the Allard beneficiaries."

Her head spun. He was right. How stupid was that? That scenario had never occurred to her at the time. She had been so assured of her own honesty that she hadn't taken into consideration that a stranger might think otherwise. She cringed, recalling that her original goal in life had been to become a criminal investigator.

"Not to worry," Aaron said, noting her chagrin. "Maybe it won't happen, but if it does, we've got you covered." He sounded a tiny bit amused as he opened the passenger side of the plane for her. Valerie was impressed, but she also found herself stifling the urge to slap the smug look off his face—smugness that penetrated even through the dark glasses.

"Did you ever personally meet Allard's grand-daughter?" he asked as she climbed cautiously into the toy masquerading as a plane.

Are you human? Do you ever come up for air? she wondered. "Once," she said.

"Any words with her?"

"Perfunctory greetings only. She spent most of her time upstairs in the library, which was odd, since she was far from the bookish sort."

Aaron leaned close to fasten her seatbelt, his hand brushing against her, causing her heart to flutter. Strong, capable, long-fingered hands—hands that should be holding her the way they had when he'd danced with her two years ago. She swallowed, irritated by her physical reaction to his close proximity. Two years ago, the occasion had been festive and he'd had a few drinks to loosen up. She was no doubt getting a dose of the real Aaron Weiss at this moment, and the real one considered her a naïve nuisance.

"You believe Mr. Allard's granddaughter is behind all of this, don't you?" she said.

"Don't you?"

A question with a question. Boy, she hated it when people did that. She wondered if he knew, or cared, that he was seriously provoking her.

Of course he didn't care. His attention was on the control panel. The engine had caught and the excuse for a flying machine was spiriting down the runway, while he was simultaneously radioing the tower. She turned her head toward the side window so he could not observe her expression as they became airborne. He was probably amused. That is, if Aaron *did* amused.

Five minutes into the flight, she felt herself relax, allowing all tensions to dissipate. It was difficult to feel resentful when below she could see the glorious expanse of God's blue ocean and brownish bits of island all laid out below her. The view was awesome. Why ruin everything by taking offense with Aaron the interrogator? Wasn't his intense personality part of the reason he'd intrigued her in the first place?

❧❧

Caye Caulker was indeed a tiny island, just four miles long. There were no cars except those used by municipal authorities. The people, a colorful mix of Hispanic, Mayan, and African roots, rode bikes, walked, or used golf carts to get around.

Once they'd disembarked, Valerie and Aaron walked silently down the unpaved sandy road that led into the village, being occasionally greeted with friendly smiles and pleasantries. Aaron was cordial, in his cool, remote way, but no one seemed put off by it. The locals appeared to be familiar with his persona.

"The people are very friendly," Valerie said.

"Yes, they are, but don't share anything confidential. Within every Belizean beats the heart of a *yenta*."

"*Yenta?*" She'd heard the Yiddish/Hebrew phrase before, but the meaning momentarily eluded her.

"A gossipy woman," Aaron said.

She forced herself not to flinch. Why did he have to throw in the disparaging woman remark? Men gossiped, too.

Oblivious to her thoughts, Aaron looked straight ahead. Even though she had protested, he carried her suitcase, setting it down only when they'd arrived at a charming pink building that proclaimed itself Annie's Inn. They were greeted by Annie herself, a sixty-ish red-haired Canadian expatriate who was courteous and helpful as she showed Valerie to a room that was neat, clean, and basic. The kitchenette had a microwave and a small refrigerator, and the tiny bathroom had an enclosed shower. The largest area was the pastel green bedroom, which boasted a queen-size bed, a ceiling fan, and French doors leading out to a charming terrace overlooking the ever-present ocean.

"Where are you staying?" Valerie asked Aaron once Annie had left them alone.

He nudged her out to the terrace and pointed toward the blue expanse of sea where she spotted the distant masts of a sailing vessel.

"You're living on a boat?" she asked, surprised.

"My boat," he corrected. "Her name is *Saniyah II*. I'll show her to you…perhaps tomorrow. You'll be more settled then."

Valerie wasn't sure she'd ever be settled. Of course she didn't think Aaron would suggest they share a room, but she'd expected him to at least have a place in the same inn, or even a nearby one. With the ocean between them, how was she going to find out what his health issues might be?

"I'm leaving now," he said. "Make sure you keep the doors locked at all times, especially the terrace ones. It's pretty safe here on this part of the island, but there's never an excuse to be careless."

She nodded mutely. In truth, she wanted to grab him and shove him down on the bed. Not for some ulterior lust-crazed purpose, but just so she could examine him and make sure he was okay. On the surface, her concern seemed unwarranted. But her underlying fear was driven by past experience. She knew the type all too well. He was the quintessential invincible male who went to bed one night, suffered a heart attack, and never woke up again.

But she kept her thoughts to herself and watched him leave. When he was gone, she obediently locked the door, returned to the bedroom, and flopped down on the bed without even bothering to unpack.

The events of the day flooded her. She'd left New York in late afternoon for the flight out to Belize on an Avian cargo jet. Belize time was at least an hour or two behind that of the United States, meaning that back home it would be well into evening. Here it was still daylight. It was disorienting, to say the least.

Get over it. The only reason she was down here was so the police, or whoever, could do their job. Then she would return to her life as quickly as possible. How they were actually going about the investigation was another story because she hadn't even bothered to ask. Her illogical lapse disturbed her since it was not in any way typical. It was Aaron's fault. If she weren't so obsessed with him, she would be her usual resourceful self.

The next day things would change. Her head would be back on straight and she would no longer feel tired and irrational. Foregoing the thought that she should probably find something to eat, she closed her eyes and drifted off to sleep.

❦

Valerie's dreams were not troubled, but they took her back to childhood as they so often did, urging her to relive vignettes of her life. Mostly she remembered the calm patience of her minister father, whom she had loved dearly.

Later, the dream drifted into winning a trophy for the high school's swim team and wanting her mother to be there to see her accept it. Her mother had congratulated her, but as usual refused to attend. "Your father will be there," she'd said confidentially.

Her father had been there for all her triumphs and her mini-tragedies. He had taken her and her brother on camping and fishing trips, taught her to swim, ride a bike, ice skate, sleigh ride, and pitch a curve ball as good as any boy.

Joel Redmond had guided her through potentially troubled waters until she went away to college with aspirations to study criminal justice. His death at the age of fifty-eight had occurred suddenly and devastatingly in her first year. The big man with the booming James Earl Jones voice—the powerful orator, whose sermons mesmerized even unruly toddlers and squalling infants—had been felled by a heart attack while shoveling snow in their driveway.

His death forever changed Valerie's course and left her with an undeniable bitterness toward her needy mother, who was totally paralyzed by widowhood. If her mother had not been so clingy and taken on more of the family's responsibilities herself, the way marriage should be, her father wouldn't have been so burdened and probably would have lived longer.

Chapter 4

Morning. Aaron awoke from a deep sleep to the gentle undulation of the sea. He rose with practiced caution from the master berth in the cramped cabin of *Saniyah II*. Every muscle in his body screamed in protest, but he ignored the sensation. The pain was expected, and it was better to feel something as a reminder instead of floating around like a brain-fogged addict, dulled by the Demerol he'd been given when he'd been released from the hospital. He had, in fact, not touched the stuff since he'd arrived in Belize three weeks ago today.

He knew that the healing process was well under way because his clarity of mind had long since returned and the physical discomfort was less. The first two weeks he hadn't even been able to go out to the boat, but had instead stayed on land in the very same room at the hotel where Valerie was. He'd paid Dodge, Annie's husband, for some assistance, and they'd sent him Estella, the pretty young woman who cleaned the rooms at their inn and worked as a waitress in the restaurant around the corner. She brought him meals and made runs to the pharmacy. The rest he'd taken care of himself without too many complications. He knew instinctively that Estella, despite being young, was a bit smitten with him and that she would have gone beyond cook and messenger duties free of charge, but he wasn't one for indulging in such dalliances.

After splashing his face with cold water, he pulled on a pair of khakis and went up on deck. The sun had not yet risen, and wispy shrouds of charcoal-colored clouds smudged the magenta sky. The air was laden with tropical humidity, the ever-present indicator of another balmy day in paradise.

He surveyed the shore and focused on the familiar pink inn. Was Valerie up yet? For a brief second he had the urge to pick up his powerful binoculars and zoom in on her terrace. Not exactly a strange notion. He had used them often for surveillance, but this was different. He frowned at the realization; this urge was driven purely by voyeurism. Clenching his teeth, he resisted the impulse and turned to go back below deck.

Unfortunately, he hadn't been as gracious a host as he'd intended, mostly because the day had been long, and pain and crankiness had set in. If Valerie had been offended by his infamous bluntness, he was sure she'd give an indication by avoiding him as much as possible, which would be disappointing, but in both of their best interests. In either case, he'd find out soon enough because his plan for the moment was to take the speedboat over to the inn, book a different room, shower, shave, and attempt to behave civilly with her.

He'd heard overnight from his contact in New York that the investigation was progressing well, and that meant she probably wouldn't have to remain in Belize very long.

❦

Valerie rose just before sunrise, and after showering and dressing in a turquoise T-shirt and bright yellow Bermuda shorts, she called Jasmine. Her friend didn't pick up, so she left her a message—a brief recap of yesterday's events. Having no clue when she would see Aaron again, she assumed she was on her own. Since Caye Caulker was only four miles long, there wasn't much danger of getting lost. She'd have a chat with Annie and acclimate herself to the place.

The lobby of the inn was small and homey with well-appointed seating and colorful island paintings on the bright tangerine walls—more like the living room of an artist's house. She found Annie wearing a wide-brimmed hat and pulling weeds from the impressive bougainvillea out back in the garden.

"I see you're an early riser like Mr. Weiss," she said, straightening.

Valerie smiled. "You've seen him?"

"Why, yes. He's in his room." She hesitated. "Isn't he?"

In his room? Apparently, Annie thought she should have known that, and for a moment Valerie almost laughed, realizing, no doubt, that the innkeeper assumed that she and Aaron were intimate.

"Mr. Weiss told me that he was spending the night out on his boat," Valerie countered. "I didn't realize until now that he had given me his room."

Annie laughed now. "Oh, but he is a cagey one, isn't he? He probably did spend the night out on the boat, but he's rented another room near yours. He was there maybe an hour ago."

"Men, who can figure them out?" Valerie gave a dismissive nod of her head. "Just wondering if you could recommend a decent restaurant."

"Sure. Assuming it's breakfast you want, try La Isla Café. It's just a short walk around the corner to your left. You can't miss it."

She thanked Annie and went back around the front. So Aaron had a room near hers. Interesting. Maybe he was still there and she should pay him a visit. No. She would keep to her original plan and go have breakfast by herself. He could easily find her if he wanted to.

At the charming café Valerie settled at a table on the terrace overlooking the sea and was poring over the morning news with a cup of coffee and an egg and cheese omelette—her cholesterol indulgence of the day—when a shadow fell over her and she looked up to see Aaron.

"May I join you?" he asked.

No, get lost. You're intruding, she thought, bemused by what a lie that definitely unspoken statement was. "Of course you may," she said.

He looked dashingly handsome in a dark blue polo shirt and spotless white linen pants, colors that set off his just a hint browner than Mediterranean-toned skin. As before, the sunglasses were present, but when he sat down, she was pleased that he propped them on top of his head aviator style, allowing her, for the first time since she'd arrived, to see his ebony eyes.

The waitress, a curvy young thing with an upswept ponytail and a flight attendant's smile, set a plate of bacon and scrambled eggs before him without even waiting for his order. He spoke a few words to her in Spanish that Valerie couldn't quite interpret. The young woman's smile deepened. She nodded courteously at Valerie and then moved to another table.

"You know her?" Valerie asked, wondering what that was about.

"Estella," he said. "You'll be seeing her often enough, since she also works at Annie's Inn during the afternoons." He proceeded to scarf down the food like a starving wolf. "I know most of the residents here. If not by name, by sight."

"Do they know you?"

"They think they do."

Typical response, Valerie thought and tried not to stare at him eating. He wasn't uncouth, lacking in etiquette, or anything, but she had never seen anyone eat that fast before.

"How about if I take you on a little sight-seeing tour later?" Aaron said.

Her cue had arrived and she made direct eye contact. She wasn't about to mince words or spare him this time. "That would be wonderful, if you're up to it."

His eyebrows arched slightly. "And why wouldn't I be up to it?"

"Suppose you tell me, Aaron. My sources have informed me that you aren't altogether on vacation in Belize either. Might rest and recuperation be more accurate?"

He smiled. The expression was slightly chilling, but boy did it come off rakish and charming. "Touché," he said.

She winked, crossed her legs and sat up straighter. "I'm willing to listen when you feel like talking."

His smile faded slowly and the way he studied her was so intense that if she were kindling, she would have ignited. "Did my good friend Noah and his lovely wife give you any specifics on how my infirmities should be dealt with?"

"No. Not at all. And I wouldn't hold it against them for being worried about you. That's what friends do. I'm sure you would feel the same if…"

"I'm aware of Noah's concerns, but they are unwarranted. Yes, I wasn't exactly in good shape a few weeks ago, but I'm just about over it."

"I'm a nurse, as I'm sure you're well aware," Valerie said. "I'm doing private duty now, but I worked for two years in an inner city hospital and almost eight years in the ER at Englewood Hospital. In other words, I've seen just about everything from amputations to third degree burns and gunshot wounds." She stirred her coffee fiercely. "When you're ready, I'd like to have a look at you so I can make that judgment call myself."

"And suppose I say no?" His eyes met hers again, and he seemed intrigued by her unyielding determination.

"I will relentlessly stalk you all over Belize and take you down with a tranquilizer dart," Valerie said. "After that I will get my way."

"You are serious, no?"

"I am serious, yes."

His eyes sparkled. Did she actually see a twisted glimmer of bad boy there?

"That might be entertaining," he said.

She glowered. "Entertaining for me, not you."

"Fine. I surrender." He raised both hands in mock defeat. "Before we go on our tour, I'll accompany you back to the hotel and you may have your way with me."

You may have your way with me? The words resounded in her head—the way he said them, with that husky accent and overbearingly proper speech. He was dropping innuendoes all over the place and she was homing in on every one, spoken and unspoken. She swallowed hard. *Don't be a nymphomaniac twit. This is strictly Nursing 101, nothing more. At least not yet, anyway.*

Aaron was on his best behavior when they returned to Annie's Inn. She took him to what was now her room. He passed through the bedroom and abruptly went out on the terrace, taking a seat on a lounge chair. Valerie lingered in the bedroom, smiling unconsciously as she removed her medical bag from her suitcase.

She was grateful that he was considerate enough to allow her some breathing space in order to get her professional act together, because at the moment, way too many bizarre thoughts and images were crossing her mind, the worst of which involved her stepping out to find him waiting for her stark naked. Aaron? She'd totally lost it. No way would Mr. Cool, Calculating, and By the Book do such a thing.

Knowing full well that the Christian side of her shouldn't even be considering such things, she went to the bathroom, washed her hands thoroughly and splashed very cold water on her face for good measure. When she joined him on the terrace, the only thing missing was his shirt. She exhaled.

What she did see was impressive—the kind of hard, sculpted body an athletic twenty-something would be proud of. His earlier artery-clogging choice of breakfast had to have been something of a fluke because it did not show on his well-toned muscular torso, which was devoid of any flab. He didn't have a bandage covering the surgical scar on the right side of his chest, though, which marred his otherwise near perfection.

"Do I appear to be on the brink of collapse?" he asked, sitting up straight.

"Hardly," Valerie admitted, placing a hand lightly on his shoulder, leaning forward to inspect his back for an exit wound.

"The bullet didn't exit," he explained when she found nothing. "The doctors fished it out of my lung."

"Did they get it all?"

"Yes."

"They took X-rays…an MRI?"

His piercing eyes met hers. "Incredible as it may seem, there really are some knowledgeable doctors in Saudi Arabia."

Valerie laughed now. "Okay, okay. I deserved that one."

She traced a finger lightly over a smaller, thinner scar where they'd inserted and removed a chest tube. It, too, was healing.

"Just one more thing," she said, taking the stethoscope out of her bag and adjusting it around her neck.

She listened to his heartbeat, which was strong, then asked him to breathe while she checked his lungs. He complied, somewhat tentatively, she noticed, but his lungs were clear. The larger scar did have some reddish areas surrounding it, but nothing to get alarmed about. A temperature check had revealed no fever.

"You need to keep a bandage on that," she told him. "It's healed enough so the wound isn't open, but when you're wearing a shirt, the material constantly brushing against it could cause problems."

Aaron nodded noncommittally. She did the honors, taping a square gauze patch in place. On closer inspection she noted that he had another barely visible, long-healed-over scar just below his ribcage. She started to question him about it, but decided not to bother. He hadn't volunteered any details concerning the event that had caused the current wound.

"I must say your bionic reputation is solid," she told him. "You're pretty amazing. You're also darn lucky."

"If I really were so lucky, I wouldn't have the scars to prove otherwise," he said.

"Well, what do you expect? He who plays with fire often gets burned."

Aaron knew her physical inspection of him was supposed to be professional only, but her close proximity was causing him to react more impulsively than he had ever done in his life. Without hesitation, he wrapped his arms around her and pulled her even closer than she had been. He had experienced a similar impulse while in the café gazing into her large almond-shaped eyes. Now the feeling was even stronger, emboldened by her scent, which was sweeter than the oleander from the garden below. Slowly his hands stroked her back, feeling the warmth of her nubile body radiating through her thin T-shirt.

Valerie stiffened slightly. "Um, Aaron."

Ignoring her voice, he fixated on her dangling silver earrings and then on her turquoise T-shirt, wondering about the taut, well-proportioned form beneath it. Engrossed in that thought, he allowed his palm to venture down the gentle slope of her backside.

"Let go of me, please."

She didn't sound like she meant it at all. Nevertheless, the negative words broke his spell.

"Why?" he asked, releasing her, not really wanting to know the answer.

"Because I'm a Christian…a serious Christian, and I think you already know that. I'm not here to behave as if we're married."

He stifled a groan. "You don't have to be married to be…friendly."

"What you were doing went beyond friendly."

At what specific point did I go beyond friendly? he thought sarcastically. Abruptly he stood up, grimacing slightly at the pulling sensation caused by the still-healing wounds, and reached for his shirt that was draped on the back of the chair.

"Might be a good idea if you would drop the machismo a notch and move a little slower," Valerie said as he pulled the shirt over his head. "It must have been excruciating for you yesterday, flinging my suitcase around like you did."

She was definitely in full nurse mode, until she tugged the shirt down in place, even though she knew full well that he could do it himself. And there was nothing strictly professional or Christian about the way her hands brushed—no, stroked the area just below his ribs as she did this. The woman was toying with him.

"You mentioned tranquilizer darts earlier," he said, his voice even thicker than usual. "Unlike *you*, I actually do own such a gun, but you may borrow it if you like."

"Sweet," Valerie said. "When I'm in the mood for stalking, I'll let you know, but right now I'd rather you be my charming tour guide."

They spent the day wandering all over the tiny island. No one on Caye Caulker seemed to be aware of time. Valerie and Aaron strolled the sandy roads, occasionally passing by barefoot people, young and old, riding bicycles or walking. Everyone smiled. Everyone relaxed.

Valerie enjoyed browsing in several small novelty shops, something she rarely did back home, and she especially loved the quirky art galleries featuring works by local artists. In one such place, she spotted a beautiful acrylic painting that depicted the Caye Caulker shoreline, the blue Caribbean fringed by pink, violet, and lime-green houses.

"Aaron, this one is gorgeous," she exclaimed, pointing. "Look, there's Annie's Inn."

"You like that one, do you?" Aaron said, somewhat sardonically.

She nudged him. "Oh, stop. I think it's beautiful. As a matter of fact, I might buy it."

He glanced at the price. "Save your money. You might be able to bargain with the gallery owner. As it is, it's too expensive."

"Hey, I'm the one to determine that," she said.

"True. But it will still be there when you come back. There are other things to do, and you don't want to be lugging a painting around, do you?"

His logic prevailed and after browsing some more, they left the gallery and had lunch at a popular seafood restaurant, followed by a short stroll down to a section known as the split. From that location, Aaron indulged Valerie's curiosity by accompanying her on a guided boat tour with a bunch of chatty British tourists out to see the island's famous manatees and other marine life.

It was nearing evening when they returned to shore, and Valerie gave Aaron silent credit for tolerance during the course of the day, because she knew the touristy excursions must have been incredibly boring for him, but at least he hadn't appeared restless and surly. True, he maintained his habitual aloofness, leaving most of the conversation for her to initiate, and twice he'd gotten calls on his cell phone and excused himself to seek privacy, but she didn't mind. After all, why would she when she was thankful to God that he was recovering so well, not to mention her extreme pleasure over the advances she'd made with him earlier.

Her real reason for being in Belize did linger at the back of her mind. What was going on with the investigation? How was it being carried out? And was there any progress? True, it was only the second day, but Aaron had to know something. As the innocent victim, Valerie felt she had a right to know some detail, and she resolved that once they got back to the hotel, she'd inquire. Right now, though, she just wanted to go slow and enjoy the island and her illusion of closeness to Aaron.

Chapter 5

Evening found them climbing from his speedboat onto the deck of *Saniyah II*. Valerie sensed that this had not been part of Aaron's plan for the day, but she had asked to see the ship and he had granted permission.

"Wow! She's gorgeous," Valerie exclaimed, genuinely impressed as she stood on the pristine teak deck, looking at the polished railings. The ship was bigger than she'd imagined and blindingly white, with two broad navy stripes on her hull. "A genuine wooden schooner, too. I should have known you wouldn't settle for fiberglass."

"Ah, an African-American woman who knows something about boats," Aaron said, watching her closely.

Valerie didn't take offense. "Not an awful lot," she admitted. "But it just so happens that when I was around ten, my father allowed me to spend a summer with friends of his from Rhode Island. That whole family was into sailing, and I learned a thing or two…even how to handle a sailboat alone…a very small, basic one, that is."

"You weren't the typical little girl, then."

Valerie glanced at him, bemused. "What is the typical little girl?"

"One who plays with dolls, has tea parties, and would never sail a boat on her own, or go fishing if she had to touch a worm."

She laughed. "For your information, I did play with dolls and have tea parties. I was also a better pitcher and a better angler than my brother."

"Just as I thought. Come. I'll show you below."

Like most sailing vessels, the living quarters below deck were tight to maximize every inch of space, but this ship definitely had more headroom than any she'd ever been aboard. The galley was neat, equipped with modern appliances; the salon area was wood paneled and a bit dark, albeit definitely masculine colors. The built-in seating had royal blue upholstery. She noticed that Aaron, at what she guessed to be around six feet, five inches tall, didn't even have to duck when he moved around.

"Custom designed?" she asked, looking at the shelving containing books, mostly navigational texts. There was also a desk with a computer, fax machine and printer.

Aaron nodded in reply. "Sit. I'll get some drinks. Does rum and coke suit you?"

"That's fine," she said.

He vanished into the galley and she noticed a bunch of art canvases stashed in a corner, facing the wall. Funny, he hadn't seemed all that interested in art when they were in town. Curious, she wandered over and peeked at one of the paintings. There was something familiar about the colorful island scene depicted—more familiar than just that it was Caye Caulker's main street with its sandy road and pastel buildings. The painting was similar in style to the one she had wanted to purchase and had probably been done by the same artist.

She selected another canvas, which looked peculiar because it was all in varying shades of aquamarine with a much deeper blue in the center of the painting, like an eye. The eye was in turn fringed by what appeared to be grainy rocks or reefs. She picked up the canvas and held it at arm's length, trying to figure it out.

Aaron returned so quietly she didn't realize he was behind her. He set their drinks on the table. " 'Curiouser and curiouser,' " he said, gently but firmly taking the painting away from her and placing it back where it had been. "What's your interpretation?"

Though perturbed by the fact that he'd taken the painting away, she decided not to fixate on it.

"Well, it kind of looked like the ocean with a giant hole in it," she said.

"Correct. That's exactly what it is. A few miles from here, there's a place in the middle of the ocean called The Blue Hole. It's a naturally formed sinkhole that's also a great diving spot. You can only get this kind of view of it from an airplane."

"Really?" She noticed something else. On the lower shelves there were paintbrushes, other art equipment, and more empty canvases. It slowly dawned on her—and she felt like a dim-witted child—that he was the artist. She inhaled deeply and then laughed.

" 'Curiouser and curiouser,' indeed," she said. "That was *your* work I was looking at in that gallery before. I'm impressed. You're very good."

"Just a hobby when I'm bored. No more, no less." He was about to retrieve their drinks to take them up to the deck when she nudged him, wanting him to comment more.

"Did you study art in college?"

"Not seriously."

Open and shut. He had no intention of engaging her with detail. *Quick*, she thought, *come up with something else.*

"Aaron?"

"Yes."

"Does *Saniyah II* have a story? I mean, is this ship named after someone, or some thing?"

"All ships have a story," he said. "*Saniyah* means 'brilliant' in Arabic. I found her years ago rotting away in some Miami shipyard. There was something about her that spoke to me, so I bought her for a steal." Aaron continued the story as he reclaimed her drink and his bottle of beer and urged her up the stairs ahead of him. "My son and I rebuilt her almost from the beams up."

Son? Valerie was glad he was behind her or she would have missed a step and fallen backward, such was

67

her surprise. Had she misunderstood him? "Did you say you have a son?"

"Andrew," Aaron said matter-of-factly, oblivious to her shock, or pretending to be. "He was eleven then, but he's all grown up now and in the navy."

Valerie's focus completely evaporated yet she didn't want him to see that she was truly astonished by that revelation. Neither Jasmine nor Noah had ever mentioned anything about Aaron having a son. If he was telling the truth, and why wouldn't he be, then there could be a wife…an ex-wife out there. She wondered if he was secretly enjoying the torture he was inflicting on her.

"Drew's mother and I never married," he said when they were seated at a table facing each other broadside on deck. "As a matter of fact, I didn't even know he existed until he was eight years old."

"That's a bit odd, isn't it?" Valerie said.

Aaron made no comment. He leaned forward and extracted a wallet from his back pocket. Flipping it open, he handed it to her. "This is Drew. He's a Navy SEAL."

Impressive, she thought, looking at the picture. The SEALs had notoriously high entrance standards. Valerie stared into the face of a young man who was clearly Caucasian and exhibited no trace of his father's more exotic breeding. Andrew Weiss was in full uniform, gorgeous as a screen idol with close-cut blondish hair, crystal clear blue eyes, a sculpted face, cleft chin — yes, the chin was like his father's. The longer she looked at him, the more she could actually see an uncanny resemblance.

"Your son looks like a movie star," she said off the top of her head. She laughed. "Almost like my mother's favorite actor."

"Who is your mother's favorite actor?"

"Paul Newman. He looks like a young Paul Newman."

Aaron smirked. "You think so?"

"His eyes are so blue," Valerie said. "Did his mother have eyes like that?"

"No. Hers were—" He shrugged. "I don't remember. Maybe they were green."

She handed the wallet back to him, waiting, hoping she wouldn't have to keep prying, hoping for once that he'd elaborate.

"Things are never as they seem," Aaron said slowly. He took a swig of beer straight from the bottle, and then he stood up and walked a few feet away from her.

She sat paralyzed, staring at the ice melting in her drink, and then raised her eyes to the glory of the sun sinking low into the azure sea. Aaron sat back across from her again.

"Look at me," he said.

Her eyes met his and she gave a start. A pair of deep blue eyes stared back at her, not crystal blue like Andrew's, but a very, very dark blue, much like the color of the ocean besieged by a storm.

Valerie forced a smile. "You so love shocking me, don't you? Those are contacts, right?"

"I was wearing contacts before," Aaron said. "Blue is my natural color. In the kind of work that I've been doing, it doesn't pay to have what some might consider odd or outstanding features. I always wear dark contacts, so most people think my eyes are black."

She shook her head. The ebony-eyed look had captivated her, but the midnight blue was even more mesmerizing and mysterious. She took a deep breath. Midnight blue like the color of the sinkhole he had painted. She felt odd and suddenly chilly, even though the breeze was balmy. *He's scary*, Denise had said. Maybe the chatterbox was right.

She toyed with her drink and attempted to sip, but somehow she couldn't swallow normally. "It's starting to get dark," she said. "Maybe I should be heading back to the inn."

He was doing it, looking at her in that reflective way again. "Of course," he said, rising, offering her his hand.

She took it and they boarded the waiting speedboat, which he had attached to *Saniyah II*. Once the bow-line was removed, they were slicing through the water at lightning speed. Valerie had never been seasick in her life, but at this moment she felt queasy.

"I'm surprised that you haven't asked about the investigation," Aaron said once they'd arrived at the inn and she was unlocking the door to her hotel room. "It's progressing quite well, and I'm sure you'll be happy to know that you won't have to stay here very long at all."

Valerie smiled at him sweetly—at least she thought it was sweetly—but the expression looked more like it belonged on the face of a piranha. "I appreciate everything you're doing, Aaron. Thank you and goodnight."

Before she could step in and close the door, Aaron's arms encircled her from behind, stopping her in her tracks. Immediately, music from the past started to play in her head as his lips heated up the back of her neck, causing her whole body to flush and tremble like a newborn kitten. Losing herself, she turned slowly in his arms, eyes closed, barely breathing.

But nothing happened. No kiss.

"Goodnight," he said, thick-voiced, releasing her and stepping back as though she'd requested him to.

Unbelievable. Valerie quickly turned on her heel, entered her room, and shut the door. Already she could hear his footsteps moving down the hall.

She threw herself on the bed, trying to figure out exactly why she was so upset. "You're crazy," she muttered to herself. "Every bit as crazy as he is."

It made no sense to be angry with him for not kissing her when she'd warned him in the beginning about taking liberties with her unmarried state. He was in a no-win situation. If he had kissed her passionately, she would have savored the moment and then been upset later on, because illusions of romance could not cover over her disturbed feelings that were prompted by his revelations onboard *Saniyah*. No, what had happened was not strange. Aaron had simply been his usual enigmatic, dismissive, and detached self. What she'd learned about him was simply too much to contain in one day, that was all. He was like putting together a challenging jigsaw puzzle and then realizing too late, after much time had been invested, that pieces were missing.

The phone rang. Valerie seized it.

"Where have you been?" Jasmine asked. "I've been trying to reach you all day."

"Sorry. I forgot to take my phone with me. I was out. You know, exploring the island."

"Alone?"

"No. I was with—" She clenched her teeth. "Aaron."

A long silence followed. "How is he?" Jasmine asked.

"Oh, he's just fine."

"Valerie? What? Why aren't you talking?"

Valerie laughed in an attempt to keep from screaming. "Don't read too much into this. I'm just tired and… and…Go on, say you told me so. That man is truly a piece of work."

"Oh, God. What has Mr. Weiss done this time? Did he completely shatter the illusion you had of him?"

Valerie thought seriously about what she was about to say and chose her words carefully. "No. He didn't exactly shatter any illusions. He's actually gone and enhanced them even more. He's such a frustrating enigma, Jas. I ask him one thing and the conversation somehow turns to something else. Trying to nail him down is like walking through a maze loaded with mines."

Jasmine sighed. "Yes, that's somehow very Aaron."

"He has a son named Andrew, who's a Navy SEAL. Did you know that?"

"A son?" Jasmine echoed. "I never knew. Wow... what's up with that? Noah never said anything about this son of his."

For a second, Valerie felt relieved. At least her best friend hadn't been keeping that tidbit from her. "Do you think Noah knows?"

"Yeah. He probably does. It would have been nice if he'd told me, but I don't find it strange. I mean, they're friends and business partners. I guess Aaron has a right to his privacy, if that's what he wants."

"I don't know, Jas, this is so crazy. I mean, he revealed a lot and then nothing at all. What's crazy is why I find the whole thing upsetting. He did tell me that he was never married to his son's mother, and certainly if he couldn't even remember the color of her eyes he couldn't have been in love with her."

"The color of her eyes?" Jasmine repeated, confused.

"Never mind. I'm tired and deranged." *And jealous.* "Let's forget about Aaron for now." She took a deep breath. "Have you seen my mother?"

"Yes. Your mother's fine. Just think, pretty soon this whole mess will be over and you can come home. I assume Aaron told you that they have a definite suspect and they're setting a trap so they can prove it."

"I know," Valerie lied. She didn't know that at all, and lying about it was even stranger. The truth was she'd been taken down a rabbit hole, or more accurately a sinkhole, and she was suffering from some kind of diver's euphoria. Part of her wanted to escape but another part wanted to remain. The crazy person who'd invaded her body didn't want to leave Caye Caulker and return to her own life until she unraveled the mystery of Aaron.

Lying flat on the deck floor, staring up at the stars and listening to the gentle whispers of *Saniyah* talking to the waves beneath her, Aaron focused on a particularly large twinkling star in the velvety expanse. The subtle flickering seemed to be transmitting an encoded message.

He was annoyed with himself, no question about that. Not in many years had he even remotely felt the urge to really talk to someone other than Noah. His art, his boat, his life, and his son were his business, and there was no clear reason to discuss them with anyone else, let alone her. But this woman actually seemed to care. She genuinely wanted to know what lay beneath his surface, and in prying, she'd probably discerned her truth about him — he was a cold, dark, uncompromising person. If indeed that was the truth, he was grateful that the evening had terminated so abruptly because he had uncharacteristically gotten way out of control and revealed more than he intended and might have revealed even more. It was not a performance he planned to repeat, and there was no reason to obsess over the lapse of judgment because the investigation would probably wrap up in a day or two and she could go back home. He wouldn't have to think about her anymore.

Chapter 6

At sunrise Valerie had breakfast at La Isla café again. No one invaded her privacy this time. She lingered longer than she intended, but Aaron didn't show. She hadn't really expected him to, but she was disappointed anyway. As she made her way back to the inn, she kept her eyes to the sea, centered on *Saniyah II* anchored out there. The ship was at such a distance that she probably wouldn't be able to make out anyone on deck, but she shaded her eyes and tried anyway. Nothing.

When she returned to her room, she looked over some tourist brochures. There were water taxis and planes to transport her to areas of interest such as the Mayan ruins at Altun Ha. She definitely wanted to see those before she left, but seeing them without Aaron made her less enthusiastic.

It was her fault. She had been overwhelmed last night and deliberately shut him out. She should have told him in words and action that it was okay to kiss her goodnight. What was he supposed to take from her cold response? Rejection, of course, even though it couldn't be farther from the truth. So what if he had a son. Aaron wasn't a kid, for God's sake, and neither was the son. Of course he would have had a woman or two in his past—maybe several. The next time she saw him she would deal with the logistics of their circumstances. She would ask him about the investigation and nothing else. If he wanted to talk about other things, that would be nice, but she had no intention of prodding.

A gentle tap sounded at her door. She unlatched it to see the pretty young woman who sometimes doubled as a waitress at La Isla Café.

"*Buenos dias*, Miss Redmond. Mr. Weiss asked me to give this message to you."

She handed Valerie an envelope.

Surprised, Valerie accepted it and thanked her. When she had gone, Valerie opened the envelope and read the printed message.

Valerie,

You will be pleased to know that Carolyn Allard, Gordon Allard's granddaughter, and an accomplice have been arrested. Ms. Allard has confessed, and when you get back home, a lawyer will probably be in contact with you to discuss the preliminaries. They may want you to appear in court at some point. Valerie gasped. She couldn't believe what she was reading. But what really sent her through the roof was that the envelope contained fare for a charter plane to take her off Caye Caulker and a plane ticket—a ticket for a regular commercial flight back home, and it was for tomorrow afternoon. She stared, aghast, at his note again. *I assumed you'd like to leave Belize as soon as possible and that you might be more comfortable on a commercial flight.*

A.W.

He assumed. She hurled the note and the tickets across the room. The papers fluttered about like confused wrens, having lost their direction. *How dare you! You don't even stop by to explain. Instead, you write me off like some raggedly Little Orphan Annie and then you have the nerve to send me back home on a commercial airliner with tickets you paid for.* Did he think she was so impoverished she couldn't even afford her own plane ticket?

"My God," she shouted aloud. "Am I really in love with that jerk? Never mind that. I'm going to kill him."

<hr />

What the—? No one ever dared come uninvited out to the spot where *Saniyah II* was anchored. In the galley, Aaron stabbed out a cigarette and automatically seized a loaded Beretta from the shelf. Shaking off an initial wave of vertigo, he vaulted the stairs two at a time. The deafening roar of a speedboat was getting nearer. He crouched on the deck, half-hidden, alert, waiting.

The approaching craft was familiar, a flashy purple boat belonging to a grizzled lobster-red guy named Zack who often shuttled tourists around the island.

Aaron relaxed, sliding the weapon into the waistband of his jeans, concealing it.

"Afternoon, Ray, mon, you got a visitor requesting permission to board," Zack hailed him, his pitch laced with island Creole.

Ray. Aaron smirked. That was one of the names the locals had given him, Ray as in Stingray. He strolled over to look down at the hovering boat. The visitor was Valerie, arms folded, glowering up at him. Glowering? What the heck was with her? She had her freedom back, why wasn't she busy in her room packing to leave?

"Permission granted," he said, taking his time lowering the mechanized boarding ladder.

Zack tossed him a line; he caught it and secured it to *Saniyah II*. Aaron then stepped back a few feet and resisted giving Valerie a hand. She didn't need it anyway. She moved easily and gracefully up the ladder like a stalking tigress homing in on her prey. Her trim but curvaceous body was poured into a pristine white T-shirt, beige-colored jeans and white sneakers. Intrigued, Aaron remained silent, watching.

❦

Intent on one purpose only, Valerie reached the deck and barely paused to take a breath. "First," she began loudly, and then swallowed hard as she confronted and absorbed the object of her wrath towering above her in raw, unkempt, and sexy splendor. She had not prepared herself for the sight of him in a black-ribbed tank top, with hands on hips, legs slightly apart, encased in ragged jeans with a hole ripped in one knee. She had not prepared herself for eyebrows slanted dangerously over narrowed cobra eyes. Blue cobra eyes.

Get over it. She struggled to regain her composure and momentum. "I came to thank you in person for having your people solve the case so quickly. Secondly, this is yours." With fire flashing in her eyes, she thrust the envelope with the plane tickets at him.

Aaron made no move to take it.

She flung the envelope and the wind sent it skittering across the deck to wedge between a nearby storage bench and a fishing rod.

"I don't need your charity, Mr. Weiss. I *will* leave you alone as you wish, but seeing that you don't own Caye Caulker or Belize, I won't leave this island until I'm good and ready, and on whatever commercial airline I *choose* to pay for."

She spun on her heel and stalked back toward the boarding ladder, the sea breeze whipping her black hair angrily in her face.

"Valerie, wait," Aaron said.

She ignored him and kept moving

"Please."

Did he actually say please? She hesitated for only a split second, wondering why she extended him even that courtesy, but it was time enough for the cobra to spring, reach out and take her by the arm, assertively, yet without aggression.

"*Mizta' eret.* I didn't mean to offend you," He said, planting both hands on her forearms, turning her gently so she was facing him again. "I thought you would be pleased to return home as quickly as possible."

"You have no right to think or assume for me, Aaron. You don't know me, and even if you did, I haven't given you that permission."

"Point well taken."

He exhaled evenly, and she literally felt his exhalation, along with a tremor-inducing hot flash that definitely was not caused by the tropical breeze, but rather by the sensation of his hands gripping her, his eyes piercing into hers, and the way the corners of his mouth curved into a scintillating slow burn of a smile, the same smile that had mesmerized her two years ago.

Speechless, she allowed the sensation to draw her in and, the next second, her arms, as if controlled by some other worldly force, locked around his waist and her head tilted upward, her lips meeting his with all the magnetic power born of desire too long deferred.

Truly surprised by the nature and the timing of the kiss, Aaron reciprocated with matching intensity, drawing her closer and closer...until her hand rose and struck him sharply across the face.

Confused and teetering on the brink of anger, he stepped back.

"You fool," she said, seething. "How can you be so stupid?"

"*Me?*" he spluttered. "Listen here, woman. You're the one who—"

Her voice rose. "Don't say anything you…you idiot. I can't believe it. I just can't believe you've been smoking. You had lung surgery a few weeks ago, and you're smoking?"

He blinked several times, as though just waking up, and then, somewhat contrite, he lowered his head and laughed, a deep throaty chuckle.

"Laugh all you want," Valerie said. "The last one will be on you. I've watched way too many patients die from lung cancer, and, believe me, it's not pretty."

"You're right," he admitted finally. "It's a bad habit, but not one that can't easily be broken."

Then break it, she wanted to say, but decided to cut him some slack. Her head spun with confusion, frustration, and everything in between, while her heart pounded with smoldering desire. And, God help her, she no longer had a clue why she was on the deck of his boat or even what she intended to say next after having initiated such an ill-timed passionate kiss—stupidly passionate and right at the moment when she was furious at him.

"We have to talk," Aaron said.

Understatement of the year, she thought and plopped down on the bench, burying her face in her hands.

"Aren't you pleased that the threats against you are over?" Aaron asked, his voice gentle. He had squatted down to her level and was looking at her earnestly. He brushed her hair away from her face with his fingers.

Did he actually think she was crying? If so, how sweet, but she most certainly was not. Her posturing was more out of frustration. She moved her hands away and sat up straight. "Of course I'm pleased," she said, "but since this…this ordeal was supposed to have been about me, I'd like details. Who? What? When? You know what I mean. How did the people involved get caught? I want to know everything."

"I'll tell you," he said. "But first let's dispense with Zack. Afterward, I'll take you back to the inn myself."

She started to protest, but he stood up and went to the railing and yelled down to the man. She sat numbly as Aaron untied the tether line and Zack was soon off, roaring and zigzagging his way back to shore, probably eager to go out of fear that Aaron might shoot him.

Were his fears really so outlandish? Valerie's chill returned. When her arms had been around him, she'd distinctly felt the telltale outline of hard gunmetal. The man was packing some serious heat.

She stood up. "Before we start this conversation, could you get rid of the weapon?"

Without batting an eyelid, Aaron turned, reached back, and pulled the Beretta into view. He placed it on the bench.

"Jeez. Is that thing loaded?"

"Not much point in carrying one if it isn't," he said.

"Why do you find it necessary to carry a gun off-duty?"

"Why don't we stick to the subject you want to hear?"

She bit her lip. He had her so flustered that she was the one stalling and drifting off base. She walked a few paces away from him and leaned over the deck railing to stare into the water as though gathering strength from its undulating blue waves.

"The box truck that tried to run you down was stolen, so it couldn't be traced," Aaron began. "Anyway, we had the FBI set up a trap using a female agent who impersonated you, drove your car, and was living in your apartment. We had her and some friends bring fake cartons of books into your apartment."

"Interesting setup," Valerie said, still staring at the water. "Very sneaky,"

"Hardly ingenious," Aaron said. "The perpetrator was a rank amateur. Had he been a professional, you wouldn't be here talking to me."

She flinched.

He ignored her reaction. "Sure enough, soon after the books were brought in, someone broke into the apartment while our decoy was out. We allowed him to steal the fake books while surveillance took pictures. As suspected, he was Evan Michaels, a low-level drug dealer and boyfriend of Ms. Allard. The next day, after he realized the books contained nothing, he made an attempt on the life of our decoy."

Valerie turned to face him now. "How did he do that?"

"Late in the evening she went out to your car and he assaulted her, demanding that she tell him where the money was. The police surrounded him and he was ordered to surrender, but he went for his gun and was shot dead."

She squeezed her eyes shut and opened them again. "Did...did they really have to kill him?"

"Yes." His eyes narrowed. "Am I missing something here? Why should you feel sorry for him when he would have killed you without a second thought?"

"I realize that," she said slowly. "But it doesn't make the loss of a life—any life—less disturbing."

Aaron's eyes bore holes into her. "I wouldn't feel too sorry for him if I were you. It turns out that Evan Michaels was an alias. He was really Daryl Bennett, who was wanted on other charges, including second-degree murder, which occurred during the holdup of a bank in Indiana two years ago. A hard-working family man was the victim."

Valerie felt a bitter sensation rise in her throat and almost regretted that she had asked him for details. She remembered her days of trauma nursing at the hospital, the tragic, innocent victims, as well as the not-so-innocent.

"And Carolyn Allard knew all this?" she said, her voice stiff, hoarse, recalling chillingly the white van that had been parked in the driveway of the Allard home the day she and Jasmine had gone there. Could Carolyn have been inside, watching?

"She claims she didn't know everything," Aaron said, moving closer to her. "But she did admit to telling her boyfriend that her grandfather often hid money in books—something about a childhood game he used to play with her in order to get her to read. She claims she just wanted what she felt was rightfully hers, but she had no idea that Bennett would try to murder you. She also found out that he had a teenage girlfriend in Denver and that he was planning to run off and keep the money himself."

"Does Carolyn have a criminal record, too?"

"No. But she is a cocaine addict who worked as a short order cook at a local diner to make ends meet. She had recently lost her job. In other words, she desperately needed the money."

Valerie turned away again and stared back at the water, appalled that the granddaughter of her friend, the educated and elegant Gordon Allard, had been reduced to groveling for drugs and slinging hash at a greasy spoon. She suspected that some of what happened wasn't entirely Carolyn's fault. She had been damaged as a toddler by the head trauma she'd suffered in the car accident that killed her parents.

"I'm sorry if what I've told you is upsetting. Life often is," Aaron said.

She felt his hand on her shoulder, comforting somehow, saying more than his cynical words implied. This was exactly why he hadn't bothered to tell her, she knew. He had assumed she would react this way. Always assuming, and the worst part was, he was right. But she would not, could not wallow in sorrow over the ails of society.

"I'm okay," she told him.

He remained standing quietly beside her, and then lightly squeezed her shoulder. "I apologize again for being so presumptuous about your return home. Of course you have the right to stay as long as you want. And…" His voice caught.

She turned to face him, waiting, curious.

"You don't have to stay away from me if you don't want to."

"I don't want to," she said softly and kissed him, gently this time.

Chapter 7

With minimal coaching from the sidelines, Aaron allowed Valerie to pilot the speedboat back to shore. She seemed to enjoy being at the helm; that was fine because it gave him the opportunity to lie back on the rear seat and watch her.

He still felt her spontaneous kiss sizzling on his lips, smooth, sensual warmth against cool ice, so unique, so unlike any kiss he'd ever experienced before. He wanted her, no question about that; and that wanting, which was really more of a yearning, terrified him. She had no idea what she was doing to his pride, his image of tight self-control, isolation, and emotional detachment.

"We're getting close to shore," Valerie shouted to him. "Maybe you better take over."

He sat up straight. "Cut back on the throttle."

When the engine calmed to a purr, he climbed over the seat and they switched places. He guided the boat into docking position at the pier and cut off the engine. Valerie smiled, an exhilarated almost childlike smile of pure delight. "That was fun."

"Wait till I teach you how to fly a plane."

She laughed. "No way. The sky is strictly your territory."

"You'll enjoy it," he insisted, balancing nimbly on the bow of the wave-rocked boat as he tied it to the dock. He turned and coughed a few times, spreading the dull ache in his chest, feeling vaguely annoyed that his body wasn't conforming to its usual high standards.

❧

Incredible how an intelligent person can be so stupid about his own health, Valerie thought, taking note of Aaron's coughing spell. She had enjoyed piloting the speedboat, true, but she had an ulterior motive as well. She wanted to give him a brief chance to rest because his sporadic coughing, along with a certain world-weary expression, disturbed her. Still, despite her concerns, the man now dressed in a black oxford shirt, gray khakis, and deck shoes moved as sure-footedly as a gymnast.

He extended a hand to help her out of the boat and she took it. When they were both standing on the pier, she looked at him intently. "Aaron," she said slowly. "Instead of going right back to the ship, why don't you stay on shore for a while?"

He studied her without blinking. *Gosh, those eyes. Wait a minute.* Had that sounded like a proposition… a call to something more intimate than she was prepared for? Why wouldn't he think that after her overly passionate kiss?

"I'm worried about you," she said, and then added quickly, "You look a little tired."

He blinked. "Guess I didn't sleep much last night."

"You weren't in pain, were you?" She reached up and touched his forehead; he felt ominously warmer than he should have.

"No. No pain."

Valerie's eyes narrowed. He probably wasn't being completely honest. "You've got a temperature check coming when we're inside."

He didn't argue with her, and she was grateful for that. Perhaps he thought he'd pushed her buttons enough for one afternoon, and he realized now that she wasn't the type who'd just cave in—definitely not when her bossy nurse side took over.

Back at the inn, Valerie took her medical bag and followed Aaron to his room, which was adjacent to hers. This room was just that, a room and a shower with no amenities and no terrace. The basic surroundings pleased her because they did not convey romantic illusions.

He sat on the edge of the bed, waiting. The thermometer revealed what she suspected—a fever. Not extremely high, but 101 couldn't be ignored. She took silent note of his temperature and then performed the stethoscope routine, whereupon she frowned in concern upon realizing that his lungs didn't sound as clear as they had the last time.

"Have you been doing anything else you're not supposed to, besides smoking?" she asked, trying to temper the sarcasm in her tone.

"Yes. I've been having intimate liaisons with every woman over the age of twenty-one in Belize. When I'm not doing that, I can be found hanging out at the bars drinking myself into oblivion and generally partying all night long."

She didn't want to laugh, but she had to. "Be serious," she said.

"What makes you think I'm not being serious?"

She rolled her eyes. "Because I know you're not."

"You think you know me, do you?"

The truth hit her. She really didn't know him at all. All she knew was the image she had built up in her head, along with whatever bone he had tossed at her. She had passionately kissed an attractive stranger and had not only been out on a boat in the middle of the ocean with him, she was now with him in his hotel room. These things alone constituted questionable behavior for any woman who considered herself a serious Christian—a serious Christian who didn't wish to compromise herself. But somehow, their strong physical attraction notwithstanding, she inwardly knew and trusted that Aaron wouldn't take advantage of her vulnerability.

She pulled up a chair and sat facing him. "You're right. All I know about you is what you've chosen to reveal. But none of that matters because right now I'm concerned as a nurse. I did see a clinic here on Caye Caulker, and I believe you should pay a visit to it today."

"Why?"

"Because adults don't run fevers for no reason. You probably could use another round of antibiotics. I'm assuming that you stopped taking your prescription way too soon."

His silence told her she had assumed right. Like a lot of patients, he had stopped taking all of his medication the moment he'd felt better.

"All right, I'll go," he agreed. "But later. I'd like to sleep first."

"Sure. You have exactly two hours. If you give me your key, I'll come back and wake you."

He merely shrugged, surrendered the key, and stretched out on the bed. Once again he had allowed her to issue a command without asking permission.

Upon returning to her own room, Valerie silently congratulated herself for resisting the urge to pay too much attention to him. She didn't have long to pat herself on the back, though, because the ringing phone distracted her. Knowing immediately who it was, she picked it up.

"Are you all packed?" Jasmine asked.

Valerie smiled slyly. "I will be in about a week."

"A week? Hasn't Aaron told you the investigation is over?"

"He did." *Boy, did he ever,* she thought.

"Valerie." Impatience radiated in Jasmine's voice. "You're not talking."

Valerie laughed aloud at her friend's frustration and realized that she was acting as evasive as Aaron, which couldn't be a good thing. "Listen up. You know how I've always been talking about taking a vacation and so far have never gotten around to it?" She didn't wait for Jasmine to comment. "It's actually beautiful here in Belize, and since I haven't seen very much of it, I'd like to spend a little more time here before coming home."

Jasmine sounded uncertain when she said, "So you're doing the tourist thing?"

"Sort of. But seriously now, don't you remember what my other mission was?"

"You told me the other day that Aaron was fine," Jasmine said.

"I did, didn't I? Well, today I'm not so sure. He's running a fever and he's got an appointment with a clinic doctor to check it out."

"Oh."

"*Oh.* Is that all you have to say, Jas?"

"Of course not. By all means, make sure he's well, but be careful. And now I'm going to really bug you

93

and say what I've always been saying. Don't get too close to him. He's big trouble and then some. Are you rolling your eyes, Val?"

"They're about to fall out of my skull."

"You'll lose them completely, along with your mind, if you seriously mess with that man. I don't care how handsome or charming he might be. He's got way too much lethal stuff going on."

Valerie sighed. "I hear you loud and clear, but rest assured, I'm neither naïve nor stupid."

"Of course you're neither of those things. You're worse. You're in love…or is that lust?"

"That's a total exaggeration. Sure, we both know I've had feelings for him for over two years, but I'm not in over my head."

"Just about," Jasmine said. "You want to hear why I think so?"

"No. But I'm sure you're going to tell me."

"Yes, I am. I know you're in over your head because you haven't asked about your mother yet."

Valerie almost dropped the phone. Normally her mother would have been the first person to come to her mind. She considered it for a second. "Has my mother asked about me?"

"Well, no…not in words."

"My point exactly. I'll be back home as soon as I'm sure Aaron is well."

Aaron dreamed he was out on the sea in a small dinghy, unarmed, defenseless, and trying to escape a posse of armed Somalian militia. Fear did not register, only a distinct sadness that his life dangled by a thread and he had never taken the opportunity to savor the aesthetic things, like the dewy mist rising from the mountains, the scent of rain, the songs of birds, the sensual rhythm of a woman's walk, all those things, plus the bitter knowledge that in the end it was always the easiest missions that got you.

He felt old, tired, and resigned. Then the gunfire rang out. Strange, a whole fusillade of bullets hit him and he didn't feel a thing, until out of nowhere materialized a doe-eyed young woman, barely an adult, with satiny smooth skin and silky black hair, who lay in his arms bleeding all over him. As he worked feverishly to stop the flow of blood, he realized he couldn't, because there were too many holes. He tried to comfort her, to console her, even though he didn't know how—even though he knew she was already gone. His eyes were swollen with something akin to tears, tears he could never release because once the floodgates were open he'd never be able to contain the raging sea.

Stillness took over, the waves ceased to rock and his stream of consciousness went black.

"Aaron, can you hear me? Wake up. Aaron, are you okay?"

The voice, taut with emotion, didn't register. Through half-opened eyes, he saw white light and blinked several times before hazily realizing that he was face-down on a bed and the plushy rectangular object blocking his vision and nearly suffocating him was a pillow. What he couldn't quite comprehend was the human touch, the undeniably feminine hands stroking his back—the warmth of her fingers radiating through the cotton material of his shirt. The touch was way too gentle to attribute to a stranger, and at the same time too wonderfully different to be the result of any fleeting intimate liaison. Where was he? What was she doing? And why did he want to wake up?

"Aaron, come on, honey. Open your eyes. The clinic. Remember? Before it closes."

Honey? And with that, he turned around so abruptly that Valerie didn't have a chance to remove her hands, which now ended up flat on his bare midsection, exposed by his unbuttoned shirt. As her face came beautifully into focus with its darkly shimmering almond eyes and softly curved cherry lips, a feeling of disorientation and surprising vulnerability overtook him. He reached up and before he was even completely aware of his own actions, he pulled her down on top of him and proceeded to cover her face with feverish, passionate kisses.

"Take it easy, baby. It's okay. It's okay," she whispered, not resisting, not struggling to get free, but merely accepting his condition.

When he realized what he was doing, Aaron released her awkwardly. "Sorry," he murmured.

"Shhh. It's okay." She traced her finger lightly over his mouth before she carefully rolled off him and sat on the edge of the bed.

"Has it been two hours already?" he asked hoarsely, attempting to recover his dignity, but his voice sounded foreign even to his own ears.

"Three, actually." He heard her exhale a sigh of relief as her hand rose to touch his forehead. "You feel cooler. The rest probably helped. Can't imagine how you could sleep facedown like that, though. Wasn't it uncomfortable?"

"Not really." He certainly didn't want to replay the death of the innocent girl again—a dream that hadn't recurred for years until now, but he longed to resume the sprawled-out, facedown position just so he could feel her hands stroking his back once more. "Maybe we can forget about the clinic," he said.

"Sorry." Her voice was firm. "You're not off the hook."

He sat up, rubbing his eyes. "I knew you would say that."

"I'm glad I didn't disappoint you."

It bothered him that she had been able to enter the room without his hearing her and awakening immediately. That had never happened to him before, because his deeply ingrained sense of awareness was normally so acute that he could hear even the quietest of footsteps outside the door.

Mercifully she didn't fixate on his perceived lapse into weakness, but she stepped back and gave him privacy while he vanished into the bathroom to freshen up. When he was ready, they walked to the clinic, which was only a block away. Dusk was starting to settle and the sun, a molten orange ball, hung low in the sky.

The clinic doctor ordered a chest X-ray and blood work performed. The results wouldn't be known until the next day, but the doctor said he would consult with Aaron's physician in New York, which satisfied Valerie because she knew everything was being done correctly. Aaron was prescribed antibiotics as a precautionary measure and reminded repeatedly that he had to continue with them until he was told to stop.

Afterward, they had dinner at a low-key restaurant specializing in Italian food.

"What are your plans for tomorrow?" Aaron asked, making direct eye contact.

"Hmm. Not sure, but you are going to do absolutely nothing but chill out and relax."

Aaron's expression did not change. "What are you going to be doing?" he asked again.

Valerie didn't want to plan anything. Just hanging out and being able to keep tabs on him was good enough, but if she did that she'd probably be intruding on his space and wear out her welcome.

"Maybe I'll take one of the tours," she said. "Cave tubing sounds like fun."

"Cave tubing?" Aaron repeated. "Do you know what's involved with that?"

She laughed at his raised eyebrows. "It involves floating down a river through underwater caves in an inner tube. I've read the brochure, and I really do have a spirit of adventure. Surely you're not taking me to be all prim, proper and civilized?"

Aaron smirked. "Civilized, maybe, but prim is hardly how I'd define you."

Not quite sure how she should take his remark, Valerie traced a finger over the rim of her wine glass. "How *do* you define me?" Uh-oh. Why did she ask that? She wasn't ready to hear what he might say.

"As a woman who definitely knows what she wants, but isn't quite convinced that she should be desiring such things. A woman who has spent most of her life struggling to conform to values society has placed upon her, and—"

"Stop," Valerie said, pushing the wine glass aside. "I know it's my fault. I asked you, but I'm just not...not in the mood to look at myself in the mirror."

He shrugged, still maintaining the disarmingly direct eye contact. "Well, if cave tubing is what you want to do, make sure you go with Danny Perez. I'll give him a call when we get back to the inn."

Incredible. In just a few seconds and with just a few words, the man had laid her out under the microscope, seen the core of her inner drama, and without missing a cue had zeroed back in on their initial mundane conversation. *Okay*, she thought, *so be it. I can play this game, too.*

"Danny Perez is a friend of yours?"

"Yes. More accurately, he's a friend of my son. He runs the best and safest tour group."

Always looking out for my safety. If he had been any other man, his protectiveness would have been irritating, but coming from him she felt irrationally flattered that she warranted his concern.

She wanted to ask him more about his son, but if she were to do that it would sound like prying and he might turn the conversation back to his assessment of her. She simply did not want to mess up the little bit of headway she had made with him regarding his health issues. Maybe when he was completely well, they'd get to have a more in-depth conversation.

When they were finished eating, Aaron paid the bill, as he had done on previous outings, dismissing her offer to do it. He was so traditional in that he always opened doors and pulled out chairs for her, and even though his countenance reflected stoicism and aloofness, he always said please and thank you to service people and tipped well.

When they were finished eating, Aaron paid the bill, as he had done on previous outings, dismissing her offer to do it. He was so traditional in that he always opened doors and pulled out chairs for her, and even though his countenance reflected stoicism and aloofness, he always said please and thank you to service people and tipped well.

Darkness had settled as they returned to the inn. Aaron needed to go back to the ship to get some things, but he decided they could wait for the morning. The clinic doctor had given him a shot and, between that and the wine, he felt sluggish and not in the mood for the hassle. He was content to just call it a night.

As he unlocked the door to his room, he glanced over his shoulder at Valerie and realized that he would be even more content to end the night with her in his room, in his bed.

"Goodnight, Aaron," she said, hesitating ever so slightly before moving to her room.

"*Lailah tov*," he said in Hebrew. And they both made long, distinct, deliberate eye contact—both sharing the same thought, yet neither willing to admit it.

Chapter 8

Valerie woke with a start and on her way to the shower, noticed a note under her door. Frowning apprehensively, she picked it up, wondering what Aaron had pulled on her this time. He could very well be on a plane halfway around the world while she had been sleeping.

She was relieved when she read that he had gone out to *Saniyah II* to get some supplies and would be back shortly. He also mentioned that he had contacted the Perez tour guy, who would be expecting her at the port in Belize City by nine o'clock, which gave her roughly two hours. The water taxi from Caye Caulker took almost forty-five minutes. She would have to hurry.

By the time she'd showered, managed her hair into an upswept ponytail, dressed in casual shorts and sneakers, and packed a swimsuit, she was just about ready; she would be completely ready if she weren't worried about Aaron. She desperately wanted to see him before leaving and would be furious if he decided to remain on the boat.

"Valerie." His voice sounded outside the door.

Good man.

She opened the door. He stood there in a black T-shirt and olive-colored khakis, looking much more rested than he had the day before.

"I see you got my note," he said, appraising her in the obvious way only a man could. "Make sure you bring along the insect repellant and use it liberally. There have been cases of malaria in the rainforest areas."

"I have it," she answered, resisting the urge to salute and say *yes, sir*.

"Whenever you're ready," he said.

She looked at him, momentarily confused. "What do you mean? You're not going…"

"On the tour, no. I'm taking you on the boat to Belize City to meet with the group."

"No. I don't *want* you to do that. I'm going to get the water taxi and you're going to spend the day right here on Caye Caulker in peace and quiet."

"But…"

"Oh, no, you don't." Her voice rose. "We had an understanding last night, and if you don't agree to do what I asked, then I'm not—"

He placed his finger lightly over her lips, silencing her. "Go get the water taxi," he said. And at the same time, his free hand went around her waist, drawing her close to him. Mesmerized, she didn't object, and as his finger trailed away from her mouth to trace the contours of her neck, he tilted his head down and kissed her, slowly, provocatively, almost indolently, on the mouth.

Don't stop. Don't stop, her heart cried out while her face flushed and her legs turned to jelly. But her hands went up, first sliding across his chest, and then planting themselves firmly there as a barrier. "Umm, Aaron, you're going to make me miss my connection."

"I'll give you a better connection."

"Aaron, please." Talk about lust; she even loved saying his name.

"Don't tell me you didn't enjoy it as much as I did," he stated huskily, releasing his grip, the wry, almost smug expression back on his face.

She had no response. What could she say to the obvious? Her reason for still being in Belize was because, God help her, she cared about him, maybe even loved him, but she was not there to make love to him—certainly not senselessly, without knowledge, trust, or commitment.

"Did you take your medicine yet?" she asked abruptly. *Now how sexy was that?*

"Yes, ma'am," he replied, amused.

"The doctor said he would call you in the afternoon to give you the test results. Make sure you get that call and…"

"Valerie, go. Have a good time."

Cave tubing was more fun than Valerie had expected. Danny Perez and the four other guides leading their party of twenty, consisting of couples, kids, and senior citizens, were above and beyond accommodating. The young Mayan knew his job, and he was an expert on the environment.

After a trek through the rainforest and the guided float through the caves, everyone was taken by bus to the Sonrisa Bar & Grill for a buffet lunch. The lunch proved even more interesting for Valerie, who had selected a lone table near a window.

Danny, who was short, sturdy, and very Mayan in appearance with a long black ponytail, came over to where she was and wanted to know if she'd had a good time. She told him she had and then he sat opposite from her and started to talk, telling her that she was a special guest because she was Aaron's friend.

"How did you get to know Aaron?" Valerie asked.

"I first met Mr. Weiss when both his son and me were fourteen and I liked hanging around the docks watching the ships come and go. That summer I fell in love with a schooner called *Saniyah*."

Valerie agreed that the boat was still beautiful and waited for him to continue the story.

"*Saniyah* was in port and I met Drew on the docks. Thought he was this rich, snooty American kid, but he turned out to be different. He told me he was spending the summer sailing with his dad, and since I was so crazy about the boat, he invited me onboard to look around." Danny smiled reflectively. "Talk about an awesome experience for a poor kid living in the ghetto section of Belize City. I also got to meet the captain."

"Captain?" Valerie said.

Danny grinned. "Drew used to call his dad Captain 'cause the dude always has this cool, kind of commanding look."

Valerie laughed in spite of herself. "Tell me about it."

"Turns out he wasn't the kind of father who tells his kid not to hang out with certain types, so Drew and me got to be really good friends—so good that when they were going to sail out to Costa Rica, the Captain went to my place and asked my mom if I could go with them."

"Did she let you?"

"Yeah. No one cared what I did. My folks were poor, and I was just another mouth to feed. Anyway, I had the time of my life on that cruise. Even got to be second mate, working on the ship right along with Drew and his father like I was part of their family."

Valerie's eyes narrowed. "Was Drew's mother ever around?"

"No. Drew had a stepfather. He told me that his mother and the Captain were never married."

Valerie breathed an inaudible sigh of relief. Danny had confirmed the truthfulness of Aaron's statement regarding his past. Even better was the revelation that Drew's mother was married to someone else.

"We went to Honduras, Nicaragua, and Costa Rica," Danny continued. "I learned a lot about sailing, and so much stuff it would take all night to tell the stories." He glanced upward. "Drew and me did get into trouble sometimes, too."

"What kind of trouble?" she asked.

"One night the Captain had some business in Costa Rica and Drew and me knew he wouldn't be back for a while, so we decided to take the ship out to a nearby port so we could meet with a bunch of girls." He chuckled. "Real stupid on my part 'cause the girls always wanted Drew, not me. Anyway, we had these fake IDs and we went to this bar pretending we were eighteen and we got totally smashed. Worst part came when we tried to sail back drunk. *Saniyah* ran aground on some rocks and was damaged."

Valerie shook her head in dismay. "That was a *terrible* thing to do. You both could have been killed."

"Yeah, it was bad. The Captain, man, he was pissed and blamed it all on Drew, even though I said it was my fault, too. They got into this really big row about drinking and being irresponsible. Drew was kinda angry anyway on account of some family stuff that made no sense to me. But you know, you get stupid sometimes when you're fourteen.

Anyway, he started cursing and throwing things and calling his father an evil bastard. Got all crazy like, and the Captain hit him, knocked him clean across the deck like he weighed two pounds." Danny laughed. "You know Captain's a big dude, but Drew wasn't no little kid, either. He was at least six feet at fourteen."

Valerie flinched, not liking the sound of what she'd heard. "Aaron hit his son?".

"Yeah, but not with his fist. More like open-handed, and Drew asked for it. I mean, I would've never talked to my father like that, and my old man wasn't worth crap." Danny laughed again. "Turns out it wasn't no big deal, though, 'cause next morning they both acted like it never happened and Drew and me did all the repairs on the ship ourselves."

Men, Valerie thought. The mental picture of Aaron really incensed and smacking his son wasn't something she'd care to witness for real, though. Of course, Danny could have exaggerated.

"I was disappointed they didn't come back the next summer," Danny said. "Didn't see them again for two years, and by then my whole life had gone down the tubes and my old man got killed in a car accident."

"I'm sorry to hear that," Valerie said softly.

"He was drunk," Danny added wryly. "Soon after that I quit school and started hangin' out with guys selling drugs. I got arrested and went to jail for a year.

When I got out, no one would hire me, so I started getting in trouble again. Then Drew and his dad came back. Drew looked me up, and the Captain told me I had to turn things around and if I was willing to work and go back to school, he'd help me out. That's when I found out that he owned Avian International, and he got me a job as a freight handler at the airport. He paid me more than I was worth, but that opportunity saved my life."

Valerie liked that part. It felt good to hear confirmation that Aaron wasn't as stone cold as people seemed to think. "So obviously you didn't remain at the airport. What happened next?"

"On weekends, Drew and me and our girlfriends would go hiking through the rainforest and canoeing on the river. We started inviting the cruise ship tourists along…taking them out to the caves and all that stuff. The tourists loved it and were willing to pay."

"Nice," Valerie said. "And this was something you actually enjoyed doing."

"Yeah. And since Belize is my country and a lot of its economy is from tourism, the Captain said I could probably make a living doing this, and I liked the idea. He then taught me a lot of important stuff about running a business, and he loaned me the capital to get started. I also ended up studying about Mayan culture and ecology, which was tough, but worth it. Now I'm sort of known as an environmental expert and I've got

two of my brothers and ten people working for me."
He smiled. "Business is good."

"Sounds like you've got a lot to be proud of," Valerie said.

Danny was about to say something else when someone called him. He excused himself, rose slowly, and flashed a crooked smile. "Don't ever let anyone tell you differently. The Captain is a good man, the best." His eyes twinkled. "And just in case you happen to be his girlfriend, don't let the tough guy, I-don't-need-nobody bull scare you off."

Way too late for that advice, she thought wryly. She felt more attracted to Aaron than ever and scared, not of him, but of what she might do if she kept seeing him.

❧

Cadmium orange, yellow, a mixture of burnt umber, and purple. Aaron preferred acrylic paint to oil these days because it wasn't as messy. Shirtless, wearing only a pair of shredded jeans, he stood on the terrace of his former room, now Valerie's, and stepped back to study the canvas. The beach at dusk had not taken long to create at all. He had capitalized on the present Belizean sunset, a mélange of smoky mauve and red fire, but the darkened sandy shore he'd created from his head, since there was no significant beachfront on Caye Caulker.

The painting seemed to have almost conceived itself, and as he studied it he realized there was an aberration apparent in the silhouetted form of a lone woman strolling by the sea. Normally he did not paint people—preferring vast landscapes undefiled by human bodies—but this subliminally sketched woman was not disturbing or defiling anything. This shadow of a female who distinctly reflected Valerie's proportions blended right in with the landscape, accepting her environment and her solitude.

He sat down on the edge of the lounge chair and rubbed his eyes. There had been only one other time he had painted a woman, a girl actually, and that was when both of their lives had been driven by youthful passion and no foreknowledge of what tragedy lay ahead.

Slowly the room and the painting blurred into a kaleidoscope of muted shadows and light, careening wildly through days, and months, and decades—decades that led to the memory of a more recent lover, a self-assured, auburn-haired beauty named Tara, who'd been an undercover agent with the CIA. He hadn't seen her die. He'd been spared that one. Her end had come in a remote area of Afghanistan when a rogue agent had blown her cover. That loss had been felt, but not as deeply as the first. Unlike the first, Tara had not been innocent. She'd known the game, played it, and lost.

Where had the years gone? Had they raced desperately down teeming cobbled streets, dodged sirens and staccato gunfire, bled onto the shore, and been washed away by the sea? Had their passing been properly wailed at the ancient wall in Jerusalem, or had they simply been ignored, forgotten, and blown away like chaff in the wind?

Aaron rose slowly and removed the drying canvas from the easel. Valerie would probably be back at any moment, and it would be in both of their best interests if they maintained a measure of distance—not miles apart, but enough so human nature wouldn't get out of control and they wouldn't end up doing something he definitely wanted, but neither of them intended. He carried the painting and some of the equipment back to his room.

He had gotten confirmation from the clinic doctor that he had developed an infection, but it had been caught in the early phase and all he had to do was continue the antibiotics and avoid strenuous activities.

A half hour after he had reclaimed his own meager space, there was a knock on the door. Aaron pulled a T-shirt on, resisted the urge to pick up his Berretta, and placed a hand on the doorknob. "Who is it?"

"Me, Valerie."

Of course he had known that, but it never paid to be careless, even while in Belize. He opened the door, allowing her to enter, but she remained in the doorway amidst the noise of other hotel guests entering their rooms, her hair tousled, her face glowing with tropical rainforest health.

"It's getting late, so I'm not going to disturb whatever you're doing," she said. "Just wanted to let you know that I had a good time on the tour and…" She hesitated for just a split second.

"And?" his eyes narrowed.

She laughed, and he liked the bordering-on-amused, slightly sarcastic sound of it. "Don't be so brusque," she said. "People tend to take it the wrong way when you don't let them finish a sentence."

A faint glimmer of a sly smile curved his mouth. "Should I care about these so-called people?"

"That depends on whether you wish to be offensive or not. But right now you need only care about the one who is standing at your door."

"And?" he repeated, folding his arms across his chest.

She shook her head. "You are truly impossible. Did you hear from the doctor?"

"Yes."

She jutted her chin and glared at him, her ebony eyes fiercely mesmerizing. "And? And?"

Aaron studied her, knowing full well he was breaking his own rule again. "It would be much easier to talk if you would just come inside and sit down. I believe I've already established that I'm not going to bite."

Rolling her eyes, she reached out and gave him a gentle but persuasive poke in the ribcage, nudging him out of the doorway. "Neither of us bites," she said entering the room, "but we do kiss quite ardently, and we both know exactly why we should stay out of each other's room."

She noticed that the TV was on even though he probably hadn't been watching it. He sat on the edge of the bed and she sat on the chair facing him, crossing her legs, aware that he was monitoring her every move.

"Now that you've finished luring the fly into the web, what about the doctor?"

He related what the doctor had said and finished by thanking her for insisting that he go. "Tell me about your day," he said.

It was agonizing for her being in such close quarters while entertaining amorous thoughts. To make matters worse, Aaron stretched out on the bed, feet crossed at the ankles, arms folded behind his head. A relaxed, seductive pose if ever there was one. "If you're tired and want to go back to your room, I'll understand," he said, apparently oblivious to what his body language was doing to her. "It's just that I've spent an entire day doing very little that could be considered productive, and I'm not handling the downtime well."

She started talking then and he did listen, his navy blue eyes not piercing in their usual confrontational way, but meeting hers at the right moments, his aesthetically pleasing eyebrows arched to perfection.

"I never realized just how much the Mayan culture influenced Central America," she babbled on enthusiastically, and then stopped upon noticing that his eyes were closed and his breathing even. Instead of being irritated, she felt a bizarre warmth spread over her. There was something ingratiating about gaining his trust to the extent that he would lower his guard and actually fall asleep in front of her. How boyishly vulnerable he looked.

Valerie rose quietly, leaned over him and brushed her lips lightly over his clean-shaven jaw, a kiss that was not lustful, but genuinely affectionate. She covered him with the blanket that lay at the foot of the bed and tiptoed out of the room, locking the door behind her.

Chapter 9

During Aaron's convalescence, Valerie came to know Caye Caulker and most of its people on a first-name basis. In fact it disturbed her to realize that the country opened up to her more than Aaron did. She was even offered a job at the clinic, which she considered flattering, but she knew she could never leave behind her place of birth and what remained of her family.

When he was well enough, Aaron took her out to see the Mayan ruins at Altun Ha, without benefit of a tour guide. None was needed because he was a wealth of knowledge and he explained all the geological and architectural wonders.

As the days rolled by, they spent the time visiting many places of interest. Once on the way back to Caye Caulker from Belize City, Aaron chose the long route and flew over the area known as The Blue Hole, giving her a plane's view of the marvel of nature. It appeared exactly as he had painted it—a huge indigo circle like a giant eye in the center of the aqua sea.

By the time the week was up, Valerie was agitated at having to return home. She still knew no more about Aaron than what others had told her, because even though she had given him plenty of opportunities, his conversations had been all about the aesthetics of geography and nature—nothing personal at all.

Sunday evening, Valerie started packing. A mechanical coldness settled over her as she sifted through clothes that were strewn all over the bed. She'd had to pick up additional luggage since she was taking back more than she'd arrived with, mostly worthless touristy junk, a few arts and crafts, and gifts purchased for Jasmine's kids.

The prospect of returning home to two million dollars should have been exciting, but it wasn't. In her opinion, it was blood money that she shouldn't have received in the first place, and she had no idea what she was going to do with it.

Aaron's last MRI had confirmed that his lungs were clear. His improvement probably meant that he wouldn't be staying in Belize much longer, either, and that he'd most likely return to New York or go off on another one of his top-secret missions and get killed. Yes, she was angry, furious, in fact, and she knew it was partially her own fault because she hadn't exactly opened up to him, either, feeling that her life was too boring to talk about.

She glared at a swimsuit, a skimpy white bikini that belonged on the body of an anorexic eighteen-year-old, not a top-heavy thirty-something with too much caboose. Why had she purchased the thing? She balled it up and threw it at the door just as it opened and Aaron, perfect reflexes and all, caught it.

"Sorry," she said, without looking at him. "I thought the door was locked."

"I knocked but you didn't answer." He dangled the offensive garment on one finger. "Have you worn this yet?"

"No. It's not for me," she lied.

She turned, sauntered over, and snatched it away from him, and then went back to what she had been doing. Rude, but she didn't care. He could think what he wanted.

"You're packing," Aaron said, helping himself to the chair nearby.

"You noticed," she replied, forgetting to ask him why he'd come to her room in the first place.

"I didn't realize you were going so soon."

"Can't stay here forever."

"Would you?"

"Would I what?"

"Stay if you could?"

"Of course not. I don't know anyone here."

"Except for Noah and Jasmine and your cousin, who do you know in New Jersey?"

She clenched her teeth, crumpled up two T-shirts, and crammed them into the suitcase.

"Aren't you going to fold them?"

"You're messing with me, Aaron." She slammed the suitcase shut and whirled to face him. "I *hate* it when you do that."

"Woman, I haven't even begun messing with you." He rose to his full height and abruptly pulled her into his arms.

Before she could wrestle herself free, the grip became a locking one, his strength so apparent she would have been completely helpless had he been an enemy. But he was not an enemy, and she knew if she really wanted him to let go he would.

"Tell me why you're so angry," he said.

"I'm not angry."

"Prevarication isn't one of your virtues, but suit yourself. Maybe you'd like to know why *I'm* angry."

His grip had not loosened, yet she felt some of her own combative tension drain. "I didn't realize you were. Why are you angry?"

"Because I'm not ready to let you go."

"I, um…" She stumbled over her words. "I guess I'm surprised to hear you say that." *Boy, what a twit.* She rarely stammered, and now here she was doing just that. "I'm not ready to let you go, either," she admitted finally.

"Good, we've reached common ground. So, what do you think of marriage?"

Her breath caught. She simply could not believe the turn the conversation had taken, the words that had come out of his mouth. "I think," she said slowly, "that in most cultures there is such a thing as engagement first."

"I'm not into customs and I don't do engagements."

She blinked. "Aaron, what exactly are you saying?

"Marry me, Valerie, here in Belize."

Speechlessness combined with numbness overtook her. A wild impulsive part of her wanted to throw all common sense out the door and say yes, but how could she? She had already had one ill-conceived marriage, and if she made another foolish mistake, she wouldn't even be able to blame it on youth.

"Have you lost your mind?" she asked him, realizing even as she said it that the question was too harsh, too cold.

He released her then, so abruptly that she nearly stumbled backward. Somehow she made it back to the bed and sat down while he paced around the room like a caged panther.

She inhaled deeply. "We can't…nobody gets married just like that. There are too many things I don't know or understand about you, and you don't really know me, either."

"I do know you," he said bluntly. "And I'm willing to tell you some things about myself."

She had a zillion things she wanted to know about him, but her mind fixated on his staunch statement regarding his so-called knowledge of her. "What do you *think* you know about me?"

He stopped pacing and began to recite as if reading a fact sheet, or, worse, a newspaper obituary. "You were born to Joel and Ruth Redmond in Middletown, New York, where you spent most of your childhood and went to school. Your father served honorably in Korea and extended his tour of duty for six years. He later resigned from the military and became a minister. You have an older brother, Greg, a corporate lawyer living in Chicago. He's married with two children. You went to college briefly in Ohio, but returned home when your father died and, soon after that, married a much older man. The marriage ended in divorce after a year. You returned home and transferred to a local college, where you took up nursing. Your mother is …"

"Enough," she said coldly, rising, ready to show him to the door. "You know statistics about me. Everything and nothing at all. Do you also know the name of the person I was married to?"

"Yes."

"Are you going to tell me his name?"

"Apparently you don't want me to."

"How did you find out all that stuff? Surely Jasmine didn't tell you." She yanked the door open wide, hoping he'd take the hint and leave. "No, wait…that's right, you have all these resources, these ways of invading a person's privacy without even asking permission."

Aaron did not move from where he stood. "I'm sorry you're offended. It's just standard procedure. When I was looking into the Allard case, I had to know a few things about you, too, in order to rule out suspects."

"You could have just asked me."

He remained silent for a few seconds, and when he spoke the mechanical tone to his voice was gone, and his pitch was lower, more emotive. "You're right. I should have asked. It just never occurred to me at the time. I'm sorry."

Valerie realized what she already suspected, that he was a man who rarely asked others for permission to do anything, and in the last few days he'd probably apologized to her more times than he'd ever apologized to anyone in his entire life. On that basis alone, she wanted to forgive him, but she was having a hard time handling everything that had been thrown at her in the last few minutes. What she really wanted to do was shove him out the door, lock it, and then get back to him in an hour when her head stopped spinning and her heart rate had returned to normal. But he clearly wasn't going any place on his own, and, unless she started screaming bloody murder, there was nothing she could do except deal with him.

"It's late," she said, trying to sound calm, hoping he'd take the hint. "We both need to think."

Aaron, who had started pacing again, stopped and moved closer to her. "Perhaps you're right about me losing my mind. I've not only lost it, but maybe I've misjudged you as well."

"Meaning?"

"What I said earlier was ridiculous. We don't have to get *married*. We can still be together without making that commitment."

"No!" She raked her fingers through her hair. "You haven't misread me at all in that regard. If I believed in no commitment, you and I would have been all over each other the first time I kissed you. The issue here is why won't you do an engagement so we can get to know each other better?"

He jammed his hands in his front pockets. "Because we both know that an engagement will give us time to think, and if we do that I will consider all the reasons why I never intended to marry and the engagement will be off."

Better to break an engagement than a marriage, she thought lamely. But, yes, the words were spoken and there was nothing romantic or intriguing about the truth—the cold, brutal truth, and now they had arrived at an impasse with no way out. Valerie avoided looking at his eyes, sat back down hard on the bed, and laughed insanely, deliriously, because it was better than screaming.

"Valerie, stay just a little while longer. A week. Three days." Aaron sat down beside her. "I'll try to answer whatever questions you might have."

Why couldn't he have just volunteered the information two or three days ago when they were relaxed and at peace? But no, he had to wait until the atmosphere was heated and volatile. "I can't discuss this anymore...not tonight," she said firmly. "I need space."

His arm slid around her, and she started to pull away, but the gesture was conciliatory, consoling. He caressed her shoulder lightly, his touch smooth as silk.

"Tomorrow morning," he said rising slowly. "We'll go for a sail on *Saniyah II*, and I won't take no for an answer."

The night stretched on endlessly. Wearing only a long T-shirt, Valerie slipped out of the bed and wandered toward the terrace. The balmy sea breeze welcomed her as she slid the screen doors open and stepped out into full view of the amber moon, which stared blatantly, luminously, and deviously at her, its leering visage reflected perfectly in the somnolent blackness of the sea.

Already she knew she'd go sailing with Aaron, for despite his arrogance and cynicism, there were many good things that she did know about him—things she'd gleaned from her own observations and things she had been told by others. Sometimes the truest portrait of a person came from their friends and associates. She'd heard that, as a very young man, he'd flown fighter jets for the Israeli Defense Force. She also knew that he was generous, heroic, fiercely protective, and loyal to those he called friends. Jasmine's husband, whose life he'd saved more than once, would readily attest to that.

Harrison Porter didn't even deserve to crawl in Aaron's shadow. Just thinking about her ex made her flush with embarrassment and humiliation. She had been so young and naïve back then. The marriage had dissolved in a year immediately after she'd suffered a miscarriage and had been told by doctors that she would never be able to have children.

After years of obligatory dating, attending church socials, and everything in between, she had never felt anything beyond brotherly affection for the other men who'd flitted in and out of her life. Only when she was around Aaron did she feel passionately alive and open to all possibilities. She absolutely owed it to herself to stay in Belize a little longer.

Chapter 10

A gentle tropic breeze caressed the sea, billowed the sails, and caused the graceful schooner to surge forward.

Standing on deck, Valerie recalled her magical childhood days on Rhode Island and the sheer delight of being on an open body of water, riding the waves, becoming a part of nature far more powerful than any human—a part that compelled even the most rebellious to follow her commands.

Aaron knew these commands intrinsically. If he had not encouraged her to work along with him raising the sails, setting the ship in motion, she would have been content just to sit back and watch him handle the lines and rigging.

They were not going very far. He had told her they would be visiting one of several atolls that dotted the coast of Belize, but the destination was not important; it was the journey that mattered.

"You've somehow managed to maintain your sea legs over the years," he said. "Are you sure you haven't been out sailing since childhood?"

"I haven't," she admitted. "But some things you just never forget. Like riding a bike, swimming, or even your first love."

"Who was your first love?" Aaron asked.

Valerie laughed. "Never mind me. I want to hear about you."

He took his place at the helm as the boat sailed effortlessly now, caught on the breeze. "Where do you want me to start?" His tone was serious.

"Most stories start at the beginning," Valerie said slowly. "Jasmine told me you were born in Africa to a Jewish father and an African mother, and that your mother died when you were very young. Is that part true?"

"Yes. But I'll start with my father, David Weiss. Contrary to what some people think, Weiss is not a Jewish name, it's German. My father's people were German Jews from Munich, and most of them died during the Holocaust. My father and his older brother, Gabriel, survived because they were living in the United States with an uncle who'd immigrated long ago."

"How did it come about that your father and his brother were living with their uncle?" Valerie asked.

"His parents, my grandparents, didn't like what was shaping up politically in Germany. They sent both of their sons to live in the United States and they planned to join them later. They waited too long."

Valerie flinched visibly. "Could you tell me more?"

"My father's uncle was involved in the diamond industry, and he often traveled to the Middle East and Africa, taking his two nephews along with him. He later moved to Africa, and that's how my father came to be associated with Cielo Vista, which was pretty much ruled by Spaniards."

"You're referring to the Arias dynasty, Noah's people," Valerie said.

"Yes."

"My father grew up there, met and married my mother, and, after she died, he left Cielo Vista and went to Israel to join his brother, who'd moved there years ago. That's where I grew up and…."

"Wait," Valerie said. "Could you tell me how your mother died?"

"She died hours after giving birth to me," Aaron said emotionlessly. "I don't know the specifics because my father never told me, but I will say that Cielo Vista was very much a third-world country back then and medical standards were primitive. It was common for women to die from childbirth-related complications."

"I'm sorry," she said.

"Don't be. It happened a long time ago," he replied in an offhand way, indicating that he was ready to move on with his story.

"Is your father still living?" she asked.

"No. He's been dead for five years now, but you're jumping way ahead. My father married again, an Israeli woman. I was raised from the age of six on a kibbutz."

"That's sort of like communal living, isn't it?"

"Yes."

"Why didn't you live with your father and stepmother?"

"I chose not to."

"At the age of six? I didn't know six-year-olds were capable of making such decisions."

"I wasn't your typical six-year-old."

"Your father wanted this for you?"

"He agreed to it. He was away on business a lot, plus he had other children with his second wife, and she and I didn't bond very well."

Valerie was alert for any signs of emotion from him, but she saw and heard nothing.

"I suppose you then joined the military as soon as you were old enough."

"I didn't join. In Israel, military service is compulsory, but I learned a lot from it. I flew bombers when the country was in conflict with Lebanon. Not too proud of some of the events that happened there."

"I heard you were outstanding."

"As a pilot and a strategist, maybe, but I was not a good soldier. Soldiers take orders. I prefer to give them, and I hated that in following orders of others, far too many civilians died."

Nothing surprising about that revelation, she thought, *especially the part about not liking to take orders.*

"Why did you leave Israel and become an American citizen?"

"I didn't leave. I was deported."

She flinched. His words were as cool and emotionless as everything he'd said thus far. "You must have done something...or been accused of something pretty terrible in order to get deported from your own country."

"I almost murdered another soldier and I was accused of treason. The treason part wasn't true."

She sighed. "Why would you attempt to kill a comrade?"

"He murdered a girl I loved."

Finally, she saw it—a miniscule flash of emotion that appeared and disappeared so quickly from his face that she almost imagined having seen it.

"She was an American citizen of Palestinian origin who lived in New York with her mother and stepfather. It just so happened that on that day she was in Lebanon visiting her biological father and her uncle. The uncle, Abdul Aziz, was a PLO terrorist. She was innocent and had no clue what he was involved in."

Valerie could see the conflict even without hearing the rest of the story. Aaron was an Israeli soldier in love with a Palestinian girl. Romeo and Juliet of the Middle East. Their story could only end tragically.

"Our assignment was to take out Abdul Aziz, and I had no problem with that. However, I didn't know that she was there with him. She survived the rocket attack on their home, and while we were on ground patrol, she ran out. She called to me and I recognized her. Ben Levy of my commando unit shot her in cold blood. She died in my arms."

Valerie covered her mouth with her hand. "He didn't know. It was an accident."

"It was no accident. He knew she was innocent." Aaron took a deep breath. "He *claimed* she had a weapon and was going to shoot. He made it look as if he killed her to protect me. He also claimed later on that I was a traitor and a double agent for the PLO. It didn't help that I am biracial and that I look more Arab than Jewish."

"Why? Why would he do all those horrible things?"

"The short version is that Levy and I grew up on the same kibbutz and from childhood there was bad blood between us. He didn't think I should have gotten as far up in the military hierarchy as I did. According to him, I wasn't Jewish enough."

She reached out and touched his shoulder "I'm so sorry, Aaron. That's awful. I…I'm almost afraid to ask. What exactly did you do to Levy?"

"After the raid, which was considered successful, by the way, there was a victory celebration in some bar. I went berserk and nearly beat Levy to death. After he was down, I just kept beating him. It took nearly ten others to get me under control. Levy was in a coma for nearly a month and suffered some permanent brain damage."

Valerie remained silent for a long time, listening once more to the sound of the sails and feeling the motion of the ship cleaving the pristine waters. The violence appalled her. She couldn't condone what he had done, yet she could understand his raging outburst. "How old were you then?" she asked.

"Nineteen. My girlfriend was only seventeen."

"What was her name?" Valerie had an eerie premonition even before she asked.

"Saniyah."

And now she knew. He hadn't built a shrine to her, but he'd crafted a ship and set her free on the seas.

"Could you go back a little? How did you and Saniyah first meet?"

"I met her a year earlier in New York. We were both taking classes at NYU."

"So your meeting Saniyah was really ironic...I mean in a bittersweet sort of way. Who would ever believe that of all the people in New York, you, an Israeli, would wind up falling in love with the niece of—"

"A terrorist," Aaron finished. "Obviously the fates have a twisted sense of humor."

Valerie sighed. "You don't really want to talk about Saniyah, do you?"

"No. But my reason for not going into detail has nothing to do with grief over a long-lost love. In reality had she lived, I'm sure Saniyah and I would have drifted apart. It's just that I don't believe in rehashing events that occurred years ago." He squinted in the bright sunlight and put his sunglasses on. "When someone dies, tears and mourning won't bring them back. If I were to dwell on all the senseless tragedies I've witnessed, I would be locked away in a sanitarium babbling incoherently."

Despite the warm breeze, Valerie shuddered involuntarily. His words made her remember the agony she'd felt when she'd learned of her father's death.

"God remembers," she said. "He will bring all the innocent ones back."

Perhaps it was the effect of his sunglasses, but Aaron looked even more distant. "I suppose some take comfort in that belief."

"And you don't?"

"In their weakness, people are willing to suspend belief in logic and turn to the supernatural as long as it sounds comforting."

Valerie was appalled by his comment, and she definitely had a comeback, but she was in no mood to start debating religion with him, although she was sure her father would have had the perfect faith-based response. She almost heard his voice, and the voice, minus the agnosticism and the accent, sounded bizarrely like Aaron's. The realization rattled her.

"Have I lost you?" Aaron asked.

"No. It's just something you said. I started thinking about my own past. Nothing anywhere near as dramatic as what you just told me, but we all have our stuff."

"Tell me."

"Not now. This conversation is supposed to be about you, remember? We'll get to me later."

"Not letting me off the hook, I see."

"Sorry. So, after you were deported, you went to live in the United States?"

"No. I returned to Cielo Vista, because I was offered asylum there by the president, my father's old friend Diego Arias."

"Noah's father."

"Yes."

"He gave me a job in security during his ill-fated regime. I didn't stay in the position very long because he didn't let me do my job."

"Meaning?"

"I warned him over and over again that members of his own family were conspiring against him...that they were the most ominous threat to his government. Noah believed me and tried to warn his father, too, but he was just a boy. Diego refused to take us seriously—wouldn't allow me to do what should have been done."

"How did you know about the conspiracy?"

"During my IDF days, I learned a lot about surveillance and covert ops through connections with Mossad, the Israeli version of the CIA."

The scary stuff, Valerie thought. "Were you still in Cielo Vista when Noah's father was assassinated?"

"No. I got fed up and went to the United States to live. A few months after I left, Diego was murdered. As you know, Noah and two others survived because they escaped to the mountain area. Later, I was able to sneak them out of the country."

Valerie nodded. Jasmine had told her that part of the story. "How did you happen to get involved in the United States military?"

A wry smile crossed his face. "They got involved with me. First of all, I no longer work directly for the U.S. or any government, unless I choose to, but in the beginning there were certain people in high places who found my skills useful. I was offered an assignment that corresponded with a need that both the U.S. and Israel had. I found the terms agreeable. I was paid well, and because this assignment was carried out to their satisfaction, I was reinstated with Israel and I can return whenever I choose."

Valerie's imagination ran wild. She knew he wasn't going to tell her just what that assignment was, and she didn't even want to hear that he was some kind of mercenary or hired assassin. But if that indeed had been the case, there obviously had to have been some justification. Even though there were things she did not know about him, she couldn't see him as a cold-blooded murderer.

"I'm glad you were pardoned by Israel," she said, trying to focus on the more positive aspects of his revelation.

Aaron shrugged. "Not that it mattered. I haven't been back since."

"Not even to see your family?"

"No."

His response was so blunt that she had no desire to take it any further. Instead, she found herself wondering at what point exactly his son and his son's mother had gotten into the picture. She remained silent for a few minutes before asking.

"Were you living in the United States when you met your son's mother?"

"No, that happened soon after my exile to Cielo Vista. She was Connie McDade, a journalist from the United States who was there on assignment. I was one of the people she interviewed."

"Apparently you gave her more than an interview," Valerie said wryly.

Aaron's expression did not change. "I'll offer no excuses for what happened between us, other than we were both reckless and irresponsible. On my part the attraction was purely physical, and when it was time for her to move on to another assignment, I was ready to let go, even though she wanted to continue the relationship. She kept writing me after she returned to the U.S., but I never answered any of her letters."

Pretty cold-hearted, Valerie thought. *But considering the circumstances, not altogether surprising.* He'd still been very young, recently exiled—and, even though he'd never admit it, seriously rebounding from the loss of Saniyah.

When she offered no comment, Aaron continued. "In case you're wondering, Connie never said anything about being pregnant in those letters. We lost contact and I didn't hear from her again until eight years later. By then I was a citizen of the United States and working as a test pilot."

"She told you eight years later. Why? Was she looking for child support?"

"No, although I would have paid it. She had a decent paying job and she came from a relatively wealthy family. I suppose she reconsidered when she got married and her husband didn't want to legally adopt someone else's kid. Maybe she realized there might come a time when the kid would want to know who his real father was."

"How *thoughtful* of her." Valerie was appalled by the idea of a woman being pregnant and not even bothering to tell the father, even if that father wanted nothing to do with the baby.

Aaron smirked. "I was shocked to learn that I had a kid. Didn't know a thing about parenthood and still don't. Never wanted a child. But I did tell her that when the boy got older, if he ever came looking for me, that

I would at least talk to him and then he could make his own decision to reject me."

"That's so cynical and assuming."

Aaron merely shrugged. "He did come looking, and much earlier than any of us expected. At eleven, his mother told me he was rebellious and causing all kinds of problems in her blue-blood society and she said that he wanted to see me."

"In what part of the country were Andrew and his mother living?"

"South Carolina."

"My mother came from South Carolina," Valerie said. "Totally different worlds, of course." She realized she had interrupted him just to say something trite. "Never mind. Please go on."

"As it turned out, I had a summer off from assignment and was spending it in Miami renovating *Saniyah II*. I was planning on alienating that kid so badly that he'd be all too eager to go back to his mom and behave himself. Instead, we bonded."

Valerie smiled, imagining how aggravated Aaron must have been dealing with an eleven-year-old. "I take it Andrew turned out to be a lot like you."

Aaron guided the helm slightly to the left. "Noah sums it up best. He says the seed didn't fall far from the tree, it just landed in better soil."

Valerie laughed openly. "That sounds like Noah."

"Drew continued living with his mother and stepfather, of course. No way he could live with me, but we spent a few more summers sailing together."

"Danny Perez mentioned something about those summers," Valerie said.

Aaron's eyes narrowed. "Did he, now? Danny always did talk too much."

"Don't blame Danny. He couldn't help being impressed, considering his relationship with his own father."

"Despite what he might have told you, my relationship with Drew is nothing like a storybook relationship. We respect each other, true, but we also keep a respectful distance…a healthy distance. It works for us."

They were rapidly approaching a small strip of land and Aaron had begun trimming the sails while she automatically moved to the helm, amazed by how quietly, how subtlety in sync they worked. She wondered if he was as aware of their joint precision as she was.

"Bannerman's Caye," he announced. "One of the most remote atolls you'll ever come across."

She didn't care about Bannerman's Caye. She wanted him to continue talking, but at the moment *Saniyah II* was between them and demanding his attention as only a jealous lover could.

Chapter 11

Powdery white sand stretched out before them as they trudged further inland, heading for the shade of the clustered palm trees. Because of the reef and surrounding rocks, they had taken an inflatable motorized dinghy to the most accessible part of the shore.

Aaron carried the cooler containing the lunch that they planned to have on the deserted island.

"Who owns this spot?" Valerie asked, scanning the horizon.

"The Belize government. Environmentalists and divers visit on occasion, but tourists rarely come out here. Nothing to interest them."

And so here she was, alone on a deserted island with the man she'd been pining after for two long years, and the only thing they intended to do was talk and eat. Could it be possible that Aaron had set her up deliberately, knowing that very few women could resist such a setting? She busied herself with the food in order to avoid looking directly into his eyes, lest she see something presumptuous and diabolical lurking there.

Being in such close proximity to each other and in such a relaxed environment, Valerie could no longer avoid looking into his eyes. First, she studied him as he half reclined, his upper body partially propped up by his elbows. Breathtaking. She swallowed hard and moved her focus up, and what she saw in his eyes both unnerved and allured her. In place of the cold, hard edge, she saw warmth and passionate desire.

"Aaron, what are you thinking?"

The wistfulness in her tone seemed to shake him out of his reverie. "The same thing you're thinking," he replied.

Valerie shook her head incredulously and laughed. "That's exactly what I was afraid of. Perhaps it's time to abandon paradise."

"Why? We don't need anyone's permission to enjoy the moment."

"That's true to a degree, but we are accountable for our actions. I'm not interested in regrets later."

His eyes studied her in that now-familiar intense way, and for a moment she saw a glimmer of humor lurking. How could he possibly find what she'd just said funny?

"So, then, you have no more questions about my life?"

His abrupt return to their earlier discussion, the reason for the outing in the first place, almost made her laugh with relief.

"I still have more. Let me think a moment. Let's see. You and Noah own one of the largest courier services in the world. Jasmine told me how the company got started but…" She hesitated for a moment, trying to gather all her thoughts. "You have alluded to your military back-ground, but how involved are you right now? What were you doing when you got shot?"

Aaron glanced at the sky. "We're known as trouble-shooters. A team of us were in Somalia when we came under fire. I was shot while trying to protect someone who had gotten careless. Other than that, I can't go into detail."

She frowned, exasperated that he wasn't going to tell her the exact purpose for the mission in Somalia. "Well, were you able to save this person?"

"Yes."

"And that's all you're going to say about it?"

"Yes. But I won't hide it from you that Avian Interna-tional has another branch, which operates secretly under a different name. Some of its backing comes from U.S. security forces and international special interest groups." He paused as though censoring his words. "Myself and the men involved are engaged in rooting out terrorists and doing what we can to maintain a level of world peace. Sometimes if our goals are the same, we work along with the CIA, Mossad, and others, but again I'll emphasize, they do not own us. More specifically they do not own me."

"That's mind-boggling. How can any organization do such a thing as maintain world peace?"

"We can't, but we do try, and while we like to think of ourselves as the good guys, it often depends on what side of the fence you're sitting on." He took a deep breath. "We don't always win, but someone has to speak and act for those who are powerless…those who have no voice."

She flinched because she wanted badly to say that the One who created the universe would one day act for the meek, the humble, and the downtrodden, but again, the timing wasn't right. Her duty was to keep quiet and listen. "And you're still actively involved in this organization?"

"Not as active as I once was, and I'm seriously considering retirement, at least from field agent status. Noah and I have enough to do just running the commercial end of Avian International."

Valerie wondered if he heard her sigh of relief when he said that. Of course she wanted him to do much more than just consider retirement, but at least what he'd said was a start down the right road.

"It's your turn to talk now," Aaron said.

Her turn to talk? She was still absorbing everything he'd just told her, and anything she might say positively paled in comparison to just one tiny episode of his life. She stretched and smiled wanly. "What could you possibly want to know about me? Yesterday you pretty much summed up my whole life in five seconds."

"Ahh, but you told me that those so-called five seconds were statistics. For starters, why did you marry a forty-year-old college professor when you were only eighteen?"

She groaned inwardly. "I was afraid you were going to ask that. And for the record, he wasn't forty."

Aaron ignored her reticence. "He was thirty-eight. A moot point, don't you think?"

His bluntness still disconcerted her, but she might as well get used to it. "My reasoning at the time was incredibly stupid," she said slowly. "I suppose I can begin by saying that I was really close to my father, and when he died so suddenly, so unexpectedly, I felt lost. And if that wasn't bad enough, no one seemed sympathetic to my pain. Friends and family were all telling me that I would have to leave college and come back home to take care of my mother, which was the last thing I wanted to do. Harrison Porter was a sympathetic friend and he asked me to marry him. I saw it as an excuse to remain in Ohio."

Aaron studied his wine glass. "Couldn't you have made the decision to stay without marrying?"

She sighed. "I could have, but guilt made it difficult. You see, I figured if I had my own family and lived in Ohio, no one would expect me to make all those sacrifices."

"So why did your mother need so much care? Surely she didn't have Alzheimer's back then."

Valerie clenched her teeth upon hearing that he knew all about the Alzheimer's, too. "No. She didn't have it then. But my mother was…was…How do I even begin to explain her? She was the most helpless, weak, clingy person you'd ever want to meet. She couldn't make even a simple decision without asking my father, and whenever my brother and I needed something, she always told us to ask him, too. If the house needed repair and my father couldn't do it himself, he was the one who had to call the plumber, the roofer, whatever, and he always had to be at home if business people came in the house." Valerie paused, annoyed by her own revelation and hoped Aaron wouldn't want to hear more.

"Why?" he asked, disappointing her.

"Because...because she was nervous around strangers. She didn't even want Greg and me to have friends over...not that we would have anyway, since she embarrassed us. The only friend my mother didn't mind having around was Jasmine. She was just so weird. Even when we had problems at school, my father was the one who had to go speak to the teachers and whatnot."

"Go on," Aaron said when she hesitated.

"I really don't want to bore you with this nonsense." Valerie twined her fingers through her hair. "I'm not a teenager anymore, and I know that there are no perfect families."

"If I were bored, I would be asleep by now," Aaron said.

Valerie sighed. "My mother wasn't a mother. I never understood her. She was always telling me not to do certain things, but she never explained why. Do you realize that it was my father who told me the facts of life...my father who explained to me the things a mother is supposed to tell a young girl. My God, Aaron, whenever I asked her something she always looked at me with this vapid expression. If a head of cabbage had an expression, that's how she looked, and she'd say, 'Ask your father.' No. Not like that, she was from the South and she had this really obvious Southern accent. She'd say 'Ask yuh fahthuh.' " Her voice rose. " 'Ask yuh fahhhthuh…ask yuh fahhh— ' "

She stopped because he was laughing and she hadn't even been aware of how melodramatically she'd been speaking. Her first reaction was embarrassment that he was making fun of her, but then she realized it was the first time she'd seen him laugh outright. His deep baritone chuckle along with his blazing smile, was so incredibly sexy it took her breath away and she had to laugh, too.

"You've got a bit of the actress in you," Aaron said.

"I tend to get carried away when it comes to discussing family dysfunctions," she replied, trying not to stare at him because her attention had suddenly focused on a silver dog tag dangling against his chest. She fought the urge to reach out and grasp it.

Aaron sat up straighter and the tag slid mercifully from sight. He glanced out to sea at the boat rocking on the waves. "And so your marriage ended in a year. Who divorced whom?"

"It was a mutual divorce, actually. No hard feelings. I know now that I didn't love him, and he just married me to have children. After I had a miscarriage, it was over."

"The fact that you even got pregnant is amazing considering that the man was gay," Aaron said.

Oh, God, he knows that part, too. "More specifically, he was bisexual," she said, embarrassed but trying not to convey her emotions. "And I didn't know that when I married him."

"I never suggested you did," Aaron said.

Valerie fought to control a grimace as she remembered that a few years after the divorce, she'd learned that Harrison had moved in with his same-sex partner. "Look, it was humiliating, okay? And you seem to know the whole story anyway."

He shrugged. "So after the divorce you ended up returning to your mother's house."

"Yes. I left Ohio University, gave up my dreams and went to a local community college and became a nurse."

"Was becoming a nurse such a bad thing?"

"No. Just the fact that I let circumstances get in the way of my original goal."

"Why *did* you go back home when your mother managed to survive a year without you?"

"She didn't survive on her own," Valerie said ruefully. "Her sister Marilyn was going through a divorce and she came to live with her during that time. Aunt Marilyn is nothing like my mother."

When the conversation finally lulled, Aaron shaded his eyes with his hand and gazed out to sea. "It's time to go," he said. "There's a boat coming, and I'm not interested in company."

Valerie didn't see anything beyond the endless blue, but she helped him gather their things and they made their way back to *Saniyah II*.

Once she was back on land and alone in her room, Valerie wondered why Aaron's first question about her personal life had been about her sham of a marriage. There were so many other things he could have started with. Could it be possible that he was concerned over whether or not she had actually been in love with Harrison Porter? If that was the case, he definitely had nothing to worry about.

But there was no point in trying to analyze him because caution and common sense had eluded her. He was the most unique person she'd ever met, and good or bad, right or wrong, she knew there was no way she was ever going to be able to simply return to her life without including him in it.

Jasmine had left a message on her cell and Valerie felt guilty that she didn't want to hear from her right now. The truth was she did not know exactly what to say. How was she going to logically explain the constant delays in her departure from Belize?

"Get a grip," she mumbled aloud. "You're a grown woman who doesn't have to give an explanation to anyone."

She knew Jasmine had good intentions and that her warnings about Aaron actually did have some validity, but her best friend simply refused to acknowledge that she could feel the same intense desire for Aaron that Jasmine felt for her own husband, Noah.

Sometimes God allowed disparate people to come into each other's lives for a reason, and no way was she going to just turn aside and let her window of opportunity slam shut, even if the person at the window had led an extraordinarily harrowing life and faced a precarious future. She was convinced that Aaron Weiss was redeemable, that he wasn't some crude, calculating warmonger, but a human being with needs, wants, and vulnerabilities, a man who maybe could use a little joy in his life. She recalled his captivating smile and his laugh. He didn't reveal that side often enough, but maybe she could encourage it.

Yes, he could be her diamond in the rough. With a little refinement and polishing, the possibilities were delectably endless.

She listened to Jasmine's message.

"Val, if you don't get back to me tonight, this is the last time I'm calling because I'm headed for Dallas on business tomorrow. You'll probably be back before I am. Your mother is all right and I had your car fixed. Oh, and your brother called me because he couldn't reach you. I told him you were on vacation in Belize, but I didn't give him any details. You might want to call him. *Ciao.*"

Her brother called? This surprised her because, aside from a holiday greeting card, she hadn't heard from Greg in nearly a year. She keyed Jasmine's number and waited until she responded, sounding slightly out of breath.

"Valerie?"

"Yup, it's me. What are you doing? You sound winded."

"I was playing with Diego, kind of chasing him around the house to get him to bed."

Valerie laughed, visualizing Jasmine's overly energetic stepson. "You said Greg called you. Did he say or give any indication what he wanted?"

"No. He didn't sound upset or anything, if that's what you're worried about. Call him. Maybe he's just realizing that he hasn't heard from his sister in a while."

"I'll call him when I get back home," Valerie said nonchalantly.

She thought about how she and her brother, despite his being much older, had been very close as children, but around his late teen years, when he was about to go away to college, he'd had a mysterious disagreement with their father and went on to alienate himself from the whole family, including her. The cold war lasted several years until Greg met and married ex-beauty queen Lisa Allen in Chicago. He'd felt no guilt whatsoever about leaving his sister with the total responsibility of their mother, so why should she be so quick to get back to him?

"I guess you're still not ready to come home," Jasmine said, sounding a bit cautious. "And don't worry, I'm not going to give you any more unsolicited grief about Aaron."

"Thanks for that, and I'll definitely be home by the end of this week."

"I'm holding you to that."

❧

Aaron had opted to spend the rest of the night on the boat. He sat on the deck watching the swells in the black water. He welcomed and embraced the solitude and distance, even though the alien being who'd possessed his heart wanted to be as physically close to Valerie as possible. He definitely needed this night out on the water to think.

From the first day he'd met her, Aaron had known that Valerie spelled trouble. For over two years his clandestine line of work and deliberate avoidance of her had made his heart accept the reality that he should remain single, but the week and a half spent in close contact with her had given him more than a glimmer of what he had been missing, especially now that he was ready to enter a different phase of his life, a more sedate and less harrowing phase that did not directly include a group called Global Defense Force.

Valerie had nearly torn down his wall of resistance and made him desire what he'd never desired before, namely warmth and companionship from another human being. He thought about the way she had mesmerized him on the private island with her understated, earthy beauty—beauty made even more apparent because she seemed so casual about it. He'd wanted to reach out and pull her body close to his—to possess her heart and soul and to lie there devoid of all physical and mental restrictions, the two of them sated, at peace, and breathing as one.

However, even though he considered his desires a weakness, he was becoming convinced that as long as she held no romanticized illusions about married life, and she agreed to a few rules, they might actually work as a couple. If she said yes, the steel doors that had slammed shut around his heart just might swing wide open, leading him into emotionally stormy skies, uncharted waters, and a set of challenges perhaps even more daunting than his current lifestyle.

Chapter 12

Valerie and Aaron had breakfast together at La Isla Café and afterward took a leisurely stroll through the town and ended up in an isolated, serene area overlooking the ocean. The sun had barely risen and was still in a vivid orange phase.

"Gorgeous," Valerie said.

Aaron sat near her, perched on a rock. She marveled at his handsome, chiseled profile. The early sun cast an interesting glow on his surprisingly long eyelashes, making them appear gold-dusted. Unable to resist, she reached up and lightly brushed her fingertips against his closely cut dark hair, tracing the precise line of his sideburn; the hair felt as smooth as velour. His hand closed around hers, gently urging it back down to her side where it belonged, but he did not release it. She felt the spreading warmth of his touch and wished they could just remain the way they were indefinitely.

"Valerie, this is the last time I'm going to ask you," he said.

She bit her lip apprehensively. "Ask?" she repeated, although she knew full well what he was going to say.

She wanted to hear it, yet feared the moment all the same.

"If you'll have me, I want to marry you this week in Belize."

Have you? I'd have you in a heartbeat, Valerie thought, but the words stuck in her throat.

She had researched Belizean laws and knew that it was possible for them to get married without much hassle at all. They could be husband and wife by the end of the week.

"There are rules," Aaron continued, while she stared straight ahead as though distracted by the sea. "Not too many, but nevertheless we can't function as a team without them."

Here come the prenuptials, she thought. "Go on," she said, finding her voice.

"Do *not* think that once we're married you'll be able to change my personality. If you can't accept me as I am right now, we don't belong together."

Guilty, Valerie thought. She did like and accept who he was, but surely some refinements and adjustments in personality would be acceptable. Everyone made compromises whether they chose to admit it or not.

"And there will be no children," he said adamantly. "And no unrealistic expectations about—"

"You don't have to worry about me having children, since I can't," she interrupted, trying to temper the hollow sarcasm in her voice. "But maybe…and I certainly don't mean anytime soon…would you consider adoption?"

"No."

And that was all he had to say. No elaboration as to why not. She squeezed her eyes shut. At some point in her single life, she had toyed with the idea of adopting a child, but it had been just that, toying. His ultimatum wasn't impossible to live with. If she ever felt the need to hear youthful laughter, there were other people's children that she could borrow from time to time. And Jasmine was going to have a new baby.

"You told me that you had a miscarriage when you were married to Porter," Aaron said. "But why did that permanently determine your inability to conceive?"

Valerie found his question jarring and invasive. But she realized that he had a right to know, and so she forced herself to get over it. "At the time of the miscarriage, I discovered that I had a bleeding disorder called Von Willebrand's."

His eyebrows rose. "Similar to hemophilia?"

"Sort of, but nowhere near as serious. I'm not in danger of bleeding to death from a paper cut or a needle puncture. It's a problem only if something traumatic happens or if I need surgery."

Aaron was silent for a second. "You had a potentially life-threatening bleeding episode during the miscarriage?"

"Yes," she admitted. "And the doctor told me I shouldn't have any children. The surgical procedure they performed resulted in scar tissue and made me unable to conceive."

"How many doctors have confirmed this?"

"Confirmed what? My inability to conceive or my having Von Willebrand's?"

"Both." Aaron's expression had a concentrated, disturbing intensity that Valerie couldn't quite read.

She clenched her hands together. "At least three. Aaron, don't look so serious, I'm a nurse, and I know the ramifications of this disorder. I told you...I'm perfectly healthy. I just can't bear children and I shouldn't chop off any fingers, toes or whatever."

His brow furrowed. "Unusual that you discovered the illness as an adult. How did you manage to survive childhood without any physical trauma? What about needing stitches from maybe falling off a bicycle, or what about having tonsils removed or dental surgery?"

"I had plenty of such incidents, and I did bleed a lot, but those episodes never turned into emergency situations, so my parents thought nothing of it. I mean, let's face it, some people do bleed more than others."

"I suppose that is true," he said.

Their discussion of rules and health issues had definitely taken a disconcerting and unromantic turn. "Can we get back to what you were originally talking about…unless…" She hesitated. "Unless my so-called *disease* has changed everything."

"It hasn't changed a thing," he said. "My other request is that you never betray my trust or enter into this alliance with any illusions that you are somehow going to be able to convert me from agnosticism to Christianity."

She flinched. *Enter into this alliance?* Was marriage a business agreement to him? But she remained silent, focusing on the latter part of his request. Somehow she could not believe that an intelligent man could refuse to acknowledge a divine being, but still she saw some hope in that at least he had not declared himself an atheist.

Aaron released her hand and stood up straight. "I'm no knight in shining armor. I'm set in my ways, and my lifestyle would not work for a clingy, needy woman, which you fortunately are not. Even if I do resign from espionage, my job with Avian will take me away from home a lot."

Valerie nodded numbly. She was well aware of all the things he'd just said, and thus far he hadn't mentioned anything that completely turned her off; also, to his credit, he hadn't even mentioned prenuptials, which she'd anticipated to be one of the major issues, since he was a wealthy man.

"Are you finished?" She rose now and stood beside him, nudging him with her elbow. When he said nothing, she breathed a sigh of relief that she wasn't going to have to go into a coldly rehearsed speech about how in the event of a separation, she had no intention of demanding anything that didn't initially belong to her.

"Are you finished?" she repeated.

Aaron nodded.

"Good." She inhaled sharply and moved around so she faced him, making direct eye contact. "I don't want to hear anything else you have to say because I have some rules, too."

There it was—that sly glimmer of a smile creasing his face. "What are your rules?" he asked.

"The first one is that you quit smoking, and I don't mean just limiting it. I mean completely."

The sly smile remained. "Not a problem. I smoke only when I'm bored."

"Then I'll have to make sure you're never bored. Secondly, I'm aware that you're not a believer, but you must never ridicule or belittle my faith." She took another deep breath. "While it wouldn't be fair for me to demand that you leave the espionage business immediately, I will highly encourage you to not just think about it, but seriously, seriously consider retirement." She reached for his hand and he offered her both of his. "Aaron, I'd like to be your friend, your love, your confidante, but don't expect me to be your doormat, the little woman, or the silent mouse who never questions her husband's decisions or…"

Aaron released her hands and slid his arms around her waist. "Are you through?"

"Gotcha, didn't I?" she said. "Seems I have more rules than you do."

"Why am I not surprised?" He tilted his head downward and met her lips with his own. "Will you?"

She savored his kiss—warm and enticing like the early sunlight filtering down on them.

"Yes," she said. "Yes."

The marriage in the town hall of Belize City was private and involved no traditional celebration. Aaron and Valerie exchanged vows before a justice of the peace and did it all in the presence of two witnesses who were little more than friendly strangers—a Belizean couple and an employee from Avian International who Aaron knew casually.

When they drove away from the town hall, he wearing a dark business suit, and she in what amounted to a fancy cocktail dress. She felt as though nothing had changed and that they were both still single.

However, on their first night together in an expensive hotel suite in ritzier Ambergris Caye, Aaron quickly vanquished that notion and left her with no doubt what the newest phase in their relationship was about. They didn't leave their hotel room for the rest of the day, because their intimate moments soared well above and beyond Valerie's most vivid imagination.

His style of intimacy was confident, unruffled, and cool—completely devoid of self-consciousness and in stark contrast to the flaming passion he ignited in her. She loved everything about being with him, including waking up in the morning entwined in such a way that even their breathing seemed to be in unison. She was fire and he was ice. Together they sizzled.

Chapter 13

On Saturday Valerie flew out of Belize alone because Aaron had some business to finalize. He'd be joining her back in the United States in another week. The brief separation was good, since there were a lot of things that she needed to do alone, the least of which involved deciding what to do with the two million dollars, which now seemed to belong to her even less.

First she had to tell her family and friends that she was a married woman, and, yes, as she stepped off the plane at JFK, she truly did feel married. A fond glance at the flawless diamond on her finger confirmed it. At least Aaron hadn't dared depart from tradition in that regard.

Once she was in the airport lobby, waiting to be picked up by a limousine, she took out her cell phone and called Jasmine. "Hey, Jas, just thought I'd give you a head's up. Are you still in Dallas?"

"Yes. I'm in a hotel room, but I'll be leaving in the morning. I hope you're calling to tell me that you're back home."

Valerie smiled. "I'm in the lobby at JFK waiting for a limo to pick me up."

"Great! We've got to go out for dinner when I get back. So tell me, how was Aaron doing when you left him?"

"Are we talking about my Aaron?" Valerie smiled again. "He's absolutely gorgeous and terrific."

"What?"

"You heard correctly. I said Aaron is absolutely gorgeous and terrific."

Jasmine chuckled uncertainly. "Still not over him, I see."

"Nope. I'm afraid not. In fact I'm so *not* over him that we are now officially married."

"Married?" Jasmine laughed outright. "Valerie, stop messing with me."

"I'm not messing with you. Aaron and I got married in Belize."

Valerie heard Jasmine's cell phone drop to the floor and she laughed out loud, ignoring a crabby woman who glared at her as if she'd coughed without covering her mouth. She slid her own phone back into her purse, knowing that Jasmine would call later when she'd had time to recover. She looked at her watch and noted that it was almost five o'clock in the evening.

When Jasmine called again, Valerie was in the backseat of a limo, heading for her modest little apartment in Englewood.

"Val, I'm like so shocked, I don't know what to say."

"Well, it's customary to start with congratulations."

"Gosh, yes. I'm sorry for being such a jerk. Congratulations. Is...is Aaron with you right now?"

"No. I left him in Belize. He'll be coming home later. Look, I understand that you're shocked. Let's face it, so am I. When I went down there, I never dreamed I'd come back married. But you know this really isn't crazy at all. I've known Aaron...sort of...for two years. I knew he was the one from the start."

"You always did say that. But why did you have to do it that way? Couldn't you have waited and got married in...in church? You're my best friend, and Aaron is Noah's. We'd love to have celebrated with you."

Valerie sighed. "I would have preferred it that way, but forget about church or a synagogue. Aaron may be half Jewish, but he's not the least bit religious."

"Didn't you think about those differences before agreeing to—"

"Yes," Valerie interrupted. "Let's not go there, okay? When it comes to that subject, Aaron and I have agreed to disagree. We'll manage."

"I'm sure you will," Jasmine said, resigned. "You know, the more I think about it, this is starting to sound good. Just imagine how we'll be able to take vacations together, without worrying about spouses who don't get along."

"Yes," Valerie agreed enthusiastically.

"And don't get the impression that I don't like Aaron because that's far from true. He's almost as gorgeous as Noah, and he's definitely got my respect. He…"

"Okay. Okay. You don't have to say anything more. I've always known that you respect him. You just have a hard time seeing him as my husband."

Jasmine laughed. "Not as *your* husband, but as anyone's husband. So tell me. Where are you going to live? At his place in Manhattan?"

"Maybe for a short while." Valerie hadn't seriously considered that yet, but she knew that she did not want to make a home of Aaron's loft above Avian's corporate headquarters, no matter how elegant it might be. She definitely wanted a house, and she would have to discuss that with him.

"If you decide on building something new, I'd love to design a home for you two. How does a shipyard or an airport hangar sound?"

"Shut up. That's so not funny."

"Sorry. Just can't control myself. Truth is, I'm getting really excited now, and I sure hope you can convince the love of your life to have a reception of some sort. We absolutely must celebrate."

Valerie didn't want Jasmine to think that her opinion had that much significance, but in reality it did. She was relieved that her friend was now seeing her marriage positively and was expressing happiness for them. Aside from her Aunt Marilyn, there was no one else who mattered. Her mother would typically have no reaction to the news, and whatever her brother's opinion, it would be irrelevant.

She ended the phone call on a cheerful note, tipped the driver for carrying her bags, and stepped out of the limo in front of her familiar two-story garden apartment complex. She collected the mail from her box and moved quickly down the hallway. She unlocked her door, went inside, and looked around. The living room was as neat as the day she had left it.

But the longer she stood in the room, the more out of place she felt, and her thoughts drifted to Mr. Allard and his final days. What was it, three months ago? Four? She was a vastly different person than that woman totally dedicated to her job, but bored, cynical, and unfocused when it came to personal fulfillment.

Carolyn Allard, the wayward granddaughter who'd had every advantage in the world and chose to squander all her opportunities, was now locked up in the county jail, awaiting trial with no one who cared enough to bail her out. Despite everything she'd done, Valerie felt sorry for her and, weirdly enough, wished she could talk to her in order to find out for herself just where this woman's head really was.

But there was no time for dwelling on someone else's misery. The first thing she had to do was go visit her mother before visiting hours ended. After all, she hadn't seen her in three weeks. It didn't even matter to her that she'd get the usual blank Ruth Ann expression. She was too happy thinking about her new husband to have Alzheimer's rain on her parade.

❧❧

"Hi, Mom. Did you miss me?"

"Yes."

"Who am I? What's my name?"

Ruth Ann Redmond, a petite figure seated in her wheelchair, even though she could walk, looked vacuously up at her daughter and continued with her methodical knitting. If she wasn't knitting she could usually be found thumbing through the Bible and quoting scriptures out of context. What was she knitting this time? Valerie wondered. Her mother had already created countless blankets and mufflers since she'd been at Friedland Manor—ever since the staff had determined that her knitting needles were no harm to herself or others.

"What's my name?" Valerie asked again.

"Valree," Ruth Ann said in her Southern accent.

Well, that's a surprise, Valerie thought. Her mother had actually gotten her name right. Now if only she'd maintain eye contact.

Despite her state of mind, Ruth Ann was still an attractive woman who appeared to be in much better shape than most of the residents in the home. Her long silver hair was combed neatly back in a chignon and her fair, almost Caucasian-toned skin was as smooth as that of a woman two decades younger.

Because of her affinity for isolation, Ruth Ann had no roommate. If she wanted to be with the other patients, she would wheel herself out into the solarium to watch her insipid soap operas on the big-screen TV and then return to her room without ever having said one word to anyone.

Valerie had tried to make the room cheerful. Ruth had her own small TV set. There were bouquets of artificial flowers on the night table and cards and gifts from the grandchildren on every piece of furniture in the room. Greg and his family were very well represented in pictures, and there was also a prominent wedding photo of Ruth and Joel Redmond.

On the mantle facing the window there was a new picture of Greg's twin sons Kyle and Kameron, identical sixteen-year-olds, in hooded parkas, posing with their well-coifed girlfriends on the steps of what appeared to be a ski lodge. As she picked up the snapshot for closer inspection, Valerie remembered that she still hadn't called her brother.

"I see Greg and Lisa sent you a new one of the boys," she said.

Ruth Ann nodded, still focused on the knitting. Valerie pulled up a chair and sank into it. "In case you wondered where I've been, I just came back from

167

Central America, a country called Belize. I got married, Mom. My name is Valerie Weiss now."

There was just a slight hitch in the knitting pattern and her mother's lip quivered. "You can't get married."

"Why not?"

"You're too young."

Valerie laughed. "I'm far from young, I'm older than you were when you married Dad."

"Don't be silly, Valree. Only mature people should get married. You need to talk to your father about this." She began to hum tunelessly as she resumed her knitting.

Valerie flinched. She wanted to shake the bland look off her mother's face and scream that her father had been dead for a long time, but there was no point, so she rose wearily from the chair and picked up her purse. "Well, I'm glad you're doing okay, Mom. I have to leave now because visiting hours are about up. You'll be meeting Aaron very soon."

The tuneless humming continued, as did the knitting. Valerie said goodbye and left the room, stopping briefly for a bit of conversation at the nurse's station. Afterwards she went out to the parking lot and dialed Greg on her cell. She was surprised that she got him directly and was pleased to hear that he and his family were doing fine. Of course Greg expressed shock when she told him that she was married, and even more surprised that she'd married a wealthy entrepreneur. Valerie successfully deflected his unspoken questions regarding her sanity. As their conversation wound down, he asked, somewhat guiltily, about their mother, and promised that he would be coming up to visit soon.

The minute they said goodbye, Valerie's thoughts went to Aaron, and a blissful smile covered her face. She wondered what he was doing at this very moment in the place that seemed half a world away. She wanted to call him, but already she'd learned that he was difficult to reach.

Chapter 14

What a senseless waste of life, Aaron thought as he erased the recorded phone message. He had accepted that the Allard inheritance investigation was over, but a law enforcement contact had just told him that there was a new development in the case. He was certain this development had no dire ramifications for Valerie, but nonetheless he planned to catch an earlier flight back to New York to make sure.

He was back in his old Caye Caulker hotel room, the one Valerie had vacated. The bed was cluttered with business papers and a few essential belongings that he was transferring to a suitcase so they'd be ready when he flew out of Caye Caulker in the morning. He had just about everything packed when he was interrupted by a knock on the door, followed by a familiar voice.

"Hey, Aaron. You there?"

Only marginally surprised, he opened the door, permitting his business partner Noah to enter, and then resumed what he was doing.

"Checking out?" Noah asked.

Aaron nodded. "Soon. What brings you here?"

Noah smiled. "Charming as ever, I see. Anything wrong with my showing a little concern for a good friend?"

"Am I a good friend?" Aaron closed the suitcase and locked it.

"I suppose that's what you've been for the last… what is it? Twenty or so years." Noah inspected him. "I'm glad to see that you look amazingly well."

"What did you expect to find? Dead man walking?"

"Actually, yes."

Aaron ignored the remark. "So where did you come from?"

"Cielo Vista." Noah strolled to the kitchenette, opened the mini-refrigerator, and helped himself to the last can of beer. "Thought I'd stop off in Belize to see how you were doing and then head back home."

"How's Simon?"

Noah popped the tab on the beer, picked up a tattered boating magazine, and sat on the edge of the bed. "He's all right. Same old problem with the refugees."

"He's going to have to close the border and put a stop to it," Aaron said dryly. "One small country can't solve the problems of an entire continent."

Simon Baraka was the African country's first democratically elected president, thanks to the aid of Aaron and Noah. By all accounts, he was doing quite well. Still, there were a lot of problems, mostly caused by outsiders who were trying to escape war-torn neighboring countries.

"Forget Simon for now," Noah said. "Tell me about you."

Quick as a cobra, Aaron swiped the beer from Noah and walked to the desk in the corner to check the e-mail on his laptop. "There's nothing to tell. I've done enough time recuperating here, and I'll be heading back home tomorrow."

Noah scowled. "Really? And what have you done with Valerie? Is she still alive and reasonably sane?"

At the mention of her name, Aaron could not conceal the smile that briefly crossed his face, and of course Noah did not miss it.

"Whoa! What was that? Was that a smile, man? Uh-oh. Now I'm really worried."

"Valerie left this morning and she is fine, a lot finer than you're going to be," Aaron said.

Noah laughed. "Not sure I like where this is going. What have I done to incur your wrath?"

"It was your idea that she look out for me. What the hell made you think I needed a nursemaid?"

"Was either that or a coroner. Get over it, Weiss. A *sabra* you may well be, but you're only human. Everyone needs help sometime."

"Your help has cost me big time."

Noah's brow rose. "How so?"

"Because I now have a wife." Aaron assessed Noah's surprised expression. "That's right. Valerie and I are married."

Noah stood up. He had been aware of the obvious chemistry between his friend and Valerie, but in all the years he had known Aaron, the man had never expressed sentimentality, minced words or acted impulsively. Chemistry not withstanding, never in his wildest dreams had he imagined that the loner, the quintessential bachelor, would end up married. He controlled his shock.

"I'm aware that Valerie is an attractive woman, but were you delirious, in pain, drunk?"

"No."

"In that case," Noah spoke slowly, "since you're not irrational like the rest of us, you married her because that's what you intended to do, and she's obviously the one you wanted."

"I did want her…and knowing that she's not the kind of woman one can just have a long term affair with, I made it legal."

Noah grinned. "I hear you. Val's an amazing woman. Gotta be in order to love the likes of you."

"My only regret is the timing," Aaron said.

"Things like love and passion can't be timed. Congratulations, *compadre*." He gave Aaron a bear-like embrace and then stepped back. "So why isn't she still here? Did she realize her mistake and dump you already?"

Aaron smirked. "Not yet. We agreed that she leave ahead of me, seeing that I have a lot of things to do here."

"Is *Saniyah II* among those things?"

"Yes. I hired someone to check up on her. Plus, Andrew has a vacation soon. He's coming down with some friends, and they plan to take her to Aruba."

"Does Drew know his old man's married?"

"I e-mailed him."

Noah shook his head incredulously. Only Aaron would e-mail his son to tell him that he was married. He probably hadn't bothered to inform him that he'd been half dead a month ago, either. Still, for the atypical family that they were, it was not strange behavior.

"You planning on being back in New York for that stockholder's meeting?" Aaron asked.

"Yeah. Are you planning on weaseling out of it again?"

"Of course. Pomp and boardroom bull are your forte." Aaron closed the laptop. "Any word on that Comoros Island deal?"

"I think we're going to get the contract, but Salazar won't work with Dalton or me. He told me he'd wait for you before he signs."

Aaron frowned. "Meaning I'll have to fly down there and hold the little rodent's paw."

"Better you than me, my man. I don't have much tolerance for rodents. The seamier sorts all take a shine to you." Noah moved toward the door and then hesitated. "Aaron, I realize this contract is important to you, but no need to jump on it right away. Salazar has waited this long, another week won't hurt. You just got married and you and Val deserve some time together."

When Aaron said nothing, Noah decided to take the man's silent response as positive. At least he hadn't brushed off the suggestion in his usual offhand way.

〜❧〜

"Hello, is this...may I speak to Valerie Redmond?" an unfamiliar and very indecisive female voice said.

"You're speaking to her," Valerie said, trying to temper the sleep-hazed irritation in her tone. The caller sounded way too unprofessional to be heralding disaster, so she did not immediately react with alarm, even though it was almost midnight and she was in bed.

"I...I'm sorry if I caught you at a bad time. I mean, I tried to get you earlier, but I couldn't. I know it's late, but this is kind of important."

Valerie sat up straight. The stranger on the other end definitely had her attention now. "What is it?"

"I'm a friend of...well, not really a friend, but related to Carolyn Allard. She asked me to call you, but I've been really reluctant to do so until now."

The woman sounded as if she were either intoxicated or on the brink of tears. Valerie's irritation and resentment levels rose, but she remained calm and continued to listen.

"You probably don't know it…or don't want to know that Carolyn has died. She hung herself in prison."

A wave of vertigo swept Valerie, and she gripped the receiver tightly as the feeling gave way to confusion tinged with anger. "I'm sorry to hear that, but who are you and why are you telling me this?"

"Umm…my name is Martha Cates, and I'm the grandmother of Carolyn's son, who is living with me."

"Grandmother? Son? Mr. Allard never mentioned a grandson."

"I don't believe the old man knew about him, not that it would have mattered. But I'm telling you the truth. My grandson's name is Brandon, and he's eleven years old. Carolyn and my son were a couple when they were young. My son is…my son is in jail for life."

Valerie took a deep breath. "Ms. Cates. I'm sorry about all this. Really, I am. But I still don't see how any of this is my business."

"I'm sorry. I understand how you feel, and I really didn't want to call you but I had to. It was the last thing Carolyn asked of me. And…and maybe she would still be alive if I'd done it sooner. She told me that her grandfather left you some things that were supposed to be hers, including a large sum of money, and she needed those things for her son."

"Oh, I get it now. Of course this is about money. Why didn't Carolyn's grandfather know about the boy?"

"Carolyn said she never told him because he wouldn't accept him. You see, Ms. Redmond, we're African-American, which makes Brandon biracial. Carolyn told me that her grandfather was a racist."

"That can't possibly be true," Valerie said, her voice rising. "I'm African- American, too, and I knew Mr. Allard for a few years. He never once gave me such an impression. Sure, he was solid conservative when it came to politics and…" She stopped. Why was she defending Mr. Allard to a complete stranger who could very well be lying? The whole story didn't sound kosher. "Listen, Ms. Cates. You need to understand that I cannot have this conversation now. If you give me your number, maybe I will call you sometime tomorrow."

The moment of silence on the line indicated that the woman was disappointed, but she did give a number and an address.

Valerie scribbled the number and address down on a notepad. "Thank you. If I don't call you, do not call me again. Is that clear?"

"Yes, but—"

Valerie put the receiver down quietly. Oddly enough, she did not feel threatened by the intrusion, just disturbed and saddened...saddened over Carolyn's death and all the events and bad choices that had led to it.

Aaron was coming home to her place tomorrow, and she wondered if she should call him in Belize and tell him what had happened. After toying with the idea for a while, she decided that it could wait.

In the morning, after checking and responding to most of her backlogged phone messages, Valerie stared at the notepad where she had written down the information about Martha Cates. She had decided that she would not call her, but already her admittedly morbid interest in the tragic case of Carolyn Allard was out of control and her finger was itching to key in the number. It also didn't help that she still had no real idea what to do with the money that was stashed away in a safe at Jasmine's fortress home.

Valerie shoved the notepad aside. Right now there were plenty of other things to do, and her husband was her priority. She pulled on a thick down coat and stepped out into the frosty February air to take a trip to the supermarket because Aaron had said he would meet her at her apartment in the evening. He had given her the keys to his penthouse in Manhattan, but he was aware of her dislike for the city and hadn't insisted that they stay there.

She wondered exactly what locality they would eventually call home. She did know for certain that she wanted the house to be in the New York/New Jersey metropolitan area, maybe not far from Jasmine and Noah. Whatever the case, it was comforting to know that money would not be an issue.

While meandering down brightly lit produce aisles and dodging other shoppers with loaded carts—not one of her favorite ways to spend a morning—she realized that she didn't even know what Aaron's favorite foods were. Why hadn't she asked him last night over the phone? Here she was married to the love of her life and left with only her imagination to figure out what would appeal to him. Well, she did at least know that he liked beer. As for brand, she was clueless because they didn't sell the same type as in Belize, so she selected a German import because she liked the design of the bottle.

After purchasing enough to feed a small nation, she returned home and immediately set to work making pot roast, potatoes, vegetables, and a salad so the meal would be ready and she could heat it up in the microwave. She had decided to give her husband a break this time, but later she hoped to be able to cajole him into a healthier diet, meaning no red meat.

At noon, she took the fifteen-minute ride to Teaneck for an impromptu visit with her aunt, hoping to catch her alone. Aunt Marilyn had long since remarried after her divorce from Denise's no-count gambling-addicted father. Frank, her current husband, was a calm, amiable sort who had no destructive vices.

"Valerie, I'm glad you're back. How was your vacation?" Aunt Marilyn asked, hugging her the minute she stepped into the living room. "Frank's working and Denise is away."

"My vacation was great," Valerie said, secretly pleased that her cousin wasn't home and aware that her aunt knew zilch about the circumstances surrounding that vacation and very little about Aaron.

Marilyn was what most people would call a handsome woman who bore no resemblance to her daintily pretty sister Ruth Ann. In fact, anyone seeing them together would never think they were even related. Marilyn was much taller, browner skinned, and fuller bodied. If anything, Valerie thought she resembled her aunt more than she did her own fragile mother.

As they sat sipping tea in the sunny kitchen of the modest split-level home, Valerie let her aunt do most of the talking. Most of the conversation was about goings-ons in the church and Denise and her so-called plans for a wedding.

"So, are you still intending to stay with private practice, or are you going back to the hospital to work?" her aunt asked.

"I definitely won't be going back to work for any hospital," Valerie said slowly. "Private duty is less restrictive. Actually, I may not have to work ever again, but I'll probably choose to."

Aunt Marilyn clinked her spoon in her teacup. "Surely you can't be serious. You're much too young to retire."

And at that point, Valerie informed her aunt that she was married. Aunt Marilyn reacted with surprise, of course, but she had learned that she couldn't control her own daughter, let alone her niece, who'd always had a sound mind and usually knew what she was doing. She told Valerie that Aaron sounded like a real catch and that she was happy for her and couldn't wait to meet him.

After leaving her aunt, she went to the nursing home to visit her mother, insuring that she and Aaron would have the whole evening uninterrupted.

As she got out of the car, pulling her scarf tighter around her neck against the arctic air, she had the strange feeling that she was being watched. Puzzled, she looked around, but nothing seemed unusual. She shrugged off the feeling and entered the building through the wide-swinging automatic doors.

Once on the third floor—the one she referred to as *The Twilight Zone*—she settled down for another dead-end conversation with Ruth Ann, who wasn't knitting this time but sitting in the solarium with two other women. One was muttering to herself, and the other seemed to be staring in a stupor at the large screen TV where a talk show host was cheerfully introducing her next guest.

Valerie had been sitting there for almost an hour when there was a tap on the open door. Expecting to see an aide, she gave a start when she saw Aaron framed in the doorway. Dressed in a belted black leather jacket and black pants, he appeared as tall and impressive as ever.

"Aaron," she exclaimed, the shrill timbre of her own voice surprising her as she rose immediately and went to him. They embraced, she without reserve and he in his cool way. She sensed by his quick release that her husband was not too keen on public displays of affection.

"Mother, this is Aaron, my—"

Valerie stopped in mid-sentence because her mother had turned away from the TV and was actually getting out of her chair. Not only was she getting out of the chair, but also her eyes were alive and gleaming. "Joel!" she cried. "Joel, where have you been?"

"*Mother*," Valerie said, mortified at what was transpiring. Until now, her mother had never, ever mistaken any male visitor for her husband. In fact, since she'd been diagnosed with Alzheimer's, she had never even mentioned his name. "Mother, that's not Joel, that's my husband, Aaron."

"I've got so much to tell you," Ruth Ann blabbered on obliviously, addressing Aaron as though Valerie were invisible. "Come talk to me."

"Valerie," Aaron said patting her shoulder, his voice tight and controlled, "it's all right." He embraced her mother quickly. "It's nice to meet you, Mrs. Redmond," he said, and then guided her carefully back to her chair as one would a toddling child. When she was seated, he knelt to her level.

"My name is Aaron. Valerie and I were married two weeks ago."

"I have to tell you about Valree," Ruth Ann said. "You must talk to her. She's liking this white boy, and you know she's way too young and that boy doesn't care about her. He's only going to make a fool out of her and throw her away."

Valerie wished the floor would open up and swallow her. Never had she imagined that her mother would behave in such a way. She had expected the usual vacant expression and lethargic apathy, but this was a most humiliating and embarrassing first introduction.

"Aaron, please don't humor her. She's babbling. She's way back in the past and she thinks you're my father."

"I know," Aaron said quietly, but he didn't move from Ruth's side.

"I'll speak to Valerie about it," he said. "I'll do everything in my power to protect her. Is there anything else?"

"Tell Greg not to be angry at me. Try to make him understand."

"I'll tell him." Aaron squeezed her hand lightly and stood up. "I'll talk to you later."

"Please come back," Ruth Ann said.

"I will. I promise."

Aaron nodded at Valerie. "I'll wait for you in the lobby."

Chapter 15

"I didn't expect you until later," Valerie said as they stood in the parking lot of the nursing home.

"I decided to catch an earlier flight. I was in Manhattan pretty much all morning."

"And you didn't call me?"

"I had business to take care of. Anyway, I'm here now."

"How did you know I was here?"

Aaron walked her slowly to her car. "Took a wild guess. I went to your place first, and when you weren't there, I assumed you'd probably be visiting your mother."

Valerie flinched without even realizing it. "Welcome to Friedland Manor and Ruth Ann's world. I'm sorry for that display. Imagine her thinking that you're my dead father. You don't even look anything like him. If…"

"Stop apologizing. It's nothing to get upset about. You told me ahead of time what her condition was."

"I know." Valerie sighed. "I'm overreacting. I suppose I wasn't prepared for your first meeting with her to be like that."

As he opened her car door, a slight twinkle appeared in his eyes—his dark eyes. He was wearing the black contact lenses again. "Are you going to tell me who the white boy was?"

"We were both twelve and that's not funny," Valerie said, kissing him and then sliding into the driver's seat.

"I'm not letting you off the hook," Aaron said, charming her with a rakish wink. "When we get to your apartment, you will tell me."

"Or else?"

"Or else you'll be sleeping alone."

"I've done that for the past ten or so years. Another day won't hurt."

He stepped back as she closed the door. She didn't turn the key in the ignition, but watched him not just walk, but stalk to his car—a sleek, black Lexus. The man's movements were silent, swift, lethal, and sexy, and he was now in her territory, coming to her apartment. How cool was that? Smiling sappily, she was jolted from her hypnotic state when she realized that he was waiting for her to back her car out first.

When they finally stood at the doorway of her apartment, Valerie good-naturedly elbowed Aaron in the side. "Well, aren't you going to carry me over the threshold?"

"No. This isn't our home and that's a ridiculous tradition."

She laughed. "In that case, maybe I should carry you, since I have nothing against ridiculous traditions."

Apparently Aaron didn't find her remark particularly funny because he followed her inside with a blank expression on his face—blank perhaps to the eyes of someone who didn't know him. He was casing the surroundings and wasn't missing a thing, not even the dust mote settling on the end table.

After they hung up their coats, and she showed him around in what took roughly five seconds, he washed his hands, went to the kitchen, and opened the refrigerator, selecting—no surprise at all—a bottle of beer.

Valerie wished Aaron would make some comment about her humble but cozy little apartment, yet she did not feel miffed that he didn't. She had adjusted enough to his persona to realize that she would be foolish to take offense with a man who always used words sparingly and mostly reserved those few for important issues, not gentility and social etiquette.

"Supper will be ready in a couple of minutes," she told him. "I hope you haven't eaten already."

"No. I haven't."

He didn't even bother to ask what she was serving. He pulled a chair up to the table and sat, picking up a newspaper that she'd abandoned there. She shrugged and busied herself attending to the microwave while at the same time inhaling the subtle, wonderful scent of his cologne, which reminded her of something far more sensual than food. *This is so bizarre*, she thought. Yes, she had gotten used to him in Belize, but here in this tiny kitchen in her own familiar environment, his presence seemed so foreign, exotic, and surreal.

She glanced at him from the corner of her eye, noting that he was much cleaner shaven than she'd been accustomed to and that he wore a black crew-necked sweater, black slacks, black shoes. Was that the only color in his wardrobe?

The microwave pinged and she painstakingly filled two plates and set one before him, resisting the urge to laugh because Aaron barely looked at it. He shoved the paper to the side as she handed him a knife and a fork. After seating herself, she conspicuously made a show of saying a quick blessing over the food, ignoring his shark-eyed stare. Then they ate in silence.

Well, he's eating. And he's not complaining, so I guess my cooking isn't too appalling. She'd never been much of a gourmet, but it was a relief to know that she wasn't the worst cook around. Still, it would have been nice to hear a compliment.

"Anything interesting happen since you've been back?" Aaron asked, still focusing on what was left of the meal.

"No. Things are pretty much the same." She suddenly remembered the phone call from Martha Cates. "Actually, something did happen."

"Tell me."

Of course she had his undivided attention now as she told him the whole story about the midnight caller and the fate of Carolyn Allard.

"Why didn't you call and tell me this last night?" he asked, a tinge of annoyance in his tone.

"It was late and you're hard to reach," she said, sounding defensive and feeling slightly stupid.

"You should have called me anyway. Did you get back to Cates?"

"No, I didn't. I kind of had mixed feelings about it." She stopped. "Aaron, you don't seem very surprised to hear about Carolyn's suicide."

"I'm not." He pushed his empty plate aside. "And I'm glad you didn't return that call. Don't. I'll check out the Cates woman tomorrow."

"Are you saying you knew what happened to Carolyn before I got the—" she started, but was interrupted because he stood up and reached for her hand, bringing her to her feet. His arms entwined around her waist, their lips met, her heart pounded, and she was a goner.

Nearly two hours later, she lay in bed with her head against his chest, his arm looped around her. "I'm sorry about earlier," Aaron whispered, his voice like a rumble in her ear. "I should have answered you."

"You're forgiven this time," Valerie said, toying with the dog tag around his neck. "What I want to

189

know is who told you about Carolyn, and why I have the feeling that you're worried that someone might still be pursuing me because of that stupid money?"

"A contact told me about Carolyn," he answered. "And I'm 95 percent positive that you're not in any danger."

"Uh-oh. I know 95 percent isn't good enough for you." She traced her finger carefully over his scar.

"You don't have anything to worry about," Aaron said, brushing her hand lightly aside.

Gathering the blankets around her, Valerie sat up straight. The finality in his voice hinted that the discussion was over and this irked her. She was not about to be placated as if she were a completely helpless child convinced that Daddy could protect her from everything—like her mother, who had always looked to her husband as if he were God Himself.

"I'm the one who will decide what I have to worry about." She clutched the blankets tighter. "Do you think Martha Cates is dangerous?"

"No. But she was the last and only person to visit Carolyn in prison. I don't want you to do anything with the information she gave you. At least not until everything about her checks out."

Valerie sighed. His logic couldn't be refuted. It definitely made sense, and it certainly wasn't that she was thrilled about getting back to the woman anyway. She glanced at Aaron, whose expression in the darkened room seemed unreadable

"But if Cates is clean, are you planning to call her at some point?" he asked.

"I don't want to." She slid closer to him again. "But at the same time, I don't feel right about keeping the money. I've never felt right about it, and in some ways I'd be happy to give it away."

"Gordon Allard wanted you to have it," Aaron said.

"Yes, but that's going on the assumption that he didn't know he had a grandson."

"Suppose he really was a bigot and deliberately shut the kid out?"

Valerie sighed for the hundredth time. "And then turned around and gave the inheritance to an unrelated black woman? Look, I know that there are some things you can never really know about another person, but I honestly don't believe he would do such a thing. If his granddaughter believed him to be a racist, it was probably due to her disagreements with him over some of the seamy characters she associated with. What parent would have nice things to say about their child associating with criminals, no matter what race they were?"

Aaron said nothing. He had moved over on his side with his back to her, and as she leaned over to look, she noticed his eyes were closed. She nudged him.

"Aaron Weiss, you better not be sleeping when I'm talking to you."

She could see that the corner of his mouth was turned up ever so slightly, prompting her to tickle him under the chin because she knew he hated that gesture. He responded by slapping her hand away.

She laughed and suddenly remembered her odd feeling earlier in the day. "Just one more question and I promise I'll let you sleep. Before you got here, did you by any chance have someone watching me, playing bodyguard?"

"Do you think I did?" He sounded amused.

"I wouldn't put it past you. And this morning I had the strangest feeling that I was being followed."

"Valerie, you worry entirely too much. Not only that, but you're getting paranoid."

"What? How dare you of all people, Mr. Cloak and Dagger, call *me* paranoid." She seized her pillow and whumped him on the side of the face.

He laughed and her own laughter quickly blended with his. He then turned around and took her in his arms again.

"Now what? I thought you were tired."

"How could I possibly be tired? The night is still young and my wife is still beautiful."

Chapter 16

The information on Carolyn Allard and Martha Cates did check out. Carolyn had given birth to a son eleven years ago and had promptly turned him over to the care of her then-boyfriend's mother after the two had broken up. There was nothing suspicious about Carolyn's death, either. It was confirmed that she had deliberately hanged herself in her jail cell, using a dress sash as a noose. She had not been considered high risk, and therefore had not been placed under suicide watch. Other than negligence by the prison guards, there was nothing left to be said.

As far as Mrs. Cates was concerned, the woman was a widow, a harmless sixty-year-old, church-going grandmother on disability, who owned a house and was raising her grandchild because her wayward son was incarcerated long term on several drug trafficking charges. The grandmother did not have much in the way of money, but neither she nor the child were in danger of starving, and they weren't totally on public assistance, either.

Satisfied that Valerie was completely safe, Aaron didn't bother to report the details to her and hoped she wouldn't ask him about it. In his opinion, getting involved with a whining stranger was an unnecessary nuisance. It would be best if she just forgot about Martha Cates and her grandkid. The two would survive. Besides, with such a nefarious background, the kid was probably going to end up behind bars like both his parents, and that being the case, Gordon Allard wouldn't have bequeathed him anything anyway.

Aaron had also had Valerie's landline phone number changed to an unlisted one, so Mrs. Cates wouldn't be able to reach her, should she get the notion to call again.

Over breakfast, a mere two hours before he was planning to fly out of JFK to cement the Comoros Island airfreight deal, Valerie mentioned it.

"Aaron, what about the Allard case?"

"Everything checked out." He rose and placed his coffee mug in the sink.

"Then Carolyn definitely committed suicide, and she really does have a son?"

"Yes."

"And you couldn't have just *told* me, instead of making me ask?"

The aggravation in her voice was clear, but he had neither the time nor patience to deal with her attitude now.

"Let's not make an issue of it. We can talk about this when I get back."

Valerie bit her lip, visibly censoring what she wanted to say. "And when do you think you'll be back?"

"Three days tops."

Yes, she was definitely displeased, and while it would be nice to make amends, there wasn't enough time.

Resigned, she took hold of his gray silk tie and drew him close. "Have a good trip," she said.

He kissed her, picked up his briefcase, and left.

Hours later, while sitting at a table in a crowded fast food eatery listening to Jasmine reprimand her four-year-old stepson, Valerie found herself feeling disgruntled. They had just gotten back from the Meadowlands after seeing a matinee performance of the Ice Capades, a show which Morgan, the well-mannered older child, had enjoyed. But it had obviously not been pleasing to Diego, who'd kept Jasmine constantly up and down during the performances.

"Diego, for the last time, I said no." Jasmine grasped the wayward child by the hood of his jacket and tugged him back to the seat. "You wanted a chocolate shake, and you haven't even finished that. You're not getting strawberry."

"Why can't I?" Diego demanded, his eyebrows knitted furiously over his angelic face. The boy was child-model gorgeous with longish blond, curly hair and aqua-colored eyes. However, that ethereal beauty could be deceptive, like right now. For once, Valerie wished Jasmine would give him a good swat on his cherubic backside. It was a good thing she and Noah had a well-trained nanny to help take care of the kid. Unfortunately, she was currently off on vacation.

"So where did you say Aaron went?" Jasmine asked, once she had Diego seated.

Valerie closed her purse as Diego's hand ventured toward it. "Comoros, or something like that. He ends up in places I never even knew existed."

Jasmine smiled mockingly. "Oh, I believe Noah said something to me about that deal. At least you can be thankful that this is just something to do with Avian International freight and not...um, some military thing."

"I'm not exactly complaining, but he could have waited. I mean, we've only been together for two days since he got back from Belize and there is so much to do right here. How does he expect me to go around checking out real estate without him? He's going to have to be happy with the choice, too, and so far I haven't seen anything that even remotely suggests us."

"My mom can have a house built for you," Morgan piped up. "She's a really good architect."

"Of course she can, sweetie," Valerie said, affectionately fingering one of the girl's long braids. "But building a house from the ground up takes a lot of time."

Jasmine beamed at her daughter. "I'm glad someone appreciates my talent."

Valerie's thoughts flickered back to Aaron. Everything had been near perfect with them as long as they stayed in the bedroom and didn't talk too much. She didn't like the implications of this. She definitely didn't want the purely physical to become the defining characteristic of their relationship. Yet she was realizing already that she was going to have to carefully pick her battles with him and time them appropriately.

"I have to go to the baf *room*," Diego announced abruptly in a half-whispered monotone, while scooping off the pickle, onions, and most of the ketchup from his cheeseburger and smearing it on the table. "I have to go to the baf room!" He shouted loudly the second time, so loudly that strangers turned to look at them and Jasmine's face flushed.

"I'll take him," Morgan volunteered quickly. She got up and tugged the sleeve of the younger one, who glowered and trotted off with her as proudly and arrogantly as a peacock. Jasmine breathed a sigh of relief and dutifully began cleaning up Diego's mess.

"He's having one of his bratty days," she said apologetically.

One? Valerie thought but didn't say. She didn't feel like rubbing it in, but Jasmine's attempts to discipline the kid were totally ineffective. Even Jasmine's nine-year-old daughter handled him better. "Maybe you should be a bit more firm," she suggested

"I'm trying, but it's hard. I don't want to have to spank him."

Valerie shook her head. "I don't know, Jas…and you're expecting another."

"Must you remind me?" Jasmine rolled her eyes. "Hopefully number three will be a lot calmer than number two. D worries me sometimes."

"Well, I wouldn't worry too much. I mean, he's only four, and kids do outgrow phases."

Valerie had been waiting for this slot when she and her friend were alone, out of the range of little ears, so they could have an adult discussion, but suddenly her own trifling issues with her new husband had diminished. Aaron was, after all, just being Aaron, and she was becoming more aware that Jasmine's life wasn't completely idyllic, either. How easy was it to be a stepmother to a little boy whose biological mother had died under very troubling and traumatic circumstances? She shuddered to think about it.

"I still want a wedding reception for you two," Jasmine said, breaking the silence. "How about at Renaissance Hall?"

"Good place," Valerie agreed. "Might be difficult to get Aaron to cooperate, though."

"Maybe Noah can talk him into it."

"We'll see. But that can wait. Right now, I'm still trying to figure out what I should do with the Allard money."

Jasmine shrugged. "How about investing it in Avian stock? Business is booming and because our guys are behind it, it's not likely to go belly-up anytime soon."

Valerie smiled. "Good idea. But I still can't help thinking about other, less materialistic options."

She went on to tell Jasmine very briefly about Carolyn and her surviving son, just as Morgan and Diego returned.

"That's a tough one," Jasmine said. "What are you going to do?"

"I've been wanting to visit an old patient of mine in Nanuet anyway, so I think I just might call her tonight to let her know I'm coming tomorrow. While I'm in Rockland County I'll pay Mrs. Cates a visit as well."

"Speaking of calling, what's with your home phone?" Jasmine asked. "I tried to call you several times this morning and was told that your number was disconnected."

Chapter 17

Valerie got out of her car and carefully navigated the walkway. She had called Martha Cates twenty minutes ago, hoping she wouldn't be up to the visit, but that had not been the case. Martha was definitely at home and eagerly waiting.

"I'm surprised but so glad to see you," Martha said, opening the door for her to enter. "I never dreamed you'd come. I appreciate it. I really do because I know most people wouldn't."

"Apparently I'm a little crazier than most people," Valerie said wryly. "As you know, I was a friend of Mr. Allard's. Because of that, I couldn't get his grandson off my mind."

Martha did not look anything like Valerie had pictured her. She was short, round, and much younger-looking than her sixty years. Her brown-skinned face was smooth and unmarred by the passage of time.

"Brandon's in school right now, so we can chat. He doesn't know anything about this. And I want to make sure that you know this has nothing to do with me. I don't want anything for myself."

Valerie nodded and accepted a seat on the couch in the modest, neat living room, which boasted a fireplace that probably had not been used in years. On the mantle were dozens of photographs. A well-worn Bible and Bible-based literature covered the coffee table.

"I want to do the right thing," Valerie said. "But before I make a decision, I need to know some things about your grandson."

"Of course. Brandon is nothing like my children." She shook her head. "I hate to say it, but every one of them went bad. Not my grandson. I guess God has a way of working things out. He's the best child I ever raised. He loves going with me to church. He gets good grades in school, and he doesn't run all over the street getting in trouble like most of the kids in the neighborhood."

"I'm so glad to hear that," Valerie said, wondering how much Martha was exaggerating. "Could I see some pictures of him?"

"Sure." From the piano, Martha removed what was obviously a recent school picture. "I don't mean to say that Brandon is an angel," she continued, as though trying to read Valerie's thoughts. "I mean, he is a boy, and he does get into mischief from time to time, but it's just small things."

Valerie didn't hear a word she'd said because her heart nearly skipped a beat when she looked at the photo. Brandon, a bespectacled mocha-complexioned boy with curly, dark brown hair, bore a very marked and uncanny resemblance to the late Gordon Allard.

There was no way anyone could have ever said that he wasn't an Allard grandchild. He looked smart—introspective without appearing nerdish.

"He's quite handsome," she said.

Martha beamed. "He gets good grades in school, but he really likes history and math, and he loves to read."

This struck her, too, because Mr. Allard was definitely a reader and a history buff. "Mrs. Cates," she said slowly, "how did Brandon take his mother's death?"

There was a silence for a moment. "Um, I still have a hard time talking about this. He was sad, but he didn't have much of a reaction at all. You see, the last time Carolyn actually came to see Brandon he was five years old." Noting Valerie's disturbed expression, Martha continued. "She was ashamed of her life. She told me she didn't want to mess him up. She did keep in contact with me, though."

Valerie felt sadness for Carolyn again, wondering why she had gotten to the point of suicide when a good lawyer probably would have been able to get the more serious charges against her dropped.

"In her last moments," Martha's voice quavered, "Carolyn just wanted to do something right for her son."

Valerie stood up and replaced the picture on the mantle. "We can probably have a trust set up for Brandon. But I just want you to know that Carolyn was wrong about her grandfather. Brandon's color would not have been an issue. If he had been allowed to know him, he would have loved him and given him the inheritance himself."

"I really appreciate this…I mean, whatever you choose to give Brandon. Thank God there are some people still left on this earth who aren't self-serving and greedy."

Valerie wondered how unselfish she would have been if she hadn't married a wealthy man. "You'll be hearing from me again, after my lawyer has sorted out the details."

"May I have your number?" Martha asked.

"I thought you already had it," Valerie said.

Martha looked embarrassed. "I remember you told me not to call you, but I kind of did once and the line was disconnected."

Aaron, Valerie thought, recalling that Jasmine had mentioned something similar about not being able to reach her home phone. The master protector had changed her number without even telling her. "Let's just keep things the way they are," she said to Martha. "I promise I'll get back to you."

Chapter 18

Four days later, Aaron returned home in the afternoon. He wasn't in the best of moods because even though the deal had been successful, it had required a lot of unnecessary negotiations. There were few things more wearisome to him than having to socialize and lay on the false charm. He detested that aspect of business—absolutely loathed being in the company of wealthy, high-minded despots, who traveled about in limousines and Lear jets and turned their noses up at the very people whose burdened backs allowed them to be in their lofty positions.

In truth, Avian International didn't need the contract at all. The small islands scattered between Mozambique and Madagascar were just a tiny feather in their huge cap, but the territory was strategically significant to Avian's covert operations division. The more access Global Defense Forces had to foreign airspace and shipping lanes, the better. And this was the last and final one sought.

Desiring to find privacy at home, Aaron touched the doorknob and heard the sound of voices inside. Valerie had company. Frowning, he fought the instinct to turn around and go straight to his much more spacious Manhattan apartment, but he realized that he was going to have to start thinking more as a couple than as an individual. He fumbled in his pocket for the key, couldn't find the right one, and knocked instead.

"Aaron!" Valerie exclaimed, opening the door and enfolding him in a welcoming embrace as they stood in the tiny foyer. "I was worried about you."

"That wasn't necessary." He held her close, breathing in her subtly citrus scent of hair shampoo and exotic perfume.

"But I was expecting you yesterday."

"The business took longer than planned."

"You didn't even call. And you know I can't reach you."

"*Valerie*," he said tersely.

He felt that she was crossing the line and being way too intrusive.

As they stepped into the living room, Aaron saw that the visitors were not strangers but Noah's wife Jasmine and their obnoxious younger kid.

"It's good to see you, Aaron," Jasmine said with a genuine smile. "Major lifestyle change since we last talked, huh?"

Aaron nodded wryly. "I suppose you could say that."

"Well, I'm not about to interfere with newlyweds. We're getting ready to leave soon."

"Don't rush on my account."

"No…seriously. I have to pick up my daughter from school in about an hour anyway."

He nodded and then smirked as the brat, Diego, who had been lying on the floor noisily flinging toy cars all over the living room, literally froze in position and then started to tremble. In his peripheral vision, he saw the kid stand shakily and back away from him, creeping cautiously to the couch where he sat down quietly and hid his face. Aaron ignored him, said a few more words to Jasmine, and then vanished down the hall to the bedroom.

He yanked off his tie and tossed it on the bed. Even temporarily living here was not going to work. The room seemed claustrophobic, which was odd because he felt none of that when he was in the cramped quarters of *Saniyah II.* Of course, there was the knowledge that the vastness of the sea surrounded him, whereas here the walls were so thin, he could hear voices—not only Jasmine and Valerie's from the living room, but conversations and music from neighboring tenants as well. And now he could hear the resumed shrieks of Noah's brat, who had recovered from his trauma and was laughing and running amuck.

He changed into casual clothes, emptied the contents of his briefcase on the bed, and began to sort through the pages of a portfolio, but he couldn't concentrate. All he could hear was Jasmine saying over and over again, "Don't do that, Diego. Stop it, Diego.

Sit down, Diego." The kid would be quiet for two seconds and then resume his annoying behavior. Aaron slammed the briefcase shut and looked at his watch. A mere fifteen minutes had passed. He stalked back into the living room and nearly collided with the tiny culprit, who had both arms extended, and was spinning wildly around. The child gasped in alarm upon seeing him, stopped in mid-spin, and staggered dizzily, nearly toppling to the floor. Aaron caught him, steadied him, and then lifted him and plunked him down none too gently on the couch beside Jasmine. "Stay!" he commanded fiercely.

Valerie stared at him in mortified surprise and Jasmine blinked, indicating slight embarrassment, but she didn't jump to the defense of her stepson, who sat rigid with his lip trembling and his eyes squeezed shut, tears dribbling from the slits. Aaron went to the kitchen without saying anything else.

"Sorry about that," Valerie mouthed, appalled.

Jasmine shrugged. "Don't apologize. Diego just got his pride wounded, that's all."

Diego, still whimpering, burrowed his head against Jasmine's arm and put his thumb in his mouth.

"It's okay," Jasmine whispered to him. "Next time remember to do what I tell you."

And for the remainder of the visit, Jasmine and Valerie resumed their conversation without a peep from Diego, who remained seated like a perfect little gentleman.

❧

"Aaron, do you mind telling me what that was all about with you and Diego?"

"I didn't hurt him," Aaron said, seated at the table, focusing on the food in his plate.

"I know you didn't, but the way you treated him was just so…so harsh."

"That kid is out of control, and he needs discipline."

"Well, I agree, but he's a little boy, not a puppy, and it disturbs me that he's so terrified of you."

"So I'll never make father figure of the year. Is that a problem?"

Valerie shook her head. Diego wasn't their child. They would never have one, so why did it matter? Jasmine certainly hadn't seemed upset by what had happened. Yet it bothered her that she was discovering more and more unflattering things about Aaron — things she knew she should have known and worked out before they got married. Was she regretting their decision? No. She still wanted him as badly as she had in the beginning, but she was becoming more nervous about what else was going to come out.

Aaron seemed totally oblivious to her thoughts, and he was also being particularly uncommunicative.

He had been gone for four days to a foreign country and one would think he would have a lot to talk about. Why did he always force her to pry everything out of him?

"So how did your business deal go?"

"It went."

Incredible. Valerie stood up and put her plate in the sink. She left him alone in the kitchen and went out to the living room to sit on the couch. Was she over-reacting? Maybe. Was it wrong to want to have a conversation with her husband? No, it definitely was not. Flouncing back into the kitchen, she swiped Aaron's plate from under him and was rewarded with such a startled, baffled expression that it was hilarious.

"What are you doing?" he asked, fork suspended in mid-air. "I'm not finished."

Valerie laughed. "Are you going to bite me? Animals have been known to do that when someone gets between them and their meal."

Aaron sat up straight and folded his arms across his chest. "Would you like me to bite?"

"No. But I would like you to talk. Where I come from, families actually have conversations over meals." She set the plate back in front of him again.

"What do you want to talk about?"

"Things, Aaron. Things." She sat down at the table again. "I've decided what to do with the Allard money, for one."

Did she see an eye roll then? She continued. "I'm setting up a trust for Gordon Allard's grandson. I went to visit Martha Cates and…"

"You *visited* her?"

Yes, she definitely had Aaron's full attention now. His eyebrows were knitted together in a scowl.

"I went to visit her," she repeated, "and found out that she's a perfectly innocent grandmother raising a young boy who's *not* a delinquent. He gets good grades in school, enjoys going to church, and, what's more, he even resembles his grandfather."

"Shouldn't you be checking out real estate instead of cruising around paying visits to strangers?"

Annoyed by his sarcasm, Valerie glared at him. "You've got some nerve. I *am* checking out real estate with no help from you, thank you. And I just took a few hours out of one day to *cruise* to Rockland County, which isn't even that far."

He stood up, pushed the chair back, and emptied the remains of his plate into the garbage. "We'll be moving to Manhattan over the weekend," he said. "This apartment is too small for the both of us, but you should keep it just in case."

Valerie froze. *Move to Manhattan? Keep the apartment?* The way he had abruptly switched topics alarmed and confused her. "What are you talking about? Keep the apartment in case of what?"

"In case you have need for it."

"Why would I have need for it?"

His expression was evasive. "In the event that you don't want to join me in Manhattan, you'll have the option of staying here when I'm away."

Valerie stood up and took hold of his arm. "You're angry, aren't you? Angry that I went to see Mrs. Cates."

"I'm not angry, but you could have given some indication that that's what you planned to do."

She stepped away from him and threw up her hands. "I didn't plan it. Okay? Some things just happen. You can't plan exactly how you're going to react in every situation. We're all human and we're all individuals. Maybe getting involved with those people wouldn't have been your decision, but I'm not you." She took a deep breath. "And as my husband, I don't recall you ever saying clearly that I shouldn't."

She had him there. She knew she did. He hadn't given her a direct ultimatum. He had merely assumed that she would sense his position and not pursue it.

"And also while we're on this subject, you had no right to change my phone number without even telling me," she continued.

Realizing that he had no verbal defense for that remark, either, Aaron concealed an escaping smile with one hand and reached out with the other to pull her close to him. "I apologize," he said huskily. "And Manhattan's really not that bad. You might even like it."

What am I going to do with you? Valerie thought, once again allowing herself to be lulled into his embrace and sated with his kiss. *Why is it that even though I might win the battle of words, you somehow always win the war?*

❧❧

Valerie's first encounter with the Manhattan loft left her speechless. The place was beyond spacious, and so expertly appointed and designed that it seemed more for show than habitation. It boasted gleaming hardwood floors, a huge living room with expensive dark leather furnishings, a modern island kitchen with stainless steel appliances and granite countertops, a small library stocked with law books, maps, and atlases, and a beautiful bathroom in onyx and gold, with a sunken-in tub and Jacuzzi. The hallway was lined with well-placed paintings of Central Park scenes in summer and autumn—Aaron's own works. And the master bedroom was enormous. There were also three additional rooms, one of which he used to store art supplies. Last, but not least, there was a small gym with workout equipment.

To sum it all up, Aaron's apartment was a man's place, designed for a man, but not by him. He told her he had neither the time nor the patience to decorate, so he had hired an interior designer. Looking around, Valerie admired the aesthetics and the space, but the clinical, museum-like coldness she absorbed from the atmosphere unsettled her.

When the theatrical curtains were drawn back in the living room, there was an awesome panoramic view of the metropolis, but all she could think about was the view he might have had if he had been home when the planes crashed into the twin towers. She stood near the windows, transfixed by the patch of blue gray from the distant Hudson River.

"Impressive, no?" Aaron said, standing beside her.

"Very." She stifled an involuntary shudder, knowing instinctively that he had not been home on September 11. Had he been, he probably would have been among the heroes who perished that day.

"What are you thinking?" Aaron asked.

She slipped her arm around his waist. "Trust me. You don't want to know."

Now she felt an urgency to find a house that would speak of home to both of them.

Sunday morning, Valerie went to church in Manhattan, rather than drive across the bridge to her old congregation. Aaron, who actually had nothing important scheduled to do that day, gave her one of his looks and declined when she invited him to accompany her. No surprise there. She left him sprawled out in the living room checking out the real estate section of the *New York Times*.

When she returned, they visited a realtor and went house shopping. The time spent on grand tours of available homes in the metro area was interesting to her, but unproductive. Aaron found it wearisome. He was bored out of his mind—so bored that she was both amused and irritated by his attitude. He accused her of being too picky.

Of course there were some decadently beautiful houses in their price range, particularly in the Connecticut area. But Valerie did not find McMansions appealing. She was convinced that she would immediately know their house when she saw it, and so far none of them had struck the right chord. The day was a washout and she didn't know if she'd ever be able to cajole Aaron into accompanying her on such a mission again. She had learned one thing, though. He honestly did not care. The choice was totally up to her.

"I'm sorry for putting you through this, but I just know the right house is out there. We just haven't seen it yet," Valerie said as Aaron drove on the Long Island Expressway, heading back home.

"Why does this have to be so difficult?" he asked. "You don't like anything, and it's not that we're on a tight budget."

She sighed. "You didn't seem impressed by anything we saw, either."

"The one in Greenwich was nice."

"That was a barn, Aaron."

"It was a restored carriage house. The place had a lot of land."

"We're not going to live on the land, and you never said you wanted to have horses."

"What's wrong with horses?"

She laughed in spite of herself and patted him on the shoulder. "Nothing. I love horses, but one thing at a time."

Snow flurries were tumbling from the sky when they neared a familiar exit sign, and a flash of sentimental nostalgia hit her. She nudged Aaron. "Could you exit here, please?"

He obliged, and they soon found themselves on a local back road entering the seaside town of Lobster Bay. "Where are we going?" he asked warily.

"I know you're going to think I'm cuckoo, but humor me. I just want to look at Mr. Allard's house to see what's going on there."

Aaron groaned. "Haven't you had enough of that place?"

"Please. I know it's crazy."

"As you like." He shrugged.

They cruised into the empty circular driveway, which still contained traces of last month's snowstorm. Valerie stared up at the abandoned house, which managed to maintain its towering elegance despite appear-

215

ing as gray, depressed, and forlorn as it had the day she and Jasmine had gone by to pick up the books. Only now there was a slight difference. Even though there was no for-sale sign, the house looked wistful, as though waiting for the resurgence of spring and, with the season of rebirth, the hope of a new owner.

Transfixed, she reached out to touch Aaron to make sure he was still there.

"Can we go now?" he asked with boyish urgency.

Valerie laughed as his odd tone of voice shook her out of her trance. Aaron whining? Imagine that.

"I wonder why there's no for-sale sign?" she said.

He yawned. "Maybe the nephew decided to keep it."

"Why would he? He's from England, remember?"

"Probably intends to rent it out."

"Aaron." She hesitated for a second. "Do you think we could possibly find out what's going on with the house?"

He inhaled deeply and looked her in the eyes. "You really are a crazy woman. You would actually consider living in this house, wouldn't you?"

Valerie bit her lip. He was right. She was being crazy. But, yes. She had always loved the house, felt drawn to it, and everything about the place spoke to her. In her mind's eye, she could see the estate restored to its original grandeur.

"Sorry, I forgot to tell you that insanity runs in my family. Yes, I do like this house, and if it's for sale and it was up to me, I'd buy it in a heartbeat."

Aaron seemed taken by her enthusiasm. "In that case, I guess we'll just have to find out what the status is. Tomorrow I'll check, but don't get your hopes up."

Valerie said nothing. She simply turned and kissed him. He smiled and her heart skipped a beat. That tentative slow burn of a grin got her all the time, because it was like a puff of smoke that always vanished so quickly that it left her wondering if it had really been there at all.

"Love you," she whispered, after he returned her kiss.

"Now let's get out of here before some neighbor calls the police and we're accused of trespassing," he said.

"Imagine that," Valerie said, as he pulled the car out of the driveway. "Someone might mistake us for teenagers making out near an abandoned house."

Aaron was not amused.

Chapter 19

Upon consulting with the lawyers, Aaron discovered that Gordon Allard's nephew, John Larsen, did intend to put the house up for sale, but he had run into problems. The house was a white elephant. It needed a lot of repairs and he had put off his decision until the summer, when he could come back to the U.S. for a longer period of time.

When the information was related to Valerie, she was disappointed that there would be a long delay. Aaron could see that she had her heart set on the house. Personally, he didn't understand her obsession at all and thought it was bordering on ridiculous, but he wanted her to be happy, so, without telling her, he obtained John Larsen's phone number and gave him a personal call. Larsen turned out to be a reasonable sort and they discussed the property over the phone. In the end, they negotiated a deal that worked for both of them. John Larsen was overjoyed to unload the house as-is, and was well satisfied with Aaron's lump sum bid. A team of lawyers handled the paperwork and, in record time, Aaron had the deed and the white elephant belonged to them.

"Stop frowning," Valerie said lightheartedly as they stood in the entrance foyer of the house.

It was late afternoon and Aaron, who looked dashing in business attire and a long overcoat, had just returned from a board meeting in Manhattan and had met her at the house. In a theatrically exaggerated gesture, he swept a cobweb out of the way as they walked into the huge, now-empty drawing room. He tilted his head up toward the antique chandelier suspended from the high ceiling. "Think that ornament's steady up there?"

Valerie elbowed him. "That *ornament* has survived generations. Why should it fall now?

"Because its new owners are of a different ethnicity."

"Very funny."

He listened with apparent amusement as she expressed her vision of how the house would look once the renovations were done, and he tolerated being dragged into a kitchen so outdated that he wouldn't have been surprised to find a colonial brick oven and pots hanging from a rack. He looked around. There was a rack, but the pots had been confiscated. He smirked.

He laughed outright when they went into the bathroom and were confronted with the enormous water-stained claw-footed tub.

"So it's old," Valerie said, "but it's now considered retro." She looked at his expression. "Don't worry, we'll definitely update the bathroom."

Next she led him up the creaky, winding staircase. There was a distinct nostalgic artistry to the curve of the staircase, but she was aware of him shaking the loose balustrades, knowing that the staircase, too, would need extensive work.

"*Voila!*" she exclaimed, switching on the light. "The greatest home library in the world."

To her relief, he looked impressed that the entire second story was nothing but a gigantic library with shelves and shelves of books and a long, well-appointed oak table in the center square, with matching chairs in which phantom patrons could sit. The library was no doubt what had caused Larsen most of the problems. True to his word, he had not touched anything here.

She watched Aaron wander down the aisles looking at the shelves. He selected a book from one. "All labeled and categorized according to the Dewey Decimal system. Amazing," he said.

He blew the dust off the book in his hand, replaced it, walked farther down the aisle, and turned a corner leading to the reference section, which contained biographies, encyclopedias, and local Long Island history. He picked up a thick ancient book of atlases with nautical charts and began thumbing through it.

"And we could..." Valerie began, but she stopped talking, realizing that he was absorbed in the book. She smiled to herself. Finally, they were in agreement. The library was of interest to both of them.

When they had at last gotten out into the blustery March sunlight, Aaron surveyed the sweeping property in the rear of the house. There were tangled winter-slumbering gardens that a decade ago must have been beautiful, an old, boarded-up well, and a crumbling trellis, which heralded the way to a cracked stone path. He followed the path to where it sloped down a bank and ended at a sea wall and boat dock overlooking the glistening Long Island Sound.

Valerie quietly trailed him down the path but remained on the bank, watching as he stepped cautiously out on the wooden dock to survey the body of water. She wished she had taken her camera to capture the way he stood, his oh-so-elegant GQ model pose, resplendent with head lifted to the horizon, exotic sculpted features, penetrating eyes, and his long gray overcoat flapping in the breeze.

On that day in Belize before they'd agreed to get married, he had warned her not to try to change him, but it delighted her to realize that without prodding or nagging, she had done just that. The changes were subtle, but he definitely smiled more and appeared more relaxed and youthful. Even his manner of dress had changed somewhat, thanks to her careful tampering. She had recently taken to buying him dress shirts in pastel colors that he normally wouldn't wear, and instead of pointing them out to him, she'd simply hung them in his closet, mixing them with his other clothes. In truth, she had the feeling that Aaron knew exactly what she was up to, but he never said a word and she was deeply flattered when he actually did wear them.

She closed her eyes momentarily and saw their home the way it would be when it was restored. Her life was becoming almost perfect. She saw her husband tying a sailboat to a brand new dock, and she heard the emotive chatter of their children running to meet him. Children? Her eyes flew open and she clenched her hands in a fist so tight the knuckles blanched.

There were not going to be any children.

Chapter 20

By the beginning of April, the remodeling plans for the house had been discussed with Jasmine and a construction team was being assembled. Aaron was out of the country again on some cargo delivery run, which Valerie found troubling. Since he owned the company and had many skilled pilots employed expressly for courier duties, she didn't quite understand why he felt the need to handle any of the deliveries himself. She also knew that his typical flight plans included third-world countries possessing some of the most hazardous runways. She had expressed her concerns, but his only response was that he enjoyed flying and wasn't about to give up his wings anytime soon.

While he was away, Valerie was staying in her old apartment again. On this particular day, she had plans to go out to Long Island to check up on the house, but first she dropped by her aunt's place and was surprised to be greeted by a disgruntled and hung-over Denise, who had the place to herself because her mother and stepfather were away for a few days.

Still in her bathrobe, hair disheveled, eyes red, and her voice slurred, Denise clearly hadn't been expecting any visitors. "There's not going to be a wedding," she announced the minute Valerie stepped in the door. "Tony and I are through." She dabbed at her eyes with a tattered tissue.

"What happened?" Valerie asked.

Tony was the third suitor Denise had almost married and then tossed to the curb, so the news came as no surprise, although the hapless Tony had advanced a lot farther than the others.

"I'm tired of him, that's all." Denise sank down on the living room sofa. "He's a first class jerk who cares more about his mother and the rest of his stupid family than he does about me. And guess what? Maybe I'm just gonna fly to some island like you did and marry a good-looking old guy with money."

"This isn't about me," Valerie said irritably. "And if you're looking for advice on how to marry your romantic fantasy, don't hold your breath, because I have none to give. I'll be the first to admit that what I did wasn't wise, but I'm okay with my decision and so far it's working for me, even though I wouldn't recommend it for anyone else."

She definitely would not recommend it for anyone else. What she had done—marrying a reclusive stranger—was in most cases a prelude to disaster.

"I'll say it's working for you," Denise said enviously. "You've got more money than you know what to do with. You'll never have to work nine-to-five again, so even if you don't love Aaron Rambo, you've still got a good deal."

Valerie put her hands on her hips. "My marriage to Aaron has nothing to do with money. Yes, he's wealthy. Yes, money can be useful, but it's…"

"The root of all evil." Denise smirked.

"That's not what I was going to say, smarty pants. But now that you misquoted it, it's the *love* of money that's the root of all evil, not money itself."

"Yes, Mommy. Are we going to get out the Bible now?"

"Maybe if you'd been reading the Bible more, you wouldn't be sitting around here half drunk and sniveling."

"Oh, shut up. You're no saint. Don't tell me you didn't sleep with Rambo before you married him. Oh…wait. No. You're too much of a self-righteous follow-the-rules type to do that. You probably married him just so you could have sex." Her face lit up. "That's *exactly* what you did, isn't it?"

"Goodbye, Denise." Valerie opened the door to leave, realizing it was the wisest move because she was on the verge of slapping her cousin across the room. "When you find where you left your one brain cell, then maybe we'll talk."

It hadn't really been all about physical attraction or sex, had it? Of course not. Why was she even considering the words of a nitwit like Denise? On the other hand, physical attraction seemed to be the most tangible thing that was holding her and Aaron together at this point. Her husband's other quirks were hardly endearing. On the days he was actually around, he got up punctually every morning and jogged the city streets, rain or shine, for about an hour. When he returned, he spent another hour in the gym lifting weights. He never let his hair grow beyond three inches, never wore any type of shoes that didn't lace up, never answered a phone call if he suspected it was for her, even if she was out of the room when it rang and he was present. He insisted on always being the driver when they were both in the car, and whenever they ate out or went to some public place he always managed to sit near the exit so he could watch the surroundings. But these habits were just petty rituals, weren't they?

"Wait." Denise hiccupped, sneezed, and then reached for another tissue. "I didn't mean to say that."

"Yes, you did," Valerie retorted icily. "And you're not going to deny it later with the excuse that you were drunk."

Denise stood up and wobbled uncertainly toward her. "Don't go. I didn't mean to put it like that. But… well…so what if it is true? You've only been wanting him for years, and now you've got him."

Valerie stepped outside and stood in the doorway blocking Denise's exit. "Listen to me, and don't come out here with your crazy drunk self. You're upset because you believe things have gone so perfectly for me and they seem to be falling apart for you. Yes, I wanted Aaron…and not only for some physical reason. Now I've got him, and no, there is no pot of gold at the end of the rainbow because the rainbow never ends. Relationships aren't perfect. Even if you love someone very much, you have to realize that joining your life with that of another who's got a whole different set of genes, and a totally different way of thinking, that things aren't always going to be in sync. You have to compromise a lot, make sacrifices, and work really hard to keep things together."

"I…I know that."

"Then prove it. I think you still love Tony, and maybe you can work things out. What was the disagreement about, anyway?"

Denise looked momentarily confused. Valerie realized, of course, that the argument had probably been over something trivial.

"You're right, it was stupid," Denise admitted. "It was over where we were going on our honeymoon."

Valerie tried not to roll her eyes. "Where does he want to go?"

"Bermuda."

"And you?"

"Hawaii. He says Hawaii's too expensive."

"Well, for goodness sake, Denise. Tony's just being sensible, and he's bent over backward for you on every other issue but this. Cut him some slack. Bermuda is a beautiful island and you might get the opportunity to do Hawaii at another time. Unless, of course, you really believe this is worth breaking up over."

"I don't want to break up." Denise blew her nose again. "He just made me so mad, that's all, and now I don't even care that much about Hawaii."

"Call him and tell him you changed your mind. See what he says."

"He...he called me this morning, but I hung up on him."

"The fact that he called means he still cares. Don't be such a brat. Call him back and apologize."

"Apologize for what? For wanting to go to Hawaii?

"No, silly. For hanging up on him."

Denise grinned sheepishly now. "I'm going to try and see what happens."

"Good. I'm out of here." Valerie stepped onto the stoop and was about to close the door when she had a second thought. "Oh, and just one more thing." She smiled sweetly. "Don't ever call my husband Rambo again, or you'll be colliding with the fist of GI Jane."

After leaving Denise snuffling in the doorway, Valerie thought about how unchallenging her cousin's relationship with her fiancé was. They quarreled about the most pedestrian things, like wedding invitations, showers, and honeymoons, whereas, in stark contrast, she hadn't even gotten a legitimate honeymoon out of Aaron, unless she chose to consider their time in Belize to be one.

They'd had a rudimentary wedding—still no reception. And then there was his staunch refusal to wear a wedding band. She'd asked him why, and he'd told her that it was nothing personal, but he never wore any kind of ring and never would. She'd determined that she would not sweat the small stuff. But was it really small stuff that he always unnecessarily used protection whenever they were intimate? And her most obvious concern was the lack of communication between them when he spent long periods of time away.

He'd insisted that he wasn't currently involved in any treacherous mercenary activity; yet, she hadn't seen or heard from him in the two weeks since she'd last kissed him goodbye. No calls. Nothing. How many marriages could survive that?

By the time she reached Long Island and stood in front of the former Allard house with its recently acquired building permit in the window, she wondered just how long it would be before her dream became a nightmare.

The phone rang just before midnight. Valerie awakened from a deep sleep with her heart pounding and her throat dry. "Hello?"

"Where are you?" Aaron asked.

The anxious thudding of her heart stilled as she murmured a thank you to God. Then her pulse rate and blood pressure increased for another reason entirely.

"What do you mean, where am I? Where are you? I haven't seen or heard from you in two weeks. You call me up in the middle of the night and that's all you can ask. Where am I?"

"I'm home in Manhattan," Aaron said calmly. "Shouldn't you be?"

Arrgh. That man. The outrageous patronizing calmness in his voice made her want to strangle him even more.

"Since you called this number, you know good and well that I'm at my apartment in Englewood. The apartment *you* suggested I hold on to."

"Are we arguing?" Aaron asked.

"What's it sound like?"

"Sounds like we are. Go back to sleep. I'll see you when you decide to come home."

Her mouth opened and she heard the phone click. *Jeez.* Had she dreamt that bizarre exchange? She sat bolt upright, flung out her arm, and nearly knocked the clock off the night table. *The nerve of that arrogant whack job, telling me to go back to sleep.* There was no way she could simply go back to sleep. She got up, paced around the room, and suddenly began to get dressed.

"You think we're having an argument, do you?" she muttered aloud. "Well, I'll come in person and show you what a real argument is."

She was absolutely livid as she launched her car like a missile across the George Washington Bridge, grateful that at this unearthly hour there was very little traffic to contend with. She reached the Manhattan skyscraper in record time, parked her car in the security-controlled underground lot, and took the elevator up to the loft.

Instead of using her key, she banged loudly on the door, shouting his name.

Aaron took his good time answering, of course, and when he did, he flung the door open so abruptly that she lost her footing and tumbled right into his arms, colliding against the brick wall of his chest—his bare chest. Even though he seemed wide-awake, he'd obviously been in bed, because he was wearing black silk pajama bottoms.

"Fiery tonight, aren't you?" he commented, pulling her inside and shoving the door shut.

"I'll have you kno—"

His mouth closed firmly on hers, muffling whatever piece of her mind she intended to give him. She floundered hopelessly for a second and momentarily succumbed, allowing him to draw her into the bedroom. Finally, regaining her senses, she planted both hands on his chest and pushed herself away.

"First," she took a deep breath, "I love you and I'm glad you're home safe. But if you think this is entertaining, think again. It's not. We seriously have to discuss this problem, and we're not going to kiss, make out, and sweep everything under the rug."

"There is no rug." Aaron sat on the bed and looked at her with intense blue eyes. "I'm not going to guarantee you a satisfactory outcome, but suit yourself. Let's talk about whatever problem you have in mind."

Talking was really the last thing she wanted to do. He had gotten her all hot, bothered, and, quite frankly, discombobulated. Her first instinct was to find him a T-shirt to wear, so his physical attributes wouldn't distract her; but doing that would only flatter his indomitable ego and provide more cause for entertainment. No, she had to confront him now, or the problems would only escalate and explode at a later date.

Unbuttoning her coat, she stripped it off and tossed it in his direction. He caught it without batting an eyelid.

"To begin with, I was worried about you. You were gone a long time and, as usual, you didn't even consider me enough to call. What am I supposed to think? Are you involved in something military again?"

Aaron regarded her for a moment, as though he were about to lecture a not-too-bright child. "I told you when I left that I was delivering cargo. If you want specifics as to places, I was in Morocco, Comoros, and

Seychelles. You seem to have forgotten that I told you back in Belize that I have little tolerance for clingy women, and my rules haven't changed." His eyes narrowed. "I'm not going to constantly update you on where I might be located at any given time of day."

Seething, she held her tongue. In her heart she knew she was only being caring, not clingy. There was a big difference between the two. But at the same time she didn't think it wise to openly challenge his insistence on freedom from accountability. Before they were married he had made that clear and she had stupidly accepted his rules.

"Okay. Okay. You call it clingy, but I call it concerned. So be it." She gestured emphatically. "Of course I don't expect you to constantly update me on everything. All I want is one compromise." She didn't wait for him to respond. "When you're away for a long period of time, just call me once in a while, okay? You don't have to do anything more than just say hello… whatever."

There was a moment of silence. "I suppose I could call," Aaron said finally, in an irritated, slightly offhand sort of way. "Is that it?"

He sounded impatient and his eyes glimmered with what could only be defined as deferred lust. She wanted desperately to say yes, that their disruptive conversation was over, but his single-mindedness struck her as manipulative and controlling. She'd hardly settled anything, and somehow it seemed that she was always made out to be the one who was in the wrong. It was also perfectly obvious that he couldn't care less about what was going on in her mind; he had only one agenda. Physical satisfaction.

"No, that's not it," she said slowly. "I have a question for you." Yes, she might as well clear the air once and for all. "Don't take this the wrong way, but why is it you always use protection when we're together? I mean, it's pointless. We're married, and neither of us has a communicable disease. We both had blood tests, and it's not like I'm going to get pregnant."

His eyes had gone cold again. "Habit," he said. "And it never bothered you before, so why now?"

"Wrong. It *has* bothered me. I just didn't say anything because I hoped you would stop doing it on your own without being asked. It's kind of...well...insulting to me. It makes me feel as if I'm contaminated in some way."

Aaron looked disgusted. "Contaminated? I don't know where you get your bizarre ideas. Maybe I'm the one who's contaminated. Have you ever thought of that?"

Aghast, Valerie glared at him. "No, I haven't thought of that because there's nothing wrong with you. I've seen your blood test results."

Aaron got up and moved over to the opposite side of the bed. "It's late," he said dryly, as if suddenly realizing that he was tired. "I have things to do tomorrow and I assume you do as well."

Nice going, Val, she thought to herself. *Now you've gone and killed his desire.* "Two things," she said. "All I mentioned were two things that can easily be rectified and now I'm the spoilsport, the evil woman."

Aaron remained silent and clicked off the lamp on his side of the bed.

"Fine. Be like that." She turned around and left the room. "Have a good night."

Valerie spent the rest of the pre-dawn hours in the spare bedroom. So much for her little talk with Denise. If her cousin had been a fly on the wall listening to that appalling exchange, Valerie truly would be eating crow right now.

Other than his morning jog, Aaron didn't have any concrete plans for the day, and he was grateful because weariness had set in. He'd had only about five hours of straight sleep in the past week. The exhaustion wasn't just from the mechanics of flying and the altering time zones, but because he also physically labored along with the rest of the crew unloading shipments. The only time he'd sit back and fly a desk would be when he was too old to bench press 350 pounds. Of course he had to admit and accept that the human body could only take so much.

Valerie had been upset with him last night. It had been wishful thinking to believe that she would fully accept his lifestyle. Still, she had been honest enough to tell him that she wouldn't just keep silent and that there were times when she would question and challenge him. After years of independence and isolation it was difficult to break old habits, but he was actually enjoying having someone in his corner who cared about him without ulterior motives. She was not only a friend and lover but a nurturer, and a good person as well; and when they were in sync, body and soul, few experiences could rival the pleasure he derived. In truth, there were only two things she could do that he would find intolerable, and those things involved issues of trust. So far she hadn't broken those rules. Surely she was worth giving up a few quirks.

By the time he'd returned to the apartment, showered, and shaved, he heard her moving around in the kitchen and could smell coffee brewing. She wasn't much of a coffee drinker herself, so at least he knew she wasn't so angry that she planned to ignore him.

"Good morning," he said, quietly entering the kitchen with the *Wall Street Journal* tucked under his arm.

She had her back turned and was wearing a long blue robe. Her hair, which she was letting grow out, hung in loose ripples around her shoulders. He wanted to touch it and kiss the back of her neck. But overt affection seemed premature, considering last night.

"Good morning," Valerie said without looking up. She was pouring something from a bowl into a skillet. Pancakes? French toast? He wasn't overly fond of either, but if she intended to serve boiled tripe, he'd eat that, too.

"Aaron, I've been thinking about going back to work."

He took a seat at the table. "You don't have to."

"I know that. But I've been missing the action lately, and since you're gone most of the time, there's no reason for me to just float around doing nothing."

She moved breezily behind him, perfuming the air with a pleasantly fruity essence, and set the plate in front of him. "Being the workaholic you are, you should understand that feeling."

"I do," he admitted, "but aren't you occupied with the house?"

"Yes, but that's not enough. There's plenty of time left to take a part-time job."

Aaron shrugged. "You might not want to start next week, though."

"Why?" She sat near him.

"I'm going back to Israel for a few days and I thought, with you being a Christian and all, that some of the historical sites might be of interest to you."

She was dumbstruck for a second, but she recovered quickly. "I'm definitely interested in going. But I'm surprised. This…this trip is pretty monumental for you, isn't it? You've avoided it for so many years."

"I'd like to see my uncle," Aaron said tightly. "Gabriel's up in years, and I figure it's about time."

Her hand reached out and closed around his wrist. "If you want me to come, of course I will."

"You'll also get to meet Andrew. He's on furlough right now, and he'll be joining us. He's never been to Israel, either."

Valerie's eyes widened. "Your son's never been?"

"He hasn't had much of an interest in that side of his roots, until now." Aaron shrugged offhandedly. "Not to mention that I haven't exactly encouraged him."

A long silence ensued, in which the ticking of the overhead clock sounded like a heartbeat. "I just want you to know," Valerie said slowly, carefully, "that I'm sorry for the way things were last night."

His eyebrows arched as he looked at her. He didn't intend to apologize and he wasn't expecting her to, either.

"I'm apologizing only because the anger was childish," Valerie said. "But I'm not sorry for what I requested of you. I meant every word of that."

"Of course you meant it. You don't seem to be in the habit of saying things you don't mean." He studied her expression. "And while I might not submit to all your requests, there's nothing wrong with speaking out, especially since you have such a dramatic, interesting way of being confrontational."

She frowned slightly, realizing that he was amused and turned on by her wrath. However, he didn't give her a chance to protest.

"Since we've been together I've been counting on you to be honest, and that's one of the things I like about you." He leaned forward and kissed her on the cheek, a nice, sweet, affectionate kiss that he hoped was devoid of innuendo.

She smiled now. "I'm just glad you're home that's all."

Chapter 21

They arrived in Israel late on a Monday afternoon on a commercial El Al flight from JFK to Ben Gurion Airport. Aaron rented a car and they sped through the modern, bustling port city of Tel Aviv.

They checked into their two-bedroom hotel suite overlooking the Mediterranean. The extra room was for Andrew, who would be arriving later. Aaron had told her that this was the only night they'd stay in Tel Aviv. The rest of the time would be spent in the Jerusalem and Galilee areas, which couldn't have pleased her more, since she was more interested in seeing firsthand the places depicted in the Bible.

An hour later, while they were settling in, Andrew telephoned Aaron, announcing that he would arrive in roughly two hours and that he had a girlfriend with him.

Even though he made no comment, Valerie knew instinctively that this annoyed Aaron, who didn't appreciate even the minutest of plan changes. To be perfectly honest, she was a bit annoyed, too. Not for the same reason, but because she'd wanted to meet and get to know Andrew as an individual, not as part of a couple. She also viewed the arrangement as inconsiderate of her traditional Christian scruples. The extra room in their hotel had been intended for a single person only, not for an unmarried couple sleeping together.

❧❧

Andrew and his girlfriend were fifteen minutes late when they joined them at the table in a restaurant that specialized in Middle Eastern cuisine. Aaron stood up and the two men clasped hands in such a rapid greeting that Valerie almost missed it. *Oh, come on,* she thought. *You two haven't seen each other in a while; doesn't that rate more than just a handshake?* But regardless of their lack of exuberance, she could see affection in the eyes of both.

The son also rose to towering heights. Standing only an inch shorter than his father, Andrew was as handsome as his picture—even more so because he had a golden, outdoorsy tan that accentuated his aquamarine eyes. Both men were attracting the none-too-subtle attention of other patrons in the restaurant.

"Valerie, we finally meet," Andrew said. With no hesitation or reservation, he bent and kissed her on the cheek. "Now I understand why my father finally changed his mind about marriage."

He possessed just the slightest hint of a Southern accent. "Nice to meet you, Andrew," Valerie said, smiling in a manner that she hoped conveyed warmth. She had never been a shy person, but now she felt stiff and she wondered if it had something to do with being in the presence of two such powerful-looking men, who were also polar opposites of each other. "I've heard many good things about you." She carefully controlled the tone and pitch of her voice.

Andrew's eyes twinkled. "Make no mistake about it, none of those good things are true."

He went on to introduce his clearly overwhelmed girlfriend, Melissa, who'd retreated to the background during the initial greetings. Melissa was a visually stunning girl with hazel eyes, waist-length strawberry blonde hair, and an impressive body with curves that were well showcased in her short little black dress.

"Oh, my gosh," she gushed as she shook Aaron's hand, while he looked as if he were contemplating either muzzling her or eating her as an appetizer. "I'm so happy to meet you. I mean, it's hard to believe that you're Drew's father." She hesitated and blushed, perhaps realizing, too late, that her mouth wasn't connected to her brain. "I don't mean that you don't resemble each other…It's funny 'cause you actually kinda do. What I'm trying to say is that you don't look old enough to be his father."

"Flattery does have its place. Thank you, Melissa." Aaron forced a smile, carefully extracted his hand, and in a manner that was clearly dismissive, focused his eyes elsewhere.

But the girl didn't stop. "You don't have to call me Melissa. All my friends call me Muffy, which is silly I know, but it's my nickname." She took a deep breath.

Enough already. Stop shooting yourself in the foot. Valerie silently willed the girl to shut her mouth, but to no avail.

"It's so absolutely amazing…you and Drew are like the dark and light versions of each other. When Drew first told me that his real father was African-Amer…I mean, African-Israeli, I thought at first that you were one of the Ethiop—"

"Let's order," Andrew interrupted as he mercifully pulled out a chair for Melissa, who looked flustered, and sat. Once everyone was settled, the conversation quickly segued into a discussion about the intense security on El Al flights.

"It was just awful," Melissa said with a pitchy giggle. "I don't ever want to fly that airline again. I mean, it should be pretty obvious to everyone that Drew and I don't look like terrorists."

No one responded to her comment. The men continued to talk as if she had said nothing at all. Valerie managed to hold her own in the ensuing conversation, but found herself feeling sorry for Melissa, who, every time she opened her mouth, however briefly, consistently managed to insert foot.

Thankfully, when the food arrived, girlfriend calmed into complete silence, but the fact that her hands shook when she unfolded her napkin didn't go unnoticed by Valerie. Halfway through the meal, Melissa got up and retreated to the ladies' room.

"So where did you meet the girl, Hooters?" Aaron asked.

"No. The club was called Knickers," Andrew responded straight-faced. "She's a waitress working her way through college."

"Clothed or unclothed?"

"Clothed." Andrew smirked. "At least she was when we met."

Aaron frowned, studying his wine glass. "Why did you bring her?"

Andrew shrugged. "Aww, c'mon, Captain, don't be like that. She's sweet and she wanted to come. Said she always wanted to see the Holy Land."

The sarcasm in Andrew's tone was unmistakable. Valerie had heard enough. "You know, it's none of my business, but talking about Melissa like that is not only rude, but cruel." She took a sharp intake of breath. "Okay, so I gather she's no Rhodes scholar, but she's still a human being with feelings." She looked directly at Andrew, making eye contact. "Your father was right to ask you why you brought her here, because I'm wondering the same thing. I mean, is she really a girlfriend? How could she be if you don't even think enough of her to defend her?" She stood up, without waiting for a response. "Excuse me, I'm going to the ladies' room to see if she's okay."

Andrew's blue eyes widened in surprise as he watched her stalk off down the hall. He glanced at Aaron, who shrugged and looked impassive.

"I'm impressed," Andrew said after Valerie had gone. "She sure speaks her mind."

"Yes," Aaron replied. "That she does."

Early the next morning they drove to Jerusalem, where Aaron tolerated everyone's gawking at the ancient city. They visited the Western Wall and mingled with ordinary tourists, Ethiopians, and bearded orthodox Jews with side curls, black suits, and big hats. Aaron was better than a tour guide because he patiently explained everything. He showed them the place where the famous temple had once stood—now the gold-crested Islamic Dome of the Rock and he told them interesting anecdotes that only an expatriate would know.

Valerie was both impressed and sobered by the historic city. With every step she took down cobbled streets she thought of her father, who had longed to take this trip, but had forfeited the opportunity because his wife was afraid to travel. Aaron was such a wealth of knowledge, yet at the same time seemed so emotionally detached from his childhood environment.

While she felt no sense of real danger as they strolled around taking in the sights, the hot air seemed to throb with the decades of tension between the Palestinians and the Jews. Although in some places the dividing line between Arab and Jewish territory was invisible, you always knew when you'd crossed over.

Valerie was secretly relieved that Andrew had not been offended by her comments about Melissa in the restaurant last night. Very much like his father, the younger man seemed to embrace conflicting opinions and assertiveness from the opposite sex. She was also pleased that she had managed to assure Melissa that she wasn't a pariah. The poor girl had been convinced that Aaron hated her. Valerie had told her that her husband was simply a quiet, stoic sort of guy, who often had an unsettling effect on people. Now Melissa had taken her advice and decided the best course of action was to be a good listener rather than a chatterer.

The second day they toured the Galilee area, and, as Drew and Melissa walked way ahead of them, Valerie got her first view of the famous Sea of Galilee.

"What do you think?" Aaron asked as they stood together on the rocky banks of the placid cobalt sea, which was barricaded by mountains.

"I can't believe I'm actually here." She spoke in a reverent whisper. "But I'm a little surprised. I expected it to be larger."

"It probably was larger way back when, but time and erosion have played havoc with the landscape," Aaron admitted. "On the other hand biblical accounts do tend to be larger than life."

Valerie scanned the horizon. "I don't quite agree with that. I guess it looks small because it's so peaceful right now…peaceful in contrast to what the Bible said about the raging storm at sea and Jesus walking on water."

"Are you disappointed because you're not seeing a glowing paranormal figure skimming the surface of the waters?"

She gave him an exasperated slap. "That's not funny."

"You're the believer," Aaron said, a teasing inflection in his voice. "But the Bible account of stormy seas is scientifically accurate. This lake is both shallow and well below sea level. Because it's surrounded by mountains, when the colder wind blows and meets the warm water temperatures, it can really stir things up. Squalls can occur suddenly without warning."

Much to her delight, he began to quote Matthew 8:24 and 14:24 without benefit of having a Bible. She was almost ashamed that he could quote scriptures more accurately than she could, and the power and resonance of his voice gave her a haunting sense of *déjà vu*. He sounded like her father.

The third and final day, Drew insisted that they had to visit Masada, and so they arrived at the base of the desert mountain in the still dark pre-dawn hours, with Melissa yawning and a bit whiney but trying hard to be a good sport. Aaron now told them that morning was best because once the sun came up the soaring temperatures became intolerable.

There was cable car access, which both Melissa and Valerie would have preferred, but Aaron and Drew, steeped in their macho roughing-it mentality, decided they had to hike the arduous winding trail, appropriately called the snake path. Valerie didn't complain, although she found the physical strain of climbing the mountain path challenging.

Both couples were dressed similarly in hiking boots, T-shirts, and khakis, although Melissa had opted for khaki shorts. They carried bottles of water and were coated in layers of sun block, courtesy of the women. Neither man had felt like arguing over the nuisances of applying the skin protection, so they'd simply complied. Melissa started out strong and enthusiastic, but within fifteen minutes of the hour-long trek, the heat nearly caused her to pass out, and Drew ended up carrying her most of the way. Valerie noted that other than sweating, neither Aaron nor Andrew showed any sign of fatigue.

At the top of the summit were the ruins of what had once been the over two-thousand-year-old palatial retreat for Herod the Great. From the heights, Valerie could see the entire valley with the Dead Sea, which seemed very much alive and glistened like a jewel. The view was magnificent.

As tourists gathered and the sun slowly began its spectacular ascent, Aaron began to tell the harrowing story of the destruction of Jerusalem by the Romans. When the sun reached its peak—a molten ball of gold in the multi-hued sky—Aaron dramatically accounted the story of Masada, of how the last survivors of the destruction held off the Romans for months, and then, when all hope was gone, refused to be taken captive and committed suicide instead. He ended his account by repeating the swearing-in oath familiar to every IDF recruit: "Masada shall not fall again."

A tragic and compelling tale, Valerie thought, but Masada did not have any biblical significance to her. What was the honor in having to resort to killing yourself and your family? She didn't get it, but she kept her thoughts to herself. The audience didn't feel that way. They were moved by the surroundings and the account.

"Wow," Melissa whispered loudly to Andrew. "Your dad's awesome. Scary, but awesome."

Drew grinned and wrapped his arm around her. "The Captain has many talents. I'll be playing catch-up for the rest of my life."

Overhearing, Valerie nudged him. "You're off to a decent start."

The mountain that had taken an hour to climb took under thirty minutes to descend. From there they visited the Dead Sea resort and Andrew and Melissa decided to linger and explore. Valerie was amazed at the warm temperature and the weird buoyancy of the salty water—so salty that it was impossible to sink in. She would have donned a bathing suit and attempted to swim, but Aaron wanted no part of that scene.

"Drew and Muffin are staying awhile," Aaron said. "Unless you're interested in rolling around in salt and covering yourself with sea mud, I suggest we go find lunch."

"No. I'm with you." She curled her finger around his belt loop and tugged gently. "The name is Muffy, hon, not Muffin."

Chapter 22

Muffy was so exhausted from Masada and the Dead Sea excursion that she decided to remain in her hotel room instead of accompanying them to El Neve Kibbutz, the place where Aaron had grown up and where his uncle Gabriel lived. No one argued with her decision and Aaron suggested that Valerie might prefer to remain behind as well, but she insisted on going.

In hindsight Valerie decided that Muffy had made a wise decision, and she wished she had done likewise.

The first warning came when Aaron's amiable mood began to head south en route to El Neve, and most of the conversation during the short drive was between Valerie and Drew.

"Aren't there other family members we could visit?" Valerie asked Aaron.

"No." He focused his attention on the road.

She shrugged. "You told me you have half-sisters and a brother."

"I also told you that we don't communicate."

"Such a warm, loving family." Drew smirked from the back seat. "There is a reason for the big chill, if you really want to know."

"What's the reason?"

"Ask *yours truly*."

Valerie glanced at Aaron, who said nothing. She turned back to Drew. "Yours truly isn't talking. Tell me."

"Four years ago when his father, whom I also never met, died, my father had the body shipped out of Israel and buried in Africa next to his mother. This was totally against the wishes of the second wife and children. He had the dastardly deed done before they could even get a court order to stop it."

Valerie shook her head. "Really, Aaron. Is that true?"

"Yes," Aaron replied coldly. "Two days before his death, my father told me that's where he wanted his remains."

Valerie wasn't sure whether to be flabbergasted, appalled, or morbidly amused. Yet at the same time she wasn't surprised. "Hmm…well, I guess I do see how that might cause a rift…just a little."

Drew laughed. "Kudos to Captain Congeniality."

The moment they set foot on the grounds of the kibbutz, Aaron became completely dour. He didn't reminisce about his childhood, encourage exploration, or offer to escort them around the sprawling farm complex. Instead, they went directly to the large private home where the uncle lived with a woman named Sarah Schulman.

Gabriel, who had long ago changed his surname from Weiss to Ben-Jacob, was formidable, looking a little like a towering Hollywood version of Moses. The man was in his late eighties but stood ramrod straight. He had a silvery beard and a head full of wavy silver hair. He greeted them in an emotionless, perfunctory manner and Valerie noticed that he possessed the same glowering stare Aaron had perfected, only there was something vitally amiss; a touch of madness lurked in his faded blue eyes. He told them that his companion—he didn't even lie and refer to Sarah Schulman as a wife—was out, and he invited them inside.

The shades were drawn in the sparsely furnished sitting room, which reeked of cigar smoke. Once the three of them were settled on an overstuffed velour couch, Gabriel sat in a separate wingback chair facing them like an interrogator and commented, sans humor, that he was surprised that Aaron was married and that Valerie resembled Aaron's Cushite mother—Cushite was exactly the word he used. Valerie wasn't too sure, but she sensed that the word was used disparagingly. He then went on to say that it was about time he met Drew, who he hadn't even realized was an adult. Afterward, he fixated on Aaron, whom he neither embraced, shook hands with, or smiled at.

"You've been away much too long," he said.

"I'm here now," Aaron said.

While Valerie fought back the urge to vocalize her displeasure, the conversation switched to Hebrew, which neither she nor Drew understood, and after a few minutes, Gabriel stood and, with a wave of his hand, dismissed her, asking that she please wait out in the garden because he wanted to have a private discussion with his family.

Valerie was all too eager to leave; in a few more seconds her mouth would get her in trouble.

Sensing her chagrin, Aaron rose and escorted her down a hallway and out into a blindingly sunny garden of climbing roses, where there was a secluded bench. "This shouldn't take long," he said. "I apologize for him. Gabriel's become even more insensitive with old age."

Valerie sat heavily on the bench. "Insensitive? He's outright rude." She sighed. "Well, I guess I was warned."

When he had gone back inside, she stood up and paced, hating having been sent outside like an ostracized child. The sunlight and flowers mocked her so terribly that she ventured back to the house and found her way into the hallway. The cathedral-like arched door to the sitting room was now closed, and all she could hear were Aaron's and Gabriel's muted voices. The hallway was actually quite fascinating.

The walls on both sides were covered with framed museum-quality photographs of people—handsome young men and women with that distinct Israeli Sabra look, all captured in various poses and various locales. She walked farther down the hall, wondering who all the people were. In the midst of the adult faces was a larger picture of two gorgeous little twin red-haired girls, holding hands and standing in a field of wild daisies. She stared at them for a long time before moving on.

At the very end of the hall, an empty picture frame hung. Puzzled, she studied it. A small bronze plaque was in the bottom edge of the frame announcing a certain year followed by a hyphen.

"Hey," Drew said, causing her to jump.

He put his hand on her shoulder. "Sorry, didn't mean to startle you. Hope that crazy old lion didn't offend you too much."

"No, I'm okay. Did he dismiss you, too?"

"Yes. I hate to imagine what you must think of this bizarre excuse for a family."

"Don't worry about me. Uncle Gabriel doesn't matter. It's your father I care about. Plus, it seems you and I are getting along okay. That's really all that matters."

Drew smiled slowly. "I'm glad you're in my father's life, and I hope you stay there. Doesn't seem he's got anything here in the way of family."

"Thanks, Drew. I'm sorry about the way your uncle is. It's kind of appalling that you came to Israel for the first time hoping to meet some family, and this is what happens."

"Means nothing to me," he said with a shrug. "But I'm learning all about where my father gets his charming disposition." He studied the pictures on the wall. "Did you know that Uncle Gabriel's a famous sculptor and photographer?"

"No. Actually, Aaron's told me very little about him."

"Gabriel Ben-Jacob has pictures in the Holocaust museum, the Smithsonian, and in quite a few galleries. Most of them are Holocaust-related."

"Interesting. Any clue who all these people are?"

Drew took a deep breath. "Before the Great One dismissed me, he told me to look at the pictures. He calls this the hallway of heroes and martyrs. All of these people were personal friends of his, who were either soldiers, special agents or loved ones who died in the struggle to keep Israel a Jewish state."

Valerie sighed. "That's sad. There are so many of them. Who are the little girls?"

Drew studied the twin redheads. "I'm not too sure, but I believe they must be Uncle Gabriel's daughters. I've been told he married really late in life and that he had twins. They were six years old when they died."

"How did they die?"

"A car bombing. Gabriel and his family were vacationing in Switzerland. The bomb was meant to kill him, but instead it killed his children and his wife's brother. His wife left him after that and I think eventually committed suicide."

"Oh, God. Does it ever end?" Valerie looked away.

"Did you wonder about the empty frame on the end?"

"Yes," she admitted warily.

"That one's waiting for Aaron. Uncle Gabriel told me a few minutes ago that he dusts it off every day."

A wave of dizziness swept her. "Drew, I think I've seen and heard enough. I'm going out to the car to wait."

❧❧

Late in the evening, in their hotel room just outside of Galilee, Valerie lay on her side of the bed, half-heartedly thumbing through a travel brochure. She was swathed in a thick lavender-colored robe, even though the room was not cold.

"I hope you're not still thinking about Gabriel," Aaron said.

She shrugged. "I'm okay. You did warn me not to go."

"I should have insisted."

She put the brochure down. "I told you I'm okay. What I really want to know is, are you?"

"Me?" He looked puzzled. "Why shouldn't I be?"

"Well, for God's sake, you're human, aren't you? You haven't been back home in what? Twenty years? And that's the kind of greeting you get? What did he say to you?"

"What he said to me is irrelevant. He's old and not to be taken seriously."

His voice trailed off as he went into the bathroom and turned the shower on full blast.

Valerie sighed, reached up, and switched off the nightlight. Lying in the dark, she couldn't shake a feeling of sadness for Aaron having grown up around such callous people, and she wondered if he really was as unruffled and detached as he led everyone to believe. When she was young she had considered her own mother to be emotionally cruel, but her life had been a stroll in the park compared to his. The feelings turned to anger. She didn't care what Gabriel Ben-Iceberg thought about her, but how dare he be so cold and hostile to his nephew and to Drew?

Aaron, a towel wrapped around his waist, returned to the bedroom and sat on the edge of the bed in the darkness.

Valerie reached out and traced a finger down the smooth length of his back. "What did he say to you?" she whispered.

"It's not important."

"Aaron, please."

"He told me I was wrong to abandon my country, and that I'm a fool for getting married."

"Oh, please," Valerie said angrily. "The *married* part is none of his business, and you didn't abandon your country. If anything, the country abandoned you and then turned around and pardoned you. Sounds like being jerked around like a puppet on a string to me."

Aaron looked over his shoulder. "You're angered by this?"

"Darn right, I'm angry." She moved closer to him. "Gabriel's just so preoccupied with death, dying, and so-called honor. Please tell me you're not even thinking about ever moving back here."

"If that's what you're worried about, don't be." Aaron sounded vaguely amused. "Israel doesn't speak to me in the way it did when I was a kid. I would never live here again."

Valerie breathed a barely audible sigh of relief. "I just don't get your uncle. I never got to meet your father, but, from what I've heard, it seems like your family has such little regard for one another. No one's appreciated until they're dead. No love at all. Did your father ever hug you...make you feel special?"

She couldn't see his expression because his back was facing her, but she sensed his surprise at her question.

259

"It's unthinkable that he would do such a thing," he said. "My father was not openly demonstrative in that sort of way, but not long before he died, he said something that surprised me a little."

"What?"

"He apologized to me. I didn't expect that...didn't even want it. He said he was proud of what I had accomplished and sorry for not being the father he should have been. It was at that point that he made me promise to have his body buried in Cielo Vista near my mother."

Valerie inhaled slowly. "I'm glad he finally told you he was proud of you, but why...why do you think he was so unavailable?

"It was my unspoken belief that he blamed me for my mother's death."

"Oh, please, that's so ridiculous. How could he blame a baby? You didn't cause your own birth."

"Ridiculous, I agree. But I imagine every time he looked at me, he remembered losing her." Aaron rubbed his eyes wearily. "None of this matters now. It's true, we didn't go around embracing and commending each other, but we still cared."

"Unacceptable. Not good enough," Valerie said. "I think it's about time someone showed you some real love."

"And I suppose you're going to do that," he said, slipping under the covers, a definite hint of a smile in his voice.

"I'm certainly going to try." She shed her thick robe, exposing bare skin, and snuggled up closer, wrapping her arms around him.

The chill of his body immediately alarmed her. "My God, you're freezing."

"You used up all the hot water."

As if he needed more cold. She embraced him tighter, rubbing him, warming him with her own body heat. Slowly her hand moved down to unknot the towel. Immediately, they flowed into the rite of lovemaking, and she noticed for the first time that there was no protection—no physical barrier between them.

❧

"Hey, Valerie. How about you and me taking a little walk," Drew said.

He had just finished helping Aaron load their luggage into the SUV and was approaching Valerie, who was standing at a slight distance from the hotel, casting her final glance at the Sea of Galilee. They would be heading for the airport soon.

"What's up?"

"Got a little surprise for you."

He held up a large brown paper bag. "Quick. I don't want the others to see."

261

What was he up to? Valerie couldn't help melting at the way his eyes lit up, his boyishly handsome smile—a smile that appeared much more frequently on his face than on his father's. She followed Drew around the back of the hotel as he ducked into a narrow alleyway where three huge garbage dumpsters were lined up.

"Nice romantic spot," Drew said cheerfully.

"Very." She wrinkled her nose at the pungent aroma of putrefying food. "Is this some kind of joke?"

"I present you with…"

He let his voice trail off as he set the bag down and extracted a large picture frame. Valerie gasped as she recognized the empty frame that had been in Uncle Gabriel's hallway of heroes.

"You *didn't.*"

"Yes, ma'am. Step back, please."

She stepped back as he swung the frame like a baseball bat against the dumpster, shattering it into a million glass shards. Valerie began to laugh deliriously—laughter that was really a mask for emotional tears. He picked up the remaining pieces and tossed them in with the rest of the trash.

"Make no mistake about it," Drew said, taking a bow. "No demented old coot is going to sit back and predict my father's death."

"Amen," Valerie said. And she hugged him for all it was worth.

They were still smiling as they returned to the car.

Chapter 23

While hanging out in the airport lobby awaiting their flight home, Aaron slouched in a chair reading the Hebrew print newspaper he'd picked up at one of the stands while Drew entertained Valerie and Muffy with a few navy stories as well as some hilarious childhood tales of growing up in Blue Heron, South Carolina. Valerie learned that Drew was the only grandson in his family and that he was close to his grandfather, Lee McDade, a wealthy retired businessman. She was especially surprised that he had grown up in Blue Heron.

"It really is such a small world," she said. "My mother and my aunt came from there. Back in the 60s, my grandmother worked as a maid for some wealthy family called Sumner." She chuckled. "That was before she realized slavery had ended."

"No kidding," Drew said. "The Sumners used to own the paper mill. Old man Sumner died years ago, but the family's still around. I used to beat the crap outa Brad Sumner when we were kids."

"Are you sure it wasn't the other way around?" Muffy asked, nudging him.

"In his wildest dreams," Drew said. "Forget those people. They were the most arrogant, bigoted bunch you'd ever want to meet. Real blue-blooded Southern stereotypes."

Aaron suddenly looked up from his paper at Valerie. "What became of your grandmother?"

"Never met her. She died before I was born. As a matter of fact, I believe the Sumners buried her. They were her whole life. She lived in a small cottage on their property."

"Your mother told you this?"

"No. My mother never told me anything. My aunt did. Both my aunt and my mother moved north, but my grandmother chose to stay in Blue Heron because she was so devoted to the Sumners."

"That's so sad," Muffy said. "Why didn't she move north with her own family?"

"I don't know." Valerie shrugged, suddenly realizing that her family background was almost as baffling as Aaron's. "I think my grandmother still had the slave mentality. People were weird back then. It was before the civil rights movement really gained momentum."

"Racial tolerance has come really slowly to Blue Heron," Drew said. "Some of the townspeople still fly confederate flags. The old ways aren't practiced anymore, but people still have their mental attitudes about segregation. I mean, on the surface everyone gets along, but many people still practice their own form of segregation by choice."

"Aaron, have you ever been to Blue Heron?" Valerie asked, noticing that he'd tuned out of the conversation.

"No. And I have no plans to."

"Then you've never met Drew's grandfather?"

"We've met. It happened when we were both in Miami on business. He's a good man. A fair one."

Valerie glanced at Drew. "What kind of business was your grandfather in?"

"He was in the navy during World War II, and after the war he managed the shipping port in Charleston. He's always been connected to the sea in some way. Still owns and sails his own ketch at eighty."

"He sounds amazing."

"You'd like him," Drew said.

"And your grandmother?"

"Gone. She died when I was a kid. He remarried."

The conversation continued with Aaron perfectly content to remain silent, until an announcement was made that they were to head for the departure gate.

Valerie wished Drew could have stayed around longer, but his leave time from the navy was limited and he didn't return with them to New York.

Valerie accepted a part-time job caring for a stroke victim that didn't interfere with her personal life, and was pleased that Aaron didn't immediately resume international travel. In the weeks that followed, he shuttled between his New York office and the two Avian hubs at JFK and Newark. She got to see him at least three nights out of the week, and on Sundays he was usually around most of the day. She was also pleased that he had put aside his cautious cynicism about Martha Cates, making it easier for the lawyer to set up the trust fund for Mr. Allard's grandson. The boy became the recipient of most of the money, with Valerie retaining only a comparatively small amount.

The renovations on the house were in full swing also. With newly erected scaffolding attached to the back and sides, the estate appeared to beam at the prospect of its resurgence into the twenty-first century.

Chapter 24

On an unusually warm Sunday morning, Valerie and Aaron began painting the living room ceiling of their soon-to-be-inhabited house. The project had been her idea because she thought it would be fun to work on something together. But instead she had to deal with his perfectionism, and he teased her for being a klutz. In the end, she became so frustrated that she threw paintbrushes at him and they wound up in a very messy play fight.

Later, Noah and Jasmine dropped by to help them paint and the serious work was undertaken. The day passed very quickly.

∗∗∗

The velvety warmth of the night wrapped around them as they lay bundled up together in a sleeping bag on the living room floor. Thanks to teamwork, the living room and the smaller parlor area had been painted and, after Noah and Jasmine departed, Aaron had conceded to Valerie's wish to spend the night.

While he appreciated her sense of spontaneity, he felt vulnerable and edgy lying in the empty room surrounded by naked windows that gave free rein to the macabre dance of shifting shadows from outside. In his mind, it was the setting for the perfect hit. He visualized a sniper crouched in the cover of the night drawing a bead. In actuality, the scene was a byproduct of his paranoid imagination. He knew it was not going to happen. Not here in the United States. Here he was simply Aaron Weiss, business mogul, not Nigel Solomon, Arif Salaam, Tarek Abdul, or whatever persona from the Middle East or Africa he chose to personify.

Valerie was not in any danger at all. He never would have married her if he had even an inkling that she would be in jeopardy by default. But at the same time, she didn't know that he had a gun with him, hidden beneath a throw rug within his reach. She also didn't know that he had two armed security people patrolling the grounds. Ridiculous, yes, but he liked the added assurance. Maybe one day he would completely drop the paranoia, but not tonight.

"I'm suddenly remembering what it was like to be ten years old and camping out in the backyard," Valerie whispered.

"Is that a good memory?" he asked.

She burrowed closer, one hand resting against the hard flatness of his bare mid-section "Yes. My next-door neighbor—her name was Meg—we had a tent in the back and her yellow lab was with us." She chuckled at the thought. "My mother was appalled, but my father allowed us to do this. Meg and I didn't sleep a wink that night. All we did was tell ghost stories and run back and forth from the tent to the house, stealing junk food. By morning we were sick."

"Must've been a lot of fun," he said wryly.

She laughed. "Trust me, it wasn't as bad as it sounds."

"Valerie," Aaron said reflectively, his mind completely out of sync with what she had been talking about.

"Yes?"

"Do you know why your father gave up his military career to become a minister?"

"Umm...I've always wondered that myself, but he never...well, almost never talked about his army days. At least not to me." She toyed with the chain around his neck. "I suspect he saw some casualties...maybe even had to kill in self-defense. And I don't think a good person can take a life without feeling remorse, even if the victim is evil."

Aaron's initial silence was deafening. "Only a socio-path can kill and feel nothing. It's never easy to be judge, jury, and executioner, even if duty calls upon you to do it."

He was horribly guilty of bloodshed, but the repercus-sions of not acting would have been far worse. Still, it was disturbing to consider the grief felt by the innocent, un-suspecting wives and children of the slain terrorists.

"I think my father realized that military strength was not the way to achieve peace," Valerie said. "And he likely became a minister because he was seeking forgiveness and redemption."

"Did he find it?"

"Yes," Valerie answered with conviction. "I'm positive that God in His goodness and mercy extended it to him."

"How do you think your father would have felt about his daughter marrying someone like me?"

This was definitely not the kind of introspective questioning he usually indulged in, and Valerie was aware of it. Up until now, she had probably gotten the impression that he didn't care one way or another what anyone dead or alive thought of him, and to a degree that was true. So why was he asking her?

"I think," she said slowly, deliberately, "I honestly think he would have liked you...in time." She searched for his expression in the darkness.

"In time," Aaron repeated and then fell silent again.

"Why?" Valerie nudged him. "Why are you talking about this?"

His arm slid around her. "No reason. Does there always have to be one?"

"Not for some people, but you rarely say or do anything without one."

"Then consider this one of those rare moments," he replied.

Her questioning silence indicated that she wanted him to elaborate, but he had no such intention.

"The moon and the stars are giving a command performance tonight," he whispered in her ear.

She looked past his shoulder at the towering windows, to share his view of the active twinkling in the onyx sky.

The stars and the full moon, fat and comfortingly yellow, reminded her that there was a cohesive force at work in the universe—a force that was far loftier than humans and very much in control.

"I wish we could just stop time and hold this moment forever," she said softly.

Aaron stared at the stalking black shadows of pine trees, visualizing what would be the best angle for a sniper to attack—what angle he would take if he were the sniper. "A moment…even a good moment held forever would get boring," he said.

"Aaron, don't say that." Valerie gripped him by the forearm "Stop being so uptight and just see the world for what it is…a beautiful work of art by a loving Creator. You make things much more complicated than they need be."

Had she read his mind? He certainly hoped not, or she would probably come to the conclusion that he was suffering from post-traumatic stress syndrome or worse; still, all cynicism aside, she was right. If he could view life the way she did, it would certainly be more joyous and definitely less stressful, but he doubted if he'd ever get the spiritual angle behind her philosophy.

"Sorry," he said. "You're right. It's a nice, peaceful moment and I'm happy to be sharing it with you."

"Much better," she said, kissing him on the mouth.

Chapter 25

On the day of Denise's wedding, Valerie awakened to a gray sky and an unsettling premonition that something was about to go wrong. She didn't normally have premonitions or panic attacks, but from the moment she stumbled out of bed feeling slightly nauseated and dizzy, her world seemed off kilter. It didn't help that Aaron was in Singapore on business—or so he told her, when he'd called two days ago. But worrying about him was an exercise in futility. Perhaps the feeling was centered on fickle-minded Denise, who might change her mind at the last moment and pull a no-show.

Fortunately, as the day progressed, her mysterious malaise lifted and she was able to write off the nonsense as rainy day superstition. Except for some easily resolved wedding gown malfunctions that occurred right before arriving at the church, everything went off without a hitch. Denise and Tony were married in Aunt Marilyn's church, even though the groom wasn't a member and Denise hadn't attended since she was a child.

The reception was as loud and obnoxious as Valerie had expected, but she was able to tolerate the endless toasting, drunken dancing, and badly behaving relatives because Jasmine was with her. Jasmine was husbandless as well, since Noah was also out of the country.

After the partying into the wee hours—long after the bride and groom had slipped off en route to the all-expense-paid Hawaiian honeymoon that Valerie and Aaron had given them as a wedding present—Jasmine returned with Valerie to her Englewood apartment instead of taking the longer drive back to her home and they spent the night there.

When Valerie woke up the following Sunday, the apartment was quiet. She pulled on a robe and slipped soundlessly into the kitchen, hoping not to awaken Jasmine in the guest room. Maybe a steaming mug of tea with ginger sprinkled in it would ward off the shaky, nauseous feeling that was plaguing her again.

"Hey." Jasmine appeared in the kitchen, startling her. "The sun's not even up yet. Why are we?"

Valerie smiled. "We? I don't know about you, but I'm up because I couldn't sleep."

"Too much partying last night, huh?"

Valerie grimaced at first, then hid a smile. Despite her obvious pregnancy, Jasmine looked like a little girl in an oversize pink Tweety Bird T-shirt and blue stretch pants.

"Are we about to pop this morning?" She addressed Jasmine's belly.

Jasmine yawned. "I wish. Feel like I've been pregnant forever. Can't wait to get this little darling on the outside."

"Less than two months to go," Valerie said. "And I'm betting it'll be a lot sooner than that."

"Hope you're right." Jasmine reached into the cabinet and pulled out a box of cereal. She glanced at Valerie, toying with the tea. "Is that all you're having?"

"Yeah. I don't know. Just the thought of food is nauseating."

Jasmine laughed. "If I didn't know better, I would think that you were pregnant, too."

Valerie rolled her eyes. "Don't even joke about that. It's probably a hangover."

"Hangover from what? You hardly drank at all. Plus, you complained of feeling nauseous before the wedding. Maybe you're coming down with something."

Valerie stirred the liquid, clinking the spoon noisily against the sides of the mug. "I'm sure it's more like something called Aaron anxiety. I'm going to have to stop worrying about him so much, but every time he leaves the country, I have this nagging fear that he won't be returning."

Jasmine's eyes met hers. "Don't say that. It's not like you to think that way. I'm the one who suffers from chronic pessimism. Besides, you knew the score when you married him."

"True, but I'll stop worrying only when he tells me straight out that he's never going to get involved in special ops again."

Jasmine sat at the table. "You don't really think he's on a mission now, do you?"

"No." She shook her head and tried to console herself. "He said the business involved Avian freight. I'm sure he wouldn't lie to me."

"Then you'll just have to take his word for it."

Valerie nodded again and sipped the tea, which tasted horrible.

"You know," Jasmine said, changing the subject, "I was hoping you'd build a house close to us, but I'm really loving your Long Island place now. That house has such character. It's actually starting to personify you and Aaron."

Valerie smiled slowly. "How do you personify Aaron and me?"

Jasmine looked puzzled, realizing that there were no words to describe the couple, and they both laughed.

"Can you believe we've been married for almost six months now, and I'm still alive and reasonably sane?" Valerie said.

"And you still love him," Jasmine added, covering a cagey smile with one hand. "I've been pretty vocal with my doubts, but now I totally get the two of you together. Oh, he's still got his dark, brooding thing going on, but he's a little more down to earth...more appealing since he's learned how to laugh, and he seems to have a higher tolerance for small talk and ordinary people in general."

Valerie adjusted her sunglasses. "So it really is noticeable? His little…er, transformations have seemed so small to me."

"Trust me, girlfriend. He is changing. Just keep working on him. Noah notices it, too."

Valerie knew she should be pleased, but instead, she felt apprehensive, the feeling she got when she realized everything was going perfectly and she knew she should brace herself for a storm to come rolling in. She did not want to discuss Aaron. Her thoughts and feelings about him were too complicated, too deep, and too wrought with emotion.

"Let's talk about your baby. I'm sure he's going to be beautiful."

"Healthy is good enough for me," Jasmine said. "And I'm praying that he's nothing like Diego."

Jasmine had learned a few months ago that the new baby was going to be a boy, and while she hadn't voiced her preferences openly, Valerie sensed that she would have preferred another daughter. The irascible Diego had no doubt influenced that sentiment.

"He'll definitely be calmer," Valerie assured her, "because this one will be yours and Noah's. Let's face it, Diego's got a whole set of genes that you didn't contribute to. But I still think he'll outgrow his behavior problems."

"Hmm. In the meantime, I think I'll give him to you and Aaron to raise."

Valerie laughed and then shuddered. "God forbid. If Aaron had him, the boy would morph into a frightened rabbit."

Jasmine frowned. "At least he'd be quiet for more than two seconds."

"Don't worry about it," she said. "Things will work out."

But even as she said the words she felt like a slightly bubble-headed Disney cartoon character. Everyone knew that things didn't always work out.

By afternoon, Jasmine had returned to her own home and Valerie felt like her old self again. She chided herself for not going to church. It seemed that she had fallen into the pattern of not attending way too easily, and she wondered how much Aaron's influence was causing that tendency. She would have to rectify this soon because losing her spiritual connection was not the way to go.

She stopped to visit her mother and found Ruth Ann sitting in her room before an untouched food tray. Surprisingly, though, her mother looked up attentively and made direct eye contact as Valerie entered.

"Hi, Mom. How are you today?"

"Fine," Ruth Ann said, squinting, craning her head, and looking somewhere beyond Valerie's shoulder.

"What? What are you looking for?" Valerie asked, realizing that the unusual alertness had little to do with her presence.

"Where's your father? Is he coming to see me today?"

The wind went out of Valerie like a deflated sail, but she quickly recouped. What did she expect?

"He can't come," Valerie said flatly. "He'd like to, but he can't." She wanted to blatantly remind her that Joel Redmond was dead, but it seemed cruel.

"He *told* me he would come," Ruth Ann said, her tone petulant. "He told me the last time I saw him."

"What do you mean last time? You haven't seen him for years…" Valerie stopped herself. Clearly, she was out of sync with her mother's delusions. Ruth Ann was not talking about Joel; she was talking about Aaron.

"The man you're talking about is *not* my father, he's my husband, and he can't come to see you right now because he's out of the country on business."

"Out of the country? Business? Why is he out of the country?"

"He does that a lot, Mom. It's his job." Valerie sat on the edge of the bed, facing her mother, who was seated in a chair with the food tray in front of her. "Here, aren't you going to eat any of this?"

"I don't like that stuff. It has no taste."

She had over-cooked fried chicken, mashed potatoes, carrots, and some kind of juice, Valerie wasn't sure
what. In truth, the meal didn't look all that appealing.

"Would you like me to get you something else instead?"

Ruth Ann shook her head mutely.

"Oh, come on, Mother. How about if I stop by that
deli down the road and get you a hero sandwich? You
used to like those." Her mother wasn't on any special
diet, so she could pretty much have what she wanted.

"No. I don't want anything, and I don't feel like talking to you right now."

And it's good to see you, too, Mother, Valerie thought,
rising abruptly. There was no point in trying to continue a conversation. "I'll see you on another day, then.
Maybe you'll be in a better mood." She started toward
the door.

"When you come back, bring your father," Ruth
Ann said.

❧

That evening, Valerie began cleaning out the medicine cabinet in the bathroom, willing the phone to ring,
hoping that Aaron would call her, yet knowing that he
probably wouldn't. She tossed an empty bottle of per-
oxide into the trash, along with a decades-old bottle of
aspirin, and then she stopped and stared at a foreign ob-

ject—an unopened box containing a home pregnancy test. She frowned. What was that doing there? Then she laughed, remembering that Denise had abandoned it after a visit nearly a year ago, when the diva had had an unwanted pregnancy scare. Denise had never used it because she had been too afraid to see the results. Good old Denise, the drama queen, now married and probably having the time of her life in Hawaii. Valerie picked up the box and was about to add it to the trash, when she remembered her earlier conversation with Jasmine.

"No," she told herself aloud. "No way could I be…" She shuddered, unable to finish the sentence, but instead of throwing the test kit away, she left it sitting on the counter.

In the morning, she tumbled out of bed, dreading that she had to go to work because the now-familiar nausea was back. What was going on with her? It was true, she had missed her period, but for her, periods were normally inconsistent and unpredictable, so she hadn't thought much about that.

Beyond frazzled, Valerie stumbled to the bathroom and picked up the pregnancy test. She followed the directions carefully and, to her shock and dismay, when she looked at the indicator stick it revealed a blue line. Positive.

Chapter 26

"Aaron, there's something I have to tell you." Never in her life had Valerie dreaded such a moment.

The lights were dim and they were sitting in the living room of their Manhattan loft with the theatrical curtains drawn back, the sparkling city skyline strung before them, on what should have been an enchanted evening. How she wished she could just forget what she had to tell him and conclude the evening wrapped blissfully in her husband's arms.

Aaron set his wine glass down on the coffee table. "What is it? For the last hour, you've been like a DC-10 in a holding pattern, circling around the runway unable to land. Are you about to bring her down or abort?"

Disturbing analogy, Valerie thought, swallowing hard. "I…I don't quite know how to say this, but I… we have a problem."

Apprehension, or was it concern, flashed in his indigo eyes. "You're not sick, are you?"

She inhaled sharply. "No. Nothing like that."

"What is it then?"

A faint ring of impatience edged his voice. She couldn't really blame him, could she? People who rambled and digressed often irritated her as well. The only thing she could do was just clear the air and brace herself for the fallout.

"It turns out I was wrong when I told you that I couldn't conceive. I went to the gynecologist two days before you got back and...and discovered that I'm pregnant."

His eyes narrowed and he didn't even attempt to conceal the smoldering rage that tensed his face. "Really?" he said. "So it turned out that you were wrong, did it? Or would it be more accurate to say that you lied in the first place?"

"I didn't lie!" Valerie stood up, wringing her hands. "I really was told that I would probably never be able to conceive and—"

"Probably?" Aaron interrupted. "So now the key word is *probably*. You knew all along that there was at least the possibility that you could get pregnant. Yet you told me that you couldn't." He rose abruptly and stalked toward the window to glare at the twinkling lights on the bridge.

To a degree, she felt he had a right to be upset. It had been years ago when she'd first been given that prognosis. She should have consulted another specialist, several even, in order to determine her fertility status, but at the same time his reaction was sparking an anger that was growing within her. "I'm sorry about this," she said tightly. "I honestly told you what I felt to be true at the time. I'm only human, Aaron. I'm not in complete control over what goes on inside my body. The doctor…the one I saw two days ago…she told me that given my condition, it was unusual for this to occur…but it happened anyway. I didn't intend for this…"

"You're a nurse," he said bitterly, accusingly. "And you have a bit more than a layman's knowledge about physiology. You should have known better." He didn't turn to face her, and she was glad because she didn't want to see his eyes.

"I said I'm sorry." She couldn't temper the anguish in her own voice. "What else can I say? It's not all about you. I'm the one who has to deal with the consequences…go through that…that procedure. I'm…"

The rest of what she was trying to say would not come out. The words stuck like a huge lump in her throat, and she knew she was in serious danger of bursting into useless tears. She turned and rushed from the room to the silence of the bedroom. Once inside, she closed the door and threw herself down on the bed, burying her face in the pillow. Pathetic, she knew. She was acting like a five-year-old, but she couldn't contain her emotions, and she couldn't bear to see that expression on his face. She clutched the pillow.

Five minutes passed. Ten. Fifteen. She heard the door open and felt the bed shift slightly as he sat on the edge.

"We can deal with this. It's going to be all right." His voice sounded tight, controlled. "I'm sorry. If anyone should apologize, it's me. What happened was my fault."

Valerie hesitated. She felt his surprisingly gentle touch, his long fingers stroking the back of her neck, as if she were a trembling kitten. She didn't want him to stop, didn't want to turn around. "What are you saying?" she half mumbled into the pillow.

"I was a fool for not using protection. That was my decision to make, not yours, and I should have stuck to it."

Ouch. He had apologized, but the apology was a double-edge sword, reminding her that she was the one who'd had such an aversion to his birth control obsession, and that he shouldn't have listened to her.

"I would imagine you're going to have to deal with this problem soon," he said.

She lifted her head, resting her chin on her arm. "The doctor said as soon as possible."

His fingers were still stroking her. "Is there much risk involved?"

"Minimal, if it's done early enough."

"Have you scheduled anything yet?"

"No. I wanted to tell you first."

"I'll be there with you, if you want me to be."

Of course she wanted him to be there, but she didn't fully understand why she was still feeling confused and angry. She knew good and well that she couldn't actually have the baby. Her physical condition would not allow her to carry full term. She would probably have a traumatic miscarriage, risking her life. She'd probably…but she was doing the probably thing again. She didn't really know for a fact. How could she? She was not God, nor was she completely in control of the workings of her own body.

That was it. All the conflicting feelings were making her crazy, and the underlying anger was on account of Aaron's presumptuous easy resolution to the dilemma. Clean it up, forget all about it, and move on.

❧❧

Dr. Kate Saunders called her in the morning, wanting to know if she could come to the office, and she accepted the afternoon appointment. Aaron came along with her. They were told that if they decided to go with the abortion, it would be done the next week. But the doctor had some other news. She informed them that she had consulted with a Dr. Lawrence, who specialized in high-risk pregnancies, and he had reviewed the test results. He wanted to speak to Valerie because he felt that it might be possible for her to carry the baby full term. Valerie didn't know how to respond to that. The news left her even more confused.

"There's no need to consult anyone else," Aaron told the doctor bluntly. "We're not going to take that risk, so let's set up the appointment."

"Yes, of course…if that's your final decision," Dr. Saunders said, looking at Valerie.

Valerie nodded her head mutely.

On the ride back home, she felt her conflicting emotions and her anger mounting. What right did he have to speak for her? Why did she just sit there like a limp rag and silently sentence the new life within her to death—and that's what it would be, the death of an innocent child. She believed, had always believed, that life began at conception. Aaron wasn't even willing to give their baby a fighting chance.

"You're making the right decision. I hope you realize that," Aaron said as they entered the apartment. He hesitated for a fraction of a second. "This is what you want, isn't it?"

"It's what you want."

"And what is that supposed to mean? You know good and well that you can't attempt to have the baby. You told me before that you almost died when you had a miscarriage."

"That was then. This is now."

She looked up at him and his expression was mostly unreadable, but she did detect a bit of patronizing tolerance. Mr. Tough Guy was trying to be patient with his silly little overly emotional wife, who was on the brink of having a hormonal temper tantrum.

"I don't want to discuss this anymore," she said, going off to the bedroom. "The problem will be solved next week."

He appeared content with that, and she resisted the overpowering urge to smack the smug look off his face, which at the moment seemed more maniacal than handsome.

The following day Aaron was out of town and Valerie did the unthinkable. She knew she shouldn't because whatever was said would only make her even more upset, but she went to see the specialist her doctor had mentioned. Dr. Lawrence talked to her for a long time, explaining the risks and what could be done to circumvent them. He spoke of his success rate with cases similar to hers. She took notes and told him that she would let him know what her final decision was.

Predictably she left his office in a quandary, even more upset than before. How could she terminate the pregnancy when there was the possibility that she could go full term? What right did she have to snuff out a life that the Creator had entrusted her with? But, on the other hand, what if it really meant sacrificing her own life?

The same day, she decided that the only person she could discuss the matter with was Jasmine, but even then, she didn't plan to tell her the whole deal. Without calling her ahead of time, she took the drive out to Ramapo, hoping she'd be home, since she wasn't working during the final months of her own pregnancy.

Jasmine's eyes widened in surprise and then alarm when she heard the news. "Oh, my God. How did that happen?"

"Well, when two people of the opposite sex…"

Jasmine laughed and slapped her. "You know exactly what I mean."

Valerie sighed heavily. "I don't know myself. I was convinced by more than one doctor that I was infertile and now…surprise."

Jasmine shook her head. "Does Aaron know yet?"

"I told him."

"Oh, boy. That must've been tough. Guess that means…since you won't be able to carry full term, that you'll have to take care of it soon."

"Next Friday. Do you think you could go with me?"

"Sure…but isn't Aaron going to be with you?

"Nope."

"Val, that's totally ridiculous. What's wrong with him?"

She hesitated. "It's not his fault. He did offer, but there's just something…I don't know. It's like I don't want him there. I'm kind of angry, and I'm not sure why."

"Okay. I think I understand," Jasmine said slowly. "You wish you could have the baby, and even though you know you can't, his eagerness to get rid of it seems cruel."

She nodded wordlessly.

"I guess it's just another one of those disappointments that you have to get over and move on. I mean, it would be totally different if you actually could have the baby, and he was pressuring you to get rid of it just because that's what he wanted."

Valerie flinched. She did not tell Jasmine that there was at least a possibility that she would be able to carry the baby. She knew the final decision was hers and hers alone to live with. She was going to be the one who would either incur Aaron's wrath or risk a guilty conscience for terminating a life.

Two days before the deadline, Valerie spoke to Aaron over breakfast. "I've decided that it's not necessary for you to be with me when I go for the…the procedure. Lots of women go through it all the time. It's no big deal."

His eyes narrowed. "I thought we'd agreed that I would be there."

"It's better if you're not with me. Please don't make the situation even more difficult than it already is."

"Are you sure?"

"Yes."

"Well, since you've made up your mind, I've got some business in Miami on that day, but I'll keep in touch."

That's exactly where you wanted to be anyway, she thought. "Yes, you do that," she said in a tone that was even icier than she had intended.

Aaron gave her an odd, raised eyebrow gaze, but he didn't question her response, which was typical of him because he hadn't spoken of the dilemma since the doctor's visit. Ever since he'd learned about the pregnancy, he hadn't encouraged any physical intimacy between them, either. She assumed that they wouldn't be in normal mode again until the issue was settled.

Chapter 27

Friday morning Valerie could not will herself to go out the door. She'd spent the night before going over and over in her head what was about to take place. She'd visualized the sterile clinic surroundings, sitting on a cold table wearing a flimsy paper gown, being anesthetized and awakening with the problem all gone. The spark inside snuffed out. She couldn't move. She couldn't budge.

The phone rang. It was Jasmine asking her if she was ready to go. Valerie told her that she had a migraine and would reschedule the appointment in a few days. Who was she fooling? She had decided that she was going to try to have the baby. It wasn't a total dismissal of Aaron's feelings or wishes, but neither of them had the right to terminate what God had entrusted her with. God would determine the outcome. Aaron would just have to accept this as another challenge in their married lives.

❧

The phone rang in the mid-afternoon, about three hours after the abortion would have been completed, had she not changed her mind. Knowing full well who the caller was, Valerie did not immediately respond. Finally, when she knew she couldn't avoid telling Aaron the truth any longer, she picked up.

"Aaron," she said, feeling awkward and cowardly. "Are you still in Miami?"

"Yes. What's going on?"

"Nothing. I…um. I know this isn't what you want to hear, but I talked to the specialist Dr. Saunders referred me to, and I changed my mind. There is a possibility that I can have our baby, and I owe it to him or her to try."

Silence on the other end. Dead silence.

She continued holding the phone to her ear, wondering if he'd actually hung up on her. She knew he was furious. Yet hanging up didn't seem to be his style.

"If you're expecting me to support this insanity, think again." His tone was glacial. "I don't care what that charlatan told you. There are extreme risks involved. Your life takes precedence over an unborn child."

Valerie squeezed her eyes shut, clutching the phone so tightly her knuckles turned white. "I understand you're worried, but I have no choice. This is a faith-based decision. I seriously believe that God intends for me to have the baby." Even as she said the words, she realized that, to an agnostic, she sounded like a lunatic.

"So your benevolent God wants you to die, while bringing another unwanted person into the world. I made it perfectly clear from the start that I have no interest in raising a child."

Her voice caught in her throat. "I'm not going to die. We can work it out. You'll see. It doesn't have to be such a terrible thing...."

"And so that's it? There's nothing I can say to convince you otherwise?"

Her voice quavered. "I've made my decision."

"So be it. When I get back tomorrow, I'll let you know what *my* decision is."

And with that he hung up. Boy, she did not like the sound of that. What if his decision was the termination of their marriage? She stared numbly at the ceiling. Okay, so he was upset—outraged, actually. But maybe he'd cool off between now and the time he got back home.

❦

The day she dreaded—it seemed she dreaded most days lately—came while she was at her old apartment in Englewood. After she unlocked the door, Aaron entered and didn't even bother to take his jacket off before he lit into her.

"There were some well-defined conditions to our marriage," he began. "You understood them, accepted them, and agreed to honor them. Now you're willing to betray my trust, go completely against my wishes, and then have the audacity to expect sympathy and acceptance. Did you think I was just playing games when I said I didn't want children? Did you?"

"No, I didn't," Valerie said. She felt like a fool and a punching bag, absorbing his rage, pain, and frustration. The worst part was she didn't really have a comeback. Right or wrong, he was entitled to his feelings, and she could understand in a twisted way that he felt betrayed. If she didn't love him so much, there was no way she would be standing there taking his tongue-lashing.

"Then why? Why are you doing this? Was our so-called relationship a fraud, and you married me just so you could have a baby? You did the same thing to me that your ex did to you?"

She clenched her teeth. "How could you think that? That's not true and you know it! I've tried over and over to explain, but you're not getting it because you have no sense of spirituality…you don't want to believe in a Creator. This is *not* about me choosing a baby over you."

His voice rose. "Then what the hell is it?"

"Aaron, don't yell at me!" She seized a pillow off the couch and gripped it tightly. "I can't stand your attitude right now, and maybe I'm insane, but I love you more than I've ever loved any other human. Do you hear that? More than any other person. But when it comes to the spiritual, I have to choose God's commands over your wishes… over my own wishes, even." She took a deep breath. "If I lacked belief, then I wouldn't think twice about getting rid of the baby. Please try to understand. Please."

Aaron shook his head, and for a moment Valerie thought she saw a glimmer of reconciliation beneath the surface of the rage. He sat down on the couch and stared at a spot on the wall just beyond her. "Whatever the outcome, you have forever changed our relationship," he said.

Perhaps she had not seen reconciliation in his eyes after all. Valerie sat down on the opposite end of the couch, burying her face in her hands. "Is this it, then? The moment you tell me you want a divorce?"

Aaron said nothing. He rubbed his eyes wearily, and in his silence and body language she sensed a profound sadness.

He doesn't want a divorce. At that moment she felt the strong urge to wrap her arms around him, but she refrained because it seemed like too much too soon. Cautiously, she moved an inch closer. "I still believe we can work this out together…without terminating the pregnancy."

She was tempted to add that there was the distinct possibility that she'd have a miscarriage anyway, but she didn't say it because she knew from past experience that that could be disastrous as well. Still, she was older and wiser now. She'd take a lot more precautions than when she'd been younger and possessed the attitude of invincibility that gripped most youth.

"I can't promise you resolution," Aaron said finally. "But we're looking at one day at a time for now."

"Yes," she said, trying to blink back tears.

Chapter 28

When Jasmine gave birth to her and Noah's son, a beautiful boy named Jonathan Robert—Jonathan being Aaron's middle name—Valerie had to force herself to celebrate. She was happy for the proud couple, but their joy was such a contrast to her own situation.

Taking the advice of her doctors, she had stopped working as a nurse and now held a part-time administrative job at Englewood Hospital, performing data entry and other clerical duties. Her co-workers thought she was crazy because they knew she didn't have to work, but they didn't understand the situation. There was no way she could just loaf around the house.

She had passed the three-month danger period—the time of the miscarriage years ago—and the outcome was looking even more positive than the doctors had anticipated. In fact, the hematologist had told her that the clotting factor in her blood had increased, due to the hormonal changes that naturally occurred in pregnancy, and it would probably stay at that improved level up until the time of birth. All of this was great news and she longed to feel optimistic and content, but she could not because Aaron's attitude had not changed and her marriage was still in limbo.

Aaron had not been exaggerating when he'd told her there would be no immediate resolution to their problem. Ever since that day at her apartment, she'd seen very little of him. He'd transformed back to the remote person she had known in the beginning—the one who felt it was unnecessary to keep in touch with a phone call. He was currently disregarding all the little concessions he had made when they'd been at peace with each other.

Although she was deeply hurt by the negative changes, she was remaining mute because she didn't have the desire or the energy to argue with him. In the back of her mind, she was hoping that eventually he'd get over his need to punish her.

Their new home, which was completely finished and furnished, mocked her. Aaron was never there to enjoy it. On the rare day or two that he was in the country, he preferred his place in Manhattan. Valerie had nightmares that he was once again involved with special ops. Why not? He had never gotten around to promising her that he would retire, and now it seemed he might use the rift in their relationship as an excuse to accept another dangerous assignment, possibly as a means of working off his anger.

On a Saturday morning in late August, Valerie unlocked the door of the remodeled Allard estate. She was back to referring to the house with an air of detachment, since it didn't feel like hers anymore. She was even considering renting the place out because neither she nor Aaron spent any time there.

The magnificence of the large living room, with its chandeliers and cathedral windows, overwhelmed her, and she recalled with heartbreaking sadness the day they had painted the room. Had it been only yesterday when they'd shared the love and the laughter? How could feelings so encompassing, so right, have vanished in a heartbeat?

She tiptoed up the winding staircase so as not to disturb the ghosts and entered the library, which still retained most of its original appearance, along with its vast assortment of books. The Bible collection that had been responsible for starting her down the narrow, twisted path of intrigue and heartbreak was displayed prominently on shelves in the reference area.

As she took a step toward the shelves, she looked up and noticed with a start that a new painting dominated the wall above the fireplace—a painting of the sea. Immediately recognizing it as the Sea of Galilee, Valerie observed that the water was far from the calm, shore-lapping serenity she'd seen when they'd visited Israel. In Aaron's artistic rendition, the sky was ominously black, the sea deeply indigo, dashed with silver, foam-crested waves that rose menacingly, threatening to engulf a small fishing boat.

She held her breath. When had he hung it? When had he actually taken the time to visit the house? Unless she was losing her mind, the painting had not been there a week ago, when she had last visited the library. There was no way she could not have noticed something so eerily mesmerizing—so hypnotic. As much as she tried to pull herself away, she could not stop staring at the tiny fishing boat that was being tossed mercilessly by the ferocious waves. She inched closer. In the enshrouded mist of the brilliantly stroked sea spray, a veiled shadow, a diaphanous figure, seemed to be strolling on the water. Jesus? She shook her head and squinted. No. There was nothing like that at all in the painting, just the waves and the fishing boat that was about to capsize.

"You're definitely losing it," she muttered aloud. "Seeing things that aren't even there." She touched the expensive gold frame, desiring to remove the large canvas from the wall because its metaphorical presence disturbed and angered her, but she could not bring herself to do it. Instead, she backed abruptly away from the painting and fled the room.

Aaron was supposedly somewhere in Algiers, due to return in two days. He had not actually said so, but she knew he was waiting for her to be the one to officially end their marriage. Perhaps he considered this to be an act of civility and grace on his part. Perhaps he thought she was pathetic. Perhaps he was right on both counts. Her doctor's advice to avoid stress was about as impossible as being told to stop laughing, crying or breathing, and Aaron's actions heightened her tension levels every passing day.

❧

After leaving Long Island, Valerie forced herself to stop at the nursing home because she felt guilty for not visiting her mother in nearly two weeks. She found her in the empty solarium.

"You told me you weren't coming today," Ruth Ann said from her wheelchair. She was near the window, where she had been basking in the blinding sunlight that streamed in from the parted curtains. An open Bible was on her lap.

"I haven't told you anything," Valerie responded mechanically. "How could I when I haven't been here for at least two weeks?"

"You told me yesterday," Ruth Ann insisted.

Valerie sighed. "It was probably your sister who told you. Aunt Marilyn said she visited you yesterday."

"My sister?"

"That's right. I'm Valerie, your daughter."

Ruth Ann narrowed her eyes. "I know who you are." She opened the Bible and began thumbing the fragile pages. Valerie observed her with defensive detachment. It was just as well she had the Bible out; maybe they could discuss that instead of sitting and looking at each other with nothing to say.

"What scripture are you reading, Mother?"

"Psalms," Ruth Ann replied.

"Are you going to read it out loud?"

"No. You don't listen like he does."

Who's he? Valerie wondered, but didn't feel like asking. *He* was probably her late husband.

"You're getting fat," Ruth Ann declared suddenly.

Valerie ran her hand defensively across the front of her T-shirt. "I'm sure it's not that obvious yet, but I'm pregnant. I've told you that before."

"Your husband's worried about you."

"My what?" Valerie repeated, trying hard to suppress an eye roll. Her mother was still confusing Aaron with Joel. "Did you say my husband, or are you talking about your husband?"

"I said *your* husband, Aaron."

Valerie laughed sarcastically. This was going to be a fun visit. Ruth Ann was as confused as ever. There was nothing for her to do but play the game. "What makes you think Aaron is worried? You haven't seen him in months."

Ruth Ann peered at her above the rims of her glasses. "He came to see me. We talked for a long time and we read the Bible."

"He did not visit you," Valerie said irritably. "You met him only once, and that was a long time ago. Aaron's not even in the country, so he didn't visit you."

"He was here," Ruth Ann insisted, her voice rising. "And don't tell me that I didn't talk to him because I did."

"When?"

"Couple of days ago."

Muttering to herself, Valerie rubbed her eyes. "Okay…fine. You talked to Aaron. What did he talk about?"

"You. He's worried."

"Mother, the only person Aaron worries about is himself. He's angry at me because he doesn't want to have this baby."

You idiot! What's wrong with you? Why had she surrendered to the ridiculous need to tell her senile mother something like that. What was she looking for? Certainly not sympathy or even commiseration.

"I didn't want babies, either," Ruth Ann said.

Valerie had been prepared for her mother to make no comment at all and the response shook her. "Thanks, Mom. Maybe you'd like to explain why Greg and I are here, since you didn't want babies."

Ruth Ann maneuvered the wheelchair around so her back was to her daughter, and she stared out the window at the distant hills. "Greg was an accident, but your father loved him anyway."

"I'm sure Greg would love to hear that." Valerie felt as though the oxygen was being depleted from the room, and she knew she should just bid her mother farewell for the day, but she remained glued to the spot, wondering what was going to be said next.

"I loved your father, and I had you because he wanted you," Ruth Ann said. "He was good to both of you."

"Yes," Valerie agreed coldly. "Our father was good to us, but you seem to be admitting that you didn't care about us at all. I know it's not a perfect world, but aren't mothers…I mean normal mothers, supposed to love their children?"

Ruth Ann said nothing. She continued to stare out the window.

Valerie stood up, clenching her purse. She wanted to cross over to the window and yank the wheelchair around to make Ruth Ann look at her, but at the same time she didn't really want to see that blank expression — that look that confirmed the reality of her scathing admission.

"Fine. So you had us just to make Daddy happy, and then you completely tuned out of our lives. Since that's how you felt about us, why should we…I…care about you?"

"You don't care about me. You put me in this home," Ruth Ann said bluntly.

Valerie felt her face flush scarlet with anger. "I what? How dare you say something so stupid and untrue. I didn't put you in this home. You put yourself here. You kept walking out of the house and forgetting

303

where you were. You refused to eat. Once the police picked you up because you were walking in traffic. And then there was the time you almost burnt the house down. You've forgotten all those things, haven't you?"

She didn't expect an answer and she didn't get one, but she couldn't control the onslaught of venom spewing from her own tongue. "I had a right to my life, and I had to work. I couldn't be there 24/7 taking care of you, especially since you never even cared about me. You..."

She managed to stop in mid-sentence, when she realized that she was shouting like a lunatic and anyone could walk in and hear the outburst. Maybe if someone actually did hear it, she would be taken away in a straitjacket. She felt crazier than her mother. "I'm sorry," she said, turning away, struggling to calm down. "I can't talk about this anymore without yelling, so I'm leaving."

"I do care." Ruth Ann maneuvered the chair around to face her again. "I did the best I could, and you shouldn't be so angry. You should be happy because God cares about you and so does Aaron. God says right here in this Bible that 'thou shalt not commit murder,' so of course you can't get rid of the baby. But you need to stop being so angry and stubborn about this. Be kinder to Aaron. Talk nicer, more ladylike, and maybe he'll..."

Valerie hesitated at the door. "Mother, stop playing games. You don't know a thing about Aaron, and what's more, you don't even know what you're talking about. Goodbye."

With her head spinning, feeling as though she were about to pass out, Valerie left the room and stumbled into the nearby bathroom, which much to her relief was devoid of people. Maybe she was about to have a miscarriage right here and now. Maybe she would have a heart attack. She pressed her back against the tiled wall and closed her eyes, resisting the urge to slide down to a squatting position because she probably wouldn't be able to get back up. She tried counting backward and gradually opened her eyes to discover that the room had stopped whirling. All she could hear was the buzz of the over-burdened air conditioning unit. No miscarriage. No heart attack.

"We're okay," she whispered aloud, hand over the slight bump that contained the new life within her. "Just calm down."

Finally able to stand straight without shaking, she went to the sink and splashed cool water over her face. She stared at herself in the mirror and was pleasantly surprised to find that her reflection didn't reveal a woman about to have a meltdown. Obviously pregnancy hormones were fueling her inner turmoil, and she would simply have to get a grip or face dire consequences.

When she felt composed enough, she left the room and continued down the hall toward the elevator.

"Valerie," Sherry Jackson, one of the nurses on the floor, called out.

Valerie looked up with a start and smiled at the pleasantly plump Jamaican native. "Haven't seen you in a while," Sherry said. "Just wanted to tell you that your mom's been doing quite well lately. She seems more alert, and she's even been socializing."

"Really?" Valerie said, trying to sound interested as she approached the nurse's station where a young aide with long, braided locks also sat, talking on the phone.

"I'm thinking it might have something to do with the visitor, the male visitor she had about two weeks ago. Was he your brother?" Sherry asked.

"My brother?" Greg had called her from Chicago a few days ago and he'd given no indication that he was planning a visit. Before Valerie could come up with a startled explanation, the aide ended her phone call and chimed in. "Talk about hot...that guy was to die for."

Sherry laughed, gave the younger woman a dismissive wave, and focused on Valerie. "Well, he was quite handsome," she admitted.

"Okay, so aside from being handsome, what exactly did this man look like?" Valerie still did not believe it was possible that her mother could have been right.

"Tall, really tall," the aide chimed in again. "He was light-skinned with black, close-cut hair. Very serious and businesslike."

"Interesting," Valerie said, swallowing hard. She turned back to Sherry. "Thanks for telling me about my mother. I hope we can talk another time, but right now I really have to run."

Sherry nodded, and Valerie made a quick exit because she most certainly did not want to answer any questions about the identity of the man. The short description had made it clear just who the visitor was, but it didn't explain why. Why would Aaron have bothered to visit her mother and then not even mention it? What kind of game was he playing, anyway? And, last but not least, why was she so angry?

Chapter 29

"Aaron, what are you doing here? I thought we were going to meet in Long Island this afternoon," Valerie said as she opened the door to her Englewood apartment, allowing him to enter. His appearance, in an open-collared white oxford shirt and gray pants, took her breath away. He was flashing an even bronze tan that made his uniquely alluring eyes dazzle even more.

"I caught an earlier flight back to New York, and I didn't know if you would feel like taking the ride out to Long Island, so I came here," he said.

It was early Sunday morning and Valerie had been intending to go to church. Her sensual, spontaneous side was elated to see him, but the rigid, stubborn side was annoyed at his timing. Now she would have to forego her plan and deal with him. The truly awful thing was that she felt defensive and awkward in his presence. Because of the circumstances, she really had nothing positive to say to her husband at this moment. She had wanted them to reunite in the neutral and more spacious environment of the Allard estate.

She was a mess—another negative—a chubby frump, devoid of makeup, in hair curlers, and clothed in a frayed pink bathrobe suitable for an indigent recluse. "I'm sorry there's no food in the house," she said, turning away, moving toward the bathroom, deflecting even the slight possibility that he might kiss her. Or, worse, that he might not. "I haven't been shopping and…"

"I'm not a stranger and I didn't come here to eat," Aaron interrupted.

You seem like a stranger, Valerie thought but didn't say. Her heart sank even lower when he made no attempt to physically rein her in.

Aaron sat on the couch, sadly realizing the profoundness of his own words. It was a difficult time for both of them. They really were like strangers, and he didn't know what to do or say to break the spell, short of lying and telling her that he'd done a complete one eighty and was now ready to accept the possibility of a child-birthing nightmare and the end result.

"So how are you doing?" he asked, sounding insincere even to his own ears.

She hesitated in the hallway. "As well as can be expected." She longed for him to come to her, sweep her off her feet, and tell her he loved her—that it didn't matter if they weren't a perfect family, but that he'd try to be a good father.

He wanted to take her in his arms and tell her everything was going to be all right, that somehow they'd get through this, but she wasn't being receptive. There was detachment in her eyes and an obvious hostility in her stance. Maybe, just maybe, he had been wrong about the depths of their relationship. Maybe she had never really cared about him as much as he had hoped.

"Have you made plans for the morning?" he asked.

"I just got up, but I was intending to go to church."

"Fine. Don't let me stop you. We can always talk later." He rose and stalked back to the door, putting his hand on the knob.

Idiot! Valerie thought. "I didn't say you had to leave."

He hesitated. "Then what are you saying?"

"Aaron. I hate this…the way we are. I can't stand it anymore."

She spun around to face him, her dark eyes glowering. Despite the pathetic robe and the hair curlers that she was angrily yanking from her hair, he could still see the curving softness of her lips and the smoothness of her skin. He inched closer to her but was stopped cold by her question.

"Did you go visit my mother two weeks ago?"

"Yes."

"Why?"

Knowing where she was headed with this and not liking it, he shoved his hands in his pockets and took an exasperated breath. "I told her a while back that I would visit her. Is that a problem?"

Valerie bit at her lip. Why did he always have to be so blunt and confrontational? *Is that a problem? Is that a problem?* She resisted the urge to imitate him.

"No. It wasn't a problem, but it just doesn't make sense. You know she has Alzheimer's and she probably thought you were my father. What could you possibly talk to her about that would make any sense?"

"We didn't talk about much at all. I had to remind her over and over again who I was, until she finally got it, and for the most part, she quoted Bible scriptures and I pretended to listen."

"Did you discuss me?"

"She asked about you and I responded."

"Well, tell me exactly what you talked about." Valerie's voice rose. "She's my mother, not yours. I have a right to know."

Aaron stepped farther back. "I find it rather amusing that you dislike her so much and all of a sudden you're telling me, with impassioned fervor, mind you, that she's *your* mother and not mine."

Boy, did he know how to push her buttons and make her feel like a demented, spoiled brat. Her voice dropped lower, but nonetheless remained rife with tension.

"If you can manage to get over your great amusement, I still want to know what you talked about."

"She asked me if we were happy and I told her the truth," he said.

"The truth? I see...the truth about your not wanting our baby. Did she sympathize with you...tell you that she never wanted me or my brother, either?" Valerie suddenly had a vision of her own child, her son or daughter, running happily to Aaron, calling him Daddy, wanting to share a special moment with him and seeing him turn coldly away, telling the child to go to her instead—or, even worse, the image of the child trembling in fear of him as Jasmine's stepson had. The vision shattered her to the core.

"Valerie, you're overreacting, blowing this whole nonsense out of proportion," Aaron said.

"Stop patronizing me!" Before she even realized what she was doing, she seized a magazine off the coffee table and hurled it across the room.

Aaron's eyebrows rose. She turned away, embarrassed by her rage.

"I'm sorry." She retreated. "This is so dumb...arguing about my mother when the real problem is us. Aaron, I don't even like myself anymore and I can't live like this. We..." her voice quavered.

"Should separate," he finished.

"Yes." She couldn't believe she was responding so unemotionally now.

"Consider the Allard house a gift," he said without missing a beat. "You can do whatever you like with it. When and if the baby is born, I will support it materially. If you need anything else from me, just ask. As for the apartment in Manhattan, that was mine in the beginning and shall remain mine."

Uninhibited tears streamed down her eyes and he swam in her hazy vision, but, even in that unfocused state, she could tell he was no longer looking directly at her—that he probably didn't even notice the tears. He had severed himself physically and emotionally from her. She struggled to catch her breath and strengthen her own wall of defense. Although his words were as cold as ice, he was being generous enough. She certainly wasn't going to challenge him in court over any of his assets. She wasn't that vindictive or stupid.

"When you decide on the divorce, I'm sure we can settle amicably," he concluded.

There, the "D" word was out and he was leaving. *No!* her inner voice screamed. *Don't walk away from me. Don't leave. Please.* But she stood frozen and mute as he opened the door and slipped soundlessly from her universe.

❦

Valerie did not make it to church that day, and she called in sick at her job for the next two days. Her phone rang incessantly, but was ignored. All she did was mope around the apartment, sobbing intermittently and polishing off a half-gallon of mint chocolate chip ice cream. When she finally got around to answering the one phone call that the voice mail didn't pick up, she was annoyed that it was a nursing home employee reminding her that she hadn't picked up her mother's laundry and asking if she would like them to do it instead.

Running a comb through her tangled hair, she got dressed in whatever frightful ensemble she could find and arrived at the nursing home.

"How's Aaron?" Ruth Ann asked the minute she stepped into the room. Valerie ignored her completely—didn't even look at her—and opened the wardrobe to remove the laundry bag. She began stuffing her mother's clothes into it.

"Are you angry?"

"I suppose you could say that," Valerie muttered, dragging the bag across the floor, preparing to leave.

"Valree...don't be angry like that. It's not good for you and the baby."

"Who cares?"

"I care."

Valerie dropped the laundry bag and dabbed at her eyes, which, courtesy of sleepless nights, resembled those of a raccoon. "You asked me about Aaron...well, you won't see him ever again because he's gone. We broke up."

"He's coming back," Ruth Ann said almost defiantly. "You can get him back."

"I don't *want* him back. He doesn't love me."

"He does love you and he loves the baby, too. Get him back."

"How?" She glared at her mother. "What should I say?"

Ruth Ann's mouth opened and closed. "Ask your father."

Ask yuh fahhhthuh. The obnoxious words tumbled out, their mocking cadence reverberating in Valerie's ears like chalk scraping on a board. *Mommy, Mommy, there's a monster in my room; can I sleep in your bed? Ask yuh fahthuh. Mommy, where do babies come from? Ask yuh fahhthuh. Mom, I need…Ask yuh fahhthuh.* She remembered the sailboat, the abandoned atoll off Belize, and she recalled very vividly Aaron laughing at this very imitation of her mother. *Ask yuh…*

Gripping the laundry bag again, she rushed out of the room and nearly collided with her Aunt Marilyn, who was about to enter.

"Valerie?" Marilyn exclaimed in surprise.

"I'm sorry," Valerie shrieked, the bag thumping behind her. "I can't talk now." She didn't stop, even though Marilyn called to her again and attempted to follow. She just kept walking until she was outside, loading the bag into the trunk. Once she was back home, she barricaded herself in the bedroom.

Chapter 30

Within an hour, her aunt showed up at the door.

"I'm sorry about what happened earlier," Valerie said as they settled in the living room. "I've been under a lot of stress lately and, at this point, my mother's getting to me."

"Your mother told me that you and your husband are having problems," Marilyn said.

Valerie frowned. Even though Jasmine had said it might be a good idea, she still did not want to discuss Aaron with her aunt. "It's nothing." She gestured flippantly. "You shouldn't take anything my mother says seriously. She's in her own world most of the time anyway, and, even before she was diagnosed with Alzheimer's, she's never shown any interest in what goes on with me."

"Valerie." Marilyn cleared her throat and looked disturbed. "I know my sister's always been a little...er, odd, but in her way she really does care about you, and your brother, too. I hope you don't get so angry that you stop visiting her."

This was the first time Valerie had ever recalled her aunt admitting that Ruth Ann was odd before the Alzheimer's diagnosis. "I wish I could stop visiting. I don't get my mother, and I've never gotten her. You say she cares about us in her way, but I don't understand what that way is. When my father was alive, she always depended on him to solve all her problems and ours. She never gave any input at all."

"There were things that happened to your mother long before you were born that made her that way," Marilyn said.

"We all have our stuff," Valerie said coldly, her mind ricocheting back to Aaron. "Just because our past lives may have been troubled doesn't mean we completely shut down and ignore the present."

"That's true," Marilyn said, "but your mother—"

"It's always about my mother, isn't it?" She stood up abruptly and went to stare out the window at the afternoon sunlight filtering through the trees. "Yes, Aaron and I are having some issues. I certainly didn't expect any advice from her, but when I got there to pick up her laundry, she kept on prying into my personal life, as if she really was concerned, and then when I finally gave in and sort of asked her what I could do, she told me to ask my dead father." Valerie laughed. "She's been saying that since I was born. She still thinks he's alive."

"You have a right to be upset," Marilyn said slowly. "But I'm trying to tell you something that you need to know. It's a secret that's been kept way too long. I'm sure your father would have told you at some point, but he died before he had the opportunity." She hesitated for a moment and then continued slowly. "Something very traumatic happened to your mother, way before you were born. It was a crime."

Valerie felt a paralyzing numbness creep silently into her bones as she tried to imagine just what that crime might have been.

"I'm telling you this only because I don't want you to hate your mother the way I hated my own mother," Marilyn said, her voice shifting into a trancelike monotone that masked emotion. "When Ruth Ann and I were very young, our father and mother lived in a nice rented house in Washington, DC, where our father worked for the railroad. He was saving to buy the house, but then he died in a train accident. My mother didn't even attempt to try any other options, just dragged Ruth and me back to Blue Heron, South Carolina, where she and her mother before her had lived—back to the Sumner estate to work as a maid for the wealthy Sumner family. Ruth Ann and I were five and seven years old and we lived in a tiny run-down cottage on their property—little more than slave quarters, actually."

"I know about that part," Valerie said.

Marilyn ignored her comment. "Joseph and Marianne Sumner had two teenage sons and three younger daughters who were around our ages. The family owned a lot of property, as well as the big paper mill where almost everyone in the town worked. Our mother worshipped the ground those people walked on. She would literally die for them. She loved them and their children more than she loved us."

I don't care about my crazy grandmother and the Sumners' lofty assets, Valerie thought, struggling to keep her mouth shut so her aunt would get to the point sooner. The only thing she could focus on was the mystery of the crime that had allegedly been committed against her mother. She dreaded hearing it, but at the same time she needed to.

"And?" She looked uncertainly at her aunt who had hesitated.

"Ruth Ann and I were always close, even though our personalities were opposites. I was the wild one," Marilyn said. "When we were little, my mother made us work with her around the Sumner estate, and we always had to say 'yes ma'am' and 'no ma'am' to the adults and, even worse, we had to call their children Miss and Master so-and-so." Marilyn flinched at the memory. "We had no childhood at all. When we weren't working or in school, we were in church. All our clothes and toys were hand-me-downs from the Sumner kids, who were like royalty. That was not the kind of life I wanted."

"Aunt Marilyn, what happened to my mother?" Valerie demanded, turning away from the window, pacing across the floor.

"Hold on. I'm getting there. By the time I was around twelve or thirteen, I started defying my mother, sneaking out of the house, hanging out with bad kids, running all over the place. When my mother's older cousin, Arleen, came from New York State to visit us, my mother convinced her to take me back with her to live. Ruth Ann wanted to go, too, but my mother wouldn't let her. I felt bad that we were separated, but it was the best thing that ever happened to me and the worst thing for her."

"Would your cousin have taken both of you?" Valerie asked.

"Yes, but my mother wouldn't part with her because Ruth Ann was this nice, sweet, obedient girl who never got into trouble and never openly defied her. She did have flaws, though. She was so pretty that grown men, black and white, would literally stop in the street to gape at her when she passed by. Some women might think beauty would be an asset, but it was more of a curse to her because she was extremely shy and she didn't know how to deal with the unwanted attention. She…she was absolutely terrified of people. When we were going to school, I was her only friend, and I was the one who always had to speak up for her and fight her battles. It wasn't that she was simple-minded or anything, she got better grades in school than I did. She was just extremely shy."

Valerie sensed exactly where this nightmare tale was heading, and she exhaled loudly.

"When Ruth Ann graduated from high school, college wasn't even in the equation and she couldn't get a job on the outside because she didn't know how to relate to people, so my mother forced her to work as a domestic for Logan, the Sumners' oldest, married son. This was in the sixties, so there wasn't much else for a black woman to do in a small town.

"Well, Ruth Ann told me she was alone in the parlor dusting one morning, when Logan came in. She said he was acting really strange and she tried to leave, but he came after her. She said she fought him, but he overpowered her and…and he raped her."

Valerie's blood ran cold and her throat went dry, even though she had prepared herself for just that revelation. "Lo…Logan Sumner?" she stammered. "Isn't he a congressman or senator?"

A long silence ensued. "Yes," her aunt finally said. "Yes, he is a senator now."

"Was he arrested?" Valerie asked, knowing exactly what the answer would be.

"No. He was never even formally accused of the crime. There was no justice for a black woman then, and Ruth Ann knew it. She didn't tell anyone the day it happened, but she quit the job, stopped talking completely, and refused to leave the cottage. The truth probably would have never gotten out if she hadn't become pregnant. When our mother found out, she said it was Ruth's fault. She accused her of being promiscuous and leading Logan on. She defended that rapist even though she knew her daughter had never flirted in her life. She kicked Ruth Ann out of the house and said she never wanted to see her again."

"Oh, my God." Valerie stood still, hands balled into fists. "No wonder you hated her. I can't stand her, either, and I'm glad we never met. How could she treat her own daughter that way?" The question was rhetorical, and, even if Marilyn had replied, the information wouldn't have registered. "What did my mother do?"

"She called me," Marilyn said. "I went down to get her and she came to live with me in Newburgh. By that time I was on my own, renting an apartment and working in a sewing factory."

"And what happened to the baby? Did she…?"

"He was born. The baby was Greg."

Valerie gasped. "Then my…my father wasn't Greg's biological—"

"Your father adopted him as his own," Marilyn interrupted. "Joel was like an angel. He came into your mother's life at the right time. She was living with me and refusing to leave the house because she was so traumatized. After the baby was born, I had to take care of him, since Ruth Ann was so removed from reality that she was incapable of doing it. Joel was the one who was able to bring her out of her depression. Sort of."

Valerie returned to the couch and sat down heavily. She didn't want to believe what she'd heard, but it was too dreadfully detailed to be a fabrication and it also explained a lot of things. No wonder she and Greg looked nothing alike—why he looked Caucasian.

"Does Greg know this?"

"Yes. Joel believed he had a right to know the truth and he told him when he was eighteen."

That explained another thing—the reason for Greg's anger, why he'd cut himself off from the family for five years. She shook her head as if to clear it.

"Greg knows about the circumstances of his birth, but Joel couldn't bring himself to tell him exactly who his biological father was," Marilyn said slowly. "I don't think it would be a good idea for you to tell him, either."

"Tell him? I'm speechless. What an awful story. And…and to think Logan Sumner got away with violating my mother and now is a state senator."

Marilyn sighed. "Life can be cruel, as I'm sure you already know, but that happened over forty years ago, and you have to let it go. I've managed to put my anger aside because I know, even when crimes seemingly go unpunished, God is watching and He will repay. Logan Sumner may be a respected state senator now, but he's had some tragic family issues over the years, including a son who died from a drug overdose and a daughter who died from leukemia."

Let it go. Let it go. The words echoed in Valerie's head. Obviously her emotionally fragile mother never had, but despite everything she'd managed to eke out some semblance of a life. "Since my mother was so… so traumatized, how did she ever get together with my father?"

"Joel's family owned the apartment building where I was renting," Marilyn said. "When he came home from the war he worked with his father for a while, maintaining the building, and that's how he got to meet your mother. It was love at first sight. He didn't care what her issues were, and he simply refused to give up on her. You should have seen them. He was so kind and gentle. He brought her flowers every day and talked to her, even though she didn't always respond. He took time with Greg and treated him like his own son. I'm sure your father's told you some of those family stories."

"Yes." Valerie still felt numb, but she now realized fully how her father had come to be her mother's knight and protector.

"After they were married, Ruth Ann was terrified of having more children," Marilyn continued. "But Joel wanted at least one biological child, and somehow he convinced her to have you. He took on all the responsibility for both you and Greg because my sister couldn't. It was an agreement they had. She loved you, but she was afraid if she got involved, she'd contaminate you in some way, that you'd end up as emotionally crippled as she was."

"That's ridiculous. I mean, I do understand how she came to feel that way, but I doubt very much that I would have been *contaminated.*" Valerie made direct eye contact. "Didn't it ever occur to anyone that my mother should have been seeing a therapist?"

"Therapy wasn't the first thing people—especially black people—availed themselves of back then. In the later years, your father did discuss the idea with her, but she never cooperated, and by then they had adjusted to using a higher power to help. They relied on God. Their lives were far from perfect, but they managed okay. And both of their children turned out well."

"I…I wish I had known," Valerie murmured, feeling emotionally drained. She still couldn't completely expel her resentment over the lack of relationship with her mother, but now the resentment could be blamed on circumstances and not the person.

Marilyn reached out and pulled her into a tight embrace. "That was so difficult. I hated telling you this, but we can't just abandon my sister. We're family."

Valerie found a degree of solace in her aunt's embrace. "I was angry, and I suppose somewhat hormonal when I ran out of the nursing home, but I doubt I'd ever completely abandon her."

Marilyn sighed. "I didn't want to think that you would, either, but since my sister hasn't really been much of a mother to you, I was afraid at some point that you might retaliate."

"Can't say that I haven't been tempted, but good families don't just abandon each other," Valerie said sadly, thinking about Aaron. Why couldn't he include that in his code of honor?

As if picking up on her unspoken vibe, Marilyn said, "It's very strange, but I think your mother sees some of the qualities in Aaron that she saw in Joel. I can't offer any marital advice because you won't discuss him with me, but there is something you need to consider."

"What?"

"When your mother told you to ask your father, maybe she wasn't talking about Joel."

Valerie looked at her with a dazed, puzzled expression. "Then who?"

"Maybe she was talking about your Heavenly Father."

Chapter 31

Five months later…

Downstairs in the large game room of his home, Noah, brandishing a cue stick, paced the floor while waiting for Aaron to make his shot. "If you accept that assignment, you're deliberately signing your death warrant," he said curtly, struggling against the mounting urge to splinter the stick on his friend's hard head.

"Eight ball, bank shot. Number two in left pocket," Aaron said, leaning forward, expertly positioning his cue stick. As he made the shot, the billiard balls clanked, scattered and dashed across the green felt table bed, all too eager to do their master's bidding.

Noah's eyes narrowed when the selected balls thudded into the targeted pockets.

"Very nice," he said dryly.

"Figured you'd appreciate it."

"I'd appreciate it even more if you'd start making sense. Tell your contact they need to find another way. Don't take that assignment, man."

Aaron stroked the cue stick, his eyes still surveying the billiard table. "You don't even know what the assignment is."

"I don't have to. *Yemen* sums it up in one word. Weren't three months in Nigeria enough for you? After you almost bought the ranch last January, I was under the impression that you were retiring from active duty. What are you trying to prove?"

"Prove?" Aaron smirked, glaring at Noah "I'm only doing what I've always done for years. This—"

"Is all about your wife," Noah finished bluntly. He knew he'd struck a nerve when Aaron's direct gaze wavered. "That's right…Valerie, your pregnant wife."

"You're wrong." Aaron made a quick recovery. "First, I haven't even officially committed to the assignment, but should I accept, it will have very little to do with my *estranged* wife."

"Very little to do? I heard that perfectly clear, man. What you *didn't* say was that she would have *nothing* to do with it. Ever since you two separated, you've been miserable…and worse…all this misery is totally unnecessary. You both still love each other. I mean, so what if you didn't want children? It happened. Get over it. Make some adjustments. I mean, I could understand if the baby wasn't yours."

Aaron let the cue stick drop to the floor. "Noah, we run a business together, but my personal life is not open for discussion and it never has been."

"In the past I've always respected your privacy, but right now your personal life is my business because it's affecting our business," Noah snapped. "You're completely insane if you think your death will not impact Avian International adversely."

Aaron chuckled sardonically. "You can find another partner and you know it. At this point, the company has taken on a life of its own and even its founders are expendable. There are several capable men who could carry on. Jake Marshall, Bill Hutchens, Craig Lawrence…shall I continue?"

"You're missing the point." Noah reached out and gripped Aaron's shoulder. "They are good men, yes, but they're not you. This is, and was, our dream…the fruit of our collective labor, not theirs. You're family, man…my big brother. Why can't you understand that?"

Aaron backed away, pulled a cigarette pack from his pants pocket, and sank into a nearby chair. He'd hoped that distancing himself physically and emotionally from his wife would have the effect he wanted — that the separation would allow him to disconnect and accept that there would eventually be a termination of their relationship. But oddly enough, just the opposite was happening. He missed her even more. Never mind that she was openly defying him and, even worse, risking her own life. He wondered chillingly if a similar situation might have occurred in his father's life, culminating with his own birth and his mother's death. There was nothing more agonizing or frustrating than having foreknowledge of an event and being blocked in your effort to prevent history from repeating itself. He wished he could tell Noah the truth about his overblown childhood fears, but of the several languages he could speak, the language of emotion eluded him; the words did not exist in his vocabulary and he had no clue where to find them. Yet he was touched by Noah's open admission of their brotherly bond.

"Thought you quit smoking," Noah said.

"I thought so, too." He stared mockingly at the cigarette he'd extracted, remembering clearly the day in Belize when he'd promised Valerie he'd quit—the same day she'd agreed they'd have no children. His promise had been broken on his last week in Nigeria and he hadn't even realized the significance of it until this moment. Was he retaliating? If so, he knew he was only hurting himself, just like he was hurting from leaving her. Tempted to ignore the ramifications, he reached for a lighter but instead frowned in disgust, crammed the cigarette back into the pack, and tossed everything into the nearby trash container.

Noah leaned against the pool table, arms folded. "Can't imagine why you think being a parent is such an awful thing. In most cultures, children are considered a blessing. Hey, Jasmine and I have three kids now. They're all different, and, yeah, they're challenging sometimes, but I love them each as individuals, and they haven't cramped my lifestyle or changed who I am."

"There's no comparison between us," Aaron said. "I'm older than you, and I already have a grown son. By the time this one, Valerie's kid, reaches twenty, I'll be more like its grandfather."

"That can't possibly be what you're really worried about," Noah said suspiciously. "Guys much older than you have kids all the time."

"Valerie's a fool for putting her life at risk to have this baby," Aaron said.

"But she's doing fine. From what I've heard, she hasn't even had one major problem. In fact, Jasmine had more issues when she was expecting Jonathan. Don't tell me you haven't even spoken to her in all this time?"

Aaron studied the Tiffany lighting above the pool table. With literally oceans between them, he had spoken to his wife via phone exactly three times since they'd agreed to separate. Each time she'd told him, without bitterness, that she was doing okay, and then she'd wanted to know how he was. During their last conversation, she'd revealed that the baby was a girl, but other than that, their conversations had been perfunctory and succinct. But he was still surprised that she hadn't even alluded to divorce.

"We've spoken," he said. "Not often, though. There isn't a lot to say at this point."

"Aaron, get over it. You're the most determined, stand-up guy I've ever known. You've done things…

risen to every challenge and made sacrifices that would leave most men quivering in the dust. It's bordering on lunacy that you're going to allow fear of a baby to—"

"I'm not afraid of a baby," Aaron interrupted, unable to resist a smirk at the ludicrousness of the remark.

Noah chuckled, lightening the tension in the room. "Tell me about it. You won't even hold Jonathan."

Aaron squinted. "And the reason for that is he'll start screaming. They all scream."

"You're passing the buck. It's something you learn, like anything else. Valerie's going to have your baby soon. She needs you to be with her, not somewhere in Yemen getting your fool head blown off."

Aaron stood up and reclaimed his cue stick. "You've made your point. Now shut up and let's get on with this game so I can finish beating the crap out of you."

Valerie had known all along that she would be having a caesarean delivery because sonograms revealed that scar tissue was narrowing the birth canal. To try for a natural birth would endanger the baby. She knew all this, but she was thrown for a loop when her aunt accompanied her on her routine checkup and she was told that her blood pressure was spiking too high and they wanted to deliver the baby earlier than originally scheduled. They wanted to do it in five days. She was a little over eight months pregnant, and the early birth would make her daughter premature.

"I'm not sure I agree with them," Valerie said on the ride back home. "My blood pressure tends to fluctuate anyway. It'll probably go back down."

"You need to take their advice," Marilyn said, focusing on the highway as she drove. "The baby is almost full term and she shouldn't have difficulties that can't be managed."

"But nothing in my life is as it should be right now," Valerie said, frustration welling. "I'd at least like for my daughter to have as perfect a start as possible."

"Her perfect start will be entering the world and knowing she has a mother to love her," Marilyn responded tersely.

Valerie glanced sideways at her aunt, catching the edge in her voice and realizing that she was worried. For the first time in months Aunt Marilyn was acknowledging the possibility that something could go wrong.

"Well, I'm certainly no pregnancy expert, so I guess I have no choice except to take the advice of those who are," she said slowly.

Her aunt was worrying for nothing. Valerie didn't—couldn't even—imagine anything going wrong at this point. It was miraculous and traumatic enough that she'd conceived in the first place. Perhaps she was being irrational, maybe even a bit presumptuous, but she was sure that God wouldn't allow her to reach this point only to take away her and Aaron's daughter. And she was talking about her daughter. She'd long since stopped viewing the little girl growing inside her as a fetus, instead recognizing her as a full human being, whom she already adored. She pictured dark, wavy hair and maybe…who knows, maybe even indigo eyes like Aaron's. But it didn't really matter what their daughter looked like; she just knew that she'd be beautiful, and every time she felt the baby move, she thanked God for His unexpected gift.

The holiday season had come and gone. Denise and Tony were temporarily living at the Long Island estate while hunting for a house of their own. Valerie had been surprised that her cousin hadn't gloated over the current state of her and Aaron's relationship. She had, to the contrary, expressed hope that they would get back together. Of course Denise being Denise, she had also stated that if she were in the situation, she would not have sabotaged her own health and happiness by going ahead with the pregnancy. Valerie had shrugged the comment off, but she couldn't help thinking about how uncomplicated Denise's self-gratifying world and its absence of accountability was.

Valerie's last few awkwardly pregnant months had been spent trying to be more understanding of her mother, working sporadically, attending church regularly, and praying to God that things would work out—that Aaron wouldn't go off somewhere and get killed—that he'd live long enough to have a change of heart. But at the same time, she had resigned herself to the fact that she probably was going to be Valerie Redmond, single mom. She had accepted this and would go on accordingly even though the feeble hope burned within her that her wayward husband would change his mind once he actually saw their daughter.

"I do hope you're planning to contact Aaron soon," Marilyn said. "He needs to know when you go to the hospital."

If he cared, he would be contacting her more frequently, Valerie thought, not wanting to dwell on that downer. She was considering getting the whole labor and birth over with on her own and then telling him after the birth.

"I'll try," she replied. "But if he's out of the country, he's going to be difficult to reach."

"Not an excuse," Marilyn said. "If you can't reach him, I'm sure Jasmine's husband can."

Five days later, Valerie was in the hospital being prepared for the caesarean. She was nervous, but glad to be in Englewood Hospital. The affiliated doctors were skilled in performing many complicated procedures without immediately resorting to blood transfusions, which was another issue for her because she had a rare blood type and finding a match was difficult. Her obstetrician and hematologist were optimistic. They'd made sure her blood count was higher than normal to offset any possible bleeding issues. Blood transfusions were a consideration only as a last resort.

Aaron received her call late at night in his spartan hotel room in Santo Domingo, where he was sprawled, completely clothed, across the bed, attempting to rest after a grueling sixteen hours entrenched in rescue and recovery efforts on a neighboring Caribbean island that had been devastated by a 7.1 magnitude earthquake.

He was so physically drained from the intense, difficult labor that it took him a while to realize that the piercing sound was not someone screaming in pain, but was in fact the phone ringing.

"Weiss," he barked into the receiver, nearly knocking the phone off the night table.

"Aaron?" The tentative, questioning voice immediately got his full attention.

"Valerie, *ma shlomekh?*" He didn't even realize he'd asked her how she was in Hebrew until she replied.

"*Lo ra.* Did I just say I'm not bad, or something to that effect?"

His heart hammered in his ears. He was surprised that she even remembered one of the few phrases he'd

taught her, since she'd told him the language was difficult.

"I'm okay," she restated, when she got no reply.
"Noah told me where to reach you, and I realize it's
late, but I just wanted you to know that I'm in the hospital and I'll be having the baby tomorrow."

"What!" He sat up straight, the erratic pounding in
his chest morphing into a distinct ache. "I thought you
had another month?"

"They decided to do it earlier." Her voice sounded
calm, too calm. "Tomorrow afternoon."

His first reaction, which had been shock, possibly
tinged with fear, transformed to a vague annoyance
and then indignation, senseless indignation. "I'll be
there," he said.

"You don't have to." She must have caught the edge
in his voice. "I mean, I heard about the earthquake…
that you're involved in relief work over there, and of
course my hysterical little world pales in comparison
to what those poor people are suffering. I called you
simply because I thought you'd like to kno—"

"I know why you called, and I *told* you I'd be there,"
he interrupted.

"Do whatever you think is best," she said.

He heard the phone click, and he considered calling her back in order to apologize for his cold, brusque
attitude, but he realized that he didn't have the hospital phone number. If he went through the effort to

find it, he'd probably only say something to dig himself deeper into a hole. *Let it go.* He'd try to be more compassionate and understanding when he saw her in person. That is, if she survived the caesarean.

Aaron stood up and paced around the room, knowing that even though he was beyond exhaustion, he'd never be able to fall back asleep. With only a small strip of sea and a crummy hotel building separating him from the chaos on the bordering island, he could still smell the scent of death hanging in the air and could still see the burned-in-his-brain images of mangled bodies, dead babies, mothers crying, and orphaned children roaming the streets in rags.

He was used to this, though, way too used to it. Only this time the form of devastation was a little different. This devastation hadn't been caused by war—mankind's own peculiar brand of barbarism—this time; it had been from nature, an act of God some called it. He'd witnessed these *acts of God* before and wondered idly why they always seemed to occur in places that were already impoverished and barely standing to begin with.

What were the believers in a divine creator saying about this one? What did pain and destruction have to do with a God who was supposed to be kind and merciful?

Except for individuals like himself, who made themselves available to assist in troubled times, who really cared about the survival of disparate humans anyway? Human lives were cheap and expendable. Routinely seeing their blood soak into the earth, their frail bodies decomposing, confirmed this.

He squeezed his burning eyes shut and opened them again. Who was he? Who was Valerie in the grand scheme of things? Yes, he might lose his wife forever. In the blink of an eye, he could lose his own life, too, right here, right at this very moment. It seemed quite probable even, because not only did his chest ache, he also felt oddly light-headed. He sat abruptly on the bed and contemplated the possibility of having a fatal heart attack—a possibility that ironically caused no sense of panic or regret, only the ludicrous thought of Noah's reaction to discovering his dead carcass slumped on the bed in a cheap hotel room. The unheralded demise of Mr. Ace Pilot, Guerilla Warrior, Can-do Rambo. He chuckled aloud and waited.

Nothing happened. The queasy feeling lifted. Stress, he concluded, or more likely the delayed reaction from the acidic glop masquerading as lasagna that he'd gulped down earlier.

Chapter 32

He'd said he would be there, but he wasn't. She realized that he probably was needed more where he was, assisting with the earthquake rescue efforts. Maybe she was even being selfish for wishing him to be at her side when God possibly wanted him there, helping countless others. And it wasn't as if she were alone. Her closest supporters, Jasmine and her aunt, were sitting in the hospital waiting room. Perhaps it was best this way. When Aaron finally did show up, his daughter would be born. He would see her and fall in love with her.

As she drifted into a hazy realm of partial consciousness from the anesthesia, her thoughts were of Aaron and their daughter. In her peaceful cocoon, she was a disembodied apparition, watching as the tall man pushed the little girl on a park swing. "Higher, Daddy, higher," the shrill childish voice rang out.

"No, that's high enough," the calm voice of the father, the protector.

She wanted to be there in the park with them, but somehow she simply could not break out of the shroud that confined her and she drifted into total unconsciousness.

❦

"Mrs. Weiss. Can you hear me? Look, you have a beautiful daughter."

Valerie felt the haze slowly lifting, and she stared in awe at the tiny miracle swaddled in pink blankets who was being presented to her like a sacred offering by a petite white-masked nurse. Valerie focused on the infant whose tiny rosy-cheeked face was contorted as she shrieked high-pitched, angry, indignant shrieks — definitely not cries of pain or even discomfort, but more akin to outrage at having been pulled from a warm, quiet environment into the loud, blinding light of the world.

Surprisingly, her beautiful daughter had silky wisps of reddish hair, and, not so surprisingly, dark blue eyes like Aaron's — at least they were blue at the moment.

"It's all right. Don't cry," she croaked hoarsely to the baby, who stopped in mid-wail, long enough to seemingly make eye contact, and then toned the shrieks down to whimpers. Valerie's arms ached to reach out and hold her, but for some reason she could barely move.

"It's okay. The baby's fine," the nurse told her, "but we can't leave her with you just now because she needs monitoring."

"Monitoring?"

"Well, she is slightly premature and her lungs are a little weak."

Weak? How could she have weak lungs and scream so loudly? "Can I go with her?"

"Not now. You're still in the recovery room and you have to rest. Your doctor will come in to explain things to you."

Explain things? She didn't like the sound of that, and she didn't understand why she felt so feeble.

"Are you sure the baby's okay?"

"Yes, Mrs. Weiss. Don't worry. You're going to be fine, too. Just rest. When the anesthesia wears off, everything will make sense."

Of course it would. She knew all about standard procedure, so why was she acting so dense? Valerie closed her eyes and allowed her thoughts to drift.

◀▶

"It's all over. Can you believe that, Val? I got to see her for only a second, but gosh, she's a living doll."

Mildly surprised that she felt very little pain, Valerie looked at a beaming Jasmine, who was standing by her bedside, gripping her hand. A few feet away, she could see her Aunt Marilyn seated in a nearby chair in the claustrophobic room. To her left, the open privacy curtain revealed that the bed next to her was unoccupied. She breathed a sigh of relief that she was in a regular room and not in ICU. She also noticed that there was only a saline solution dripping into her veins from the towering IV and no trace of blood being transfused. The doctor had talked to her while she was in the recovery room and she knew her baby was okay in the neonatal unit, but, for the life of her, she couldn't remember what else had been said and there was only one major thought on her mind.

"Where…where's Aaron? Did he come?"

"He's here," Jasmine said. "Just got in a little over an hour ago. He was in your room but you were asleep and he didn't want to wake you."

Aaron had flown back. He had been in her room. Her heart thudded so loudly, she wondered if Jasmine heard it. "But that's so ridiculous. He should have awakened me. He is coming back, isn't he?"

"Of course he is." Her aunt joined Jasmine at the bedside.

Confused, Valerie looked at her aunt. "What time is it?"

"Almost nine o'clock."

"What?" She stared incredulously at the black slit of night sky that was exposed by the window curtain. "But it's dark."

"That's right. It's nine at night," Aunt Marilyn said. "You had the caesarean in the afternoon around three o'clock, remember? There were some complications, and…"

"What complications?"

"Nothing too obvious," Jasmine said calmly. "Besides, you have a beautiful little girl."

"I bled a lot, didn't I?" Valerie asked, starting to remember what she had been told in the recovery room.

"Yes," her aunt admitted, "but the doctor's got it under control and you're okay now. You might have to stay in the hospital a few days longer than you intended, though."

Valerie let it sink in and shrugged. What she had been told was hardly a surprise. Her mind wasn't really on her own health issues anyway, because her heart ached with frustration over not being able to hold her newborn; she felt sorry for her tiny daughter who was among strangers. "Where's my baby?" she asked, momentarily forgetting what the doctors had told her. "Why can't I hold her?"

"You need to rest," her aunt said, "and the baby is being taken care of. She's perfectly okay."

"She's just a little premature, like Jonathan was," Jasmine added. "They have to monitor her. You know about that stuff."

"Jasmine, did Aaron say when he was coming back?"

"No. But I'm sure he's hanging around nearby and he'll be in any minute."

Hanging around. She grimaced. She'd just had his baby and he was *hanging around.* Well, what did she expect? Nothing had changed for him. She was, after all, still his estranged wife, so his feelings would be twisted, not to mention that he'd been yanked away from the trauma of rescuing earthquake survivors in a foreign country. Surely there was reason enough for her to extend to him a measure of empathy and consideration.

"Did…did he say anything to you?"

"I didn't really see him long enough to have a conversation," Jasmine said uneasily. "But of course he's coming back. It wouldn't make sense to fly all the way here and just leave without speaking to you."

"Sense?" Valerie muttered in an undertone, realizing that it was quite possible that Aaron could have done just that. "Remember, we're talking about a man who has no common sense."

Aunt Marilyn sighed. "I know it's difficult, honey. Pray for him and just try to be patient."

Valerie inhaled deeply, felt a burning pain from where she had been stitched, and exhaled more cautiously. "I must look like the Wicked Witch of the West," she said, licking her dry lower lip.

Jasmine laughed. "Now you're starting to sound like yourself." She fumbled in her bag for a compact. "Take a look. The mirror won't break."

Nervously, Valerie glanced at her reflection and noted that she didn't look as hideous as she'd imagined. True, her skin was rather pale, and her lips were slightly chapped, but her hair was neatly combed and shiny, her eyes clear. Aaron shouldn't be overly appalled by her appearance.

"Noah's here with me," Jasmine said. "They're not allowing too many people in your room at one time, so he's waiting outside."

"That's sweet of him to come." Valerie smiled, remembering Noah's reaction upon seeing his own newborn, and at that moment her heart warmed as the thought occurred to her that Aaron was probably in the neonatal unit right now visiting their daughter. Of course that's where he was, and when he returned he'd have that same ingratiating smile on his face.

❦

Grateful to her friends and family for affording them the moment of privacy, Aaron, dressed conservatively in black pants with a gray shirt and tie, entered Valerie's room, bearing a vase of exquisitely formed red and white roses. He set them on the nightstand and studied the gorgeous woman who had literally enraptured his world and then shattered it, all in the course of one year.

The nurses at the station had told him that she was doing very well, all things considered, and that they were checking on her frequently. She certainly didn't look bad; she was delicately beautiful, actually. Her eyes were shut, as they had been when he'd glanced in the room earlier, but he knew she was awake, and he beheld in reverence the artistry of her long eyelashes fanning against her flawless sienna skin. Yet, relieved as he was to see her looking so well, he knew better than to trust appearances.

"Hey, angel." He gently kissed her on the forehead and watched as her eyelashes fluttered. "How are you feeling?"

"Aaron." She breathed his name, her eyes wide open, gazing lovingly into his. "I'm glad you came."

"I told you I would." He held her hand and she squeezed his. "I still care deeply about you. That hasn't changed," he said.

"You look so tired." She reached up to trace her finger lightly across his jaw, making him aware that he had done a lousy job shaving.

"I'm fine," he replied.

"Isn't she gorgeous?" Valerie murmured, taking his hand again.

"What?" He leaned closer, momentarily confused by her soft-spoken question.

"Her name's Aisha Joelle. Joelle is for my father... unless you have an objection."

"No," he said, suddenly realizing that she was talking about the baby. "That's a good name."

"She's just got the sweetest little face, and she has your eyes." Valerie smiled in pure bliss. "Did you notice her red hair?"

"Well…no." He blinked involuntarily. "Actually, I haven't seen the baby yet."

"What!" Her hand went limp in his and she withdrew it, as if she'd touched something vile and contaminated.

"Hey, listen, it's okay. I *am* going to see her. It's just that I wanted to see you first."

Valerie's eyes darkened in emotional turmoil and she turned her face away from him. "Jasmine told me you were here an hour earlier." She spoke through clenched teeth. "Your daughter's right on this floor, and you've had plenty of time to go see her."

Surprised by the fierce intensity of her response, Aaron placed a hand on her shoulder. "Val, relax, there's nothing to get upset about. I told you I'm go—"

She turned to look at him again. "Get out!"

He hesitated, momentarily stunned.

"I said get out of my room!"

Aaron recovered and instantly stepped back, giving her space. "Valerie, listen…"

"I don't care what you have to say!" Her smoldering eyes burst into flame, reducing him to a heap of ash where he stood. "Don't call me, and don't you dare come back until you've seen your daughter." Her eyes filled with tears, which began spilling down her face. "Get out now!"

Speechless, he did an about-face and exited just in time to see Jasmine and Valerie's aunt coming down the aisle.

"Aaron?" Jasmine started, bewilderment in her eyes.

"Excuse me," he said curtly, emotionlessly "I think she would like you both to go back in."

"But…but," Jasmine started, "aren't you…?"

"Later." Aaron continued down the hall without looking back.

By the time he reached the neonatal unit, some of his shock had dissipated and changed into resentment at her audacity in ordering him around. He didn't take orders from anyone—particularly anyone using that tone, and in most cases no one dared. What was the big deal? He really had intended to see the baby, eventually. Why such overwrought anger and urgency? He'd been told the kid was healthy, and it wasn't like it was going anywhere for the next eighteen or so years. As long as he lived, he didn't think he would ever understand women.

He hesitated near the door that had a buzzer and was opened only upon showing ID. There was a plaque on the wall nearby that heralded all the rules: All visitors must wash hands, wear provided mask and gown, no smoking, no cell phones, etc., etc. Rules, rules, rules. Frowning irritably, he resisted the urge to leave.

He started to push the buzzer but his cell phone rang. Distracted, he went farther down the hall to answer it.

The call was long distance. Ron Bennett, one of Avian's pilots who was involved in the volunteer rescue, was asking for advice on what specific transport plane should be used to run food and medical supplies to the stricken island. The call was like a lifeline and Aaron was all too eager to assist. This was his territory, his comfort zone.

Carrying on the conversation, he chose the privacy of the stairs instead of the elevator and made his way down to the hospital's main entrance lobby and stepped out the door. Standing outside, he took a deep breath of the cold, clean air and listened to the rest of Bennett's report on what was going on. It would take months, maybe even years, before the island would recover, but individuals and allied relief organizations were doing whatever was possible, and more rescue workers were pouring in from the U.S. and Europe. He didn't physically have to be there anymore, but as tough as that assignment was, it was far easier than being in the predicament he was in now.

After the call ended, he returned the phone to his pocket and re-entered the building, feeling volatile and edgy. He'd go see the kid now, and then he'd report back to Valerie what she wanted to hear—that the baby was beautiful and all that stuff, even if it wasn't. Or maybe he shouldn't even bother to see her again tonight, since his presence had upset her so badly. He hoped Jasmine and the aunt had managed to calm her down. It couldn't possibly be good for her to get that upset over nothing.

His phone buzzed again and a clinical voice greeted him. "Mr. Weiss, are you still in the hospital?"

"Yes," he said apprehensively.

"Please return to Obstetrics ASAP."

His heart thudded. He recognized that urgent, pointed tone, and as he headed quickly for the elevator, he wished he were anywhere on earth except here. Even Yemen sounded like paradise.

Chapter 33

Valerie had started hemorrhaging again and had been rushed into surgery. In the small room near the nurse's station, Aaron stared numbly at the papers he was being asked to sign granting permission to perform another procedure. What procedure? He could barely read the print, and even though it had been explained to him that his wife was extremely critical and they were doing all they could, he wanted to toss the forms into the trash and strangle the fool doctors who had encouraged her to have the baby. They had told her she would be okay, but he had known better. If only she had listened to his logic instead of trusting so blindly, so foolishly, in faith.

It was too late for rehashing what could have been, though. His worst fears were exploding in his face. Just like his own father, he'd lose his wife and be left with a helpless infant.

"Aaron."

He started slightly, standing paralyzed and gripping the pen, as Noah entered the office to stand beside him. "The forms, man. You have to sign them."

"For what? So they can finish killing her?"

"No." Noah's voice sounded very calm. "They're trying to save her life."

"Why bother? She's going to die."

Noah seized him by the shoulder and shook him. "Stop saying that. You're not God. You don't know."

Aaron scribbled his signature on the bottom line of the form and stalked out of the room as one of the office personnel claimed it. Immediately he found himself in the waiting room before the ashen faces of Jasmine and Valerie's aunt. Jasmine stood up and gave him a look that would have stopped Mt. Vesuvius from erupting.

"What happened?" Jasmine cried. "She was doing so well before you—"

"Jasmine," Noah began sharply, bringing up the rear a few paces behind Aaron.

"What's wrong with you!" Jasmine shrieked. Her hand shot out and landed with a fierce resounding smack against the side of his face.

Aaron barely flinched. He had seen it coming and he could have easily deflected the blow, but he felt that he deserved it. He turned away from the hysterical woman, and out of the corner of his eye, saw a visibly rattled Noah trying to console his wife.

"I'm sorry, Noah...I'm so sorry," she blubbered, "but all Valerie wanted was to love him and he's just so...so cold and stubborn."

Aaron kept walking until he was near the large window at the end of the hall, where he stared bleakly out into a darkened courtyard that somehow reminded him that his life should have remained solitary. What a fool he had been to think it could be otherwise.

"Aaron, listen to me." Noah joined him near the window. "I'm sorry about my wife. She was out of control and she had no right—"

"Do you think I care about that?" Aaron interrupted sharply. He wondered if Noah really had any clue just how lost he felt at this moment—how much he wished he could simply stop breathing, cease to exist.

"You've already given up, haven't you?" Noah sounded disgusted.

Aaron looked at him blankly. "What?"

"You've already accepted that Valerie's going to die."

"I'm standing here helpless while those…those surgeons are in there. I know the odds. What the hell can I do?"

"Plenty. For one thing, you can go see your daughter, and even more importantly, you can do what we're all doing…praying to God. He's always listening. He always hears."

Aaron had never come to grips with his best friend's spiritual side; he'd always mentally tuned out whenever Noah became even slightly preachy. However, at this moment, tuning out was impossible, and the prayer suggestion seemed so inane and simplistic that it angered him. He fought to resist the twisted rage, the powerful urge to slam Noah right through the window.

"I know you don't believe, but try Him anyway," Noah continued, oblivious to the threat of physical harm. "Give God a chance. You have nothing to lose and a lot to gain."

Aaron felt the rage dissipate, and he didn't even realize that he was shaking until he flinched when Noah placed his arm firmly around his shoulders. "If...," he began haltingly. "If He really exists, why should this God of yours listen to me? I haven't done anything to please him."

"You're saying that because you're thinking like a human. He's not just my God, or Valerie's...he's everyone's. God's thoughts are higher than human thoughts, and so is His mercy."

Aaron said nothing. He continued to stare out into the blackness while Noah continued to talk.

"You say you haven't done nothing for God? Well, guess what? You're wrong. Jesus said if you do it to the least of them, you've done it to Him. In your way, you've spent most of your life trying to improve the lives of countless others...even if you claim you don't care about them. Actions speak louder than words. You're a gatekeeper, man. What kind of world would we be living in without heroes like you?"

"Are you through with your speech?"

"Not quite. There's a chapel on the first floor. Why don't you go down there now? Even if the worst-case scenario does unfold, God will give you the strength you need to deal with the outcome. And just remember that I'm still in your corner, no matter what anyone else—even my own wife—thinks. I'll try to help you in whatever way I can."

"Thank you," Aaron murmured, shocked by the tremor in his voice and ashamed that he could ever have imagined striking his best friend.

Slowly, he turned away from the window and began the long walk toward the elevator.

❧

The empty Catholic-influenced chapel was a close facsimile to a small, silent church, complete with a double row of wooden pews. A large gold crucifix hung above the altar, and as Aaron glanced around, he noticed luminescent light radiating from the ornate stained glass windows and wondered if there was a confessional booth tucked away somewhere. *Forgive me Father, for I have sinned.*

The common symbols of Christianity were not unfamiliar to him—he had been inside way too many churches, mosques, and synagogues while attending the funerals of fallen comrades. The alienation he'd always felt being in man-made temples was present now and stronger than ever.

A buzzing sound filled his head as he forced a step toward the altar, and he realized that the sound was the speaker-driven simulation of a tinkling waterfall. Piped in sound effects, meant to induce relaxation. He stared again at the heavy gold crucifix and imagined it crashing down on his head. Enough.

He fled the hospital and the night claimed him. Once in his car and on the open road, he crossed the George Washington Bridge, gliding seamlessly in and out of traffic that appeared to be standing still. Driven, focused, eyes straight ahead, he pressed forward until he found himself pulling into the private gate at the airport. He flashed his badge, and barely noticed the security guard's face as he was granted access.

He sped well off the beaten path and down a narrow service road that led to a small warehouse and a private hangar. Beyond that, there was nothing but a chain link fence separating civilization from an oasis of tangled weeds, marsh, saw grass, and peace.

Completely unmindful of the fact that he'd left his coat at the hospital, he parked the car near the fence and got out. The frigid air blasted him as he inhaled, his lungs filling with the brackish scent of mucky, decaying earth. He tilted his head up to the velvet universe and observed a blue-tinged half moon and a dizzying array of shimmering stars, their celestial glow undiminished by the artificial lights of the city. In the heavens, far from the crushing bonds of earth, everything appeared so structured and cohesive.

Seized by impulse, he scaled the fence and nearly tumbled to the ground on the opposite side. After regaining his balance, he ran madly down a slight hill through the tall grassy wetlands, all the while keeping his head tilted toward the universe, beholding the stars swirling around him. Oblivious to the cold, mucky ground saturating his feet and the cuffs of his pants, he continued to run.

Are you really up there, God? Allah? Yahweh?

That couldn't be right. He knew there had to be a reverence, a certain order in which to pray, but although fundamentals eluded him, he felt as if he really was being heard.

If You are up there, I know You don't have to listen to the likes of a fool like me, but please don't let my wife die. She trusted and believed that You would make things right. I don't know how she feels about me right now, but she wants to live for the baby. She went through this whole nightmare because she has such strong faith in You, and so do my friends. I want to have faith too, but it's hard because I've seen too much...too much death and misery and pain. And in trying to make things right, I've done some terrible things, too. Why am I trying to carry the weight of the world anyway? I'm only a man, less than a microscopic dot in Your universe. Please be merciful. The Bible says You are. Please give me a chance to appreciate the small things…the really important things, like my family and friends.

Family. He stood still, breathing hard, recognizing the significance behind his mental acceptance of family. He'd never truly embraced the concept before. He'd always kept a physical, emotional distance from everyone, but he really, truly did have a family. He had Andrew, Valerie, and now Aisha. Andrew seemed to accept him unconditionally. Maybe Aisha would, too. After all, she shared his blood as well.

The stars winked and signaled. He resumed running, luxuriating in his own madness until a root or stump sprang from the mire and sent him sprawling on his hands and knees in the sludge of the earth. He stood shakily and laughed, not even bothering to wipe the muck off his clothes and body, because he found the stench of decayed earth oddly pleasing. If only Valerie could see him now.

He stared at the sky again and remembered clearly being an inquisitive nine-year-old in an Israeli synagogue. An elderly rabbi, who had known about his love for astronomy, had pointed out a passage from Isaiah 40:26 written in the ancient Tanakh, which said something to the effect of raising one's eyes and acknowledging the energy and power of the One who created the heavens, the One bringing forth the army of stars, all of which He calls by name.

The child he was back then had considered it so awesome that the Creator could actually number and call all the stars by name. It was still awesome. When had he grown into a man so ignorant that he'd stopped seeing the surrounding magnificence for what it truly was?

A familiar roar rattled the silence and he looked to the right to see a 747 rising from the distant tarmac, slivered moonlight dancing on its wings. Passenger Flight 42, no doubt, headed for Rome. Aaron ran with it, mentally savoring the thrust of engine power and the lift off. He watched the plane climb higher and higher until it settled into proper altitude and became a blip of flashing red lights that paled before the stars.

By the time he returned to the car, his heart rate had slowed and he felt a relative peace. His cell phone was buzzing frantically, but he ignored it and drove back to his apartment, where he quickly showered and changed into a casual black sweater and gray slacks. He was about to leave the bedroom when his peripheral vision detected a small object gleaming on top of the dresser. Realizing what it was, he stepped back and picked up his wedding band—the one he had worn only once, the day they'd exchanged their vows. He fingered it for a few seconds, started to slip the ring on, but instead let it drop into his pocket.

His return drive to the hospital was disquieting but he was calm, accepting, and prepared to face whatever awaited him.

❧❧

The attending nurse looked at him as if he had two heads when he requested entrance to the neonatal unit, but after he showed his ID and explained his urgency to see the baby, she relented. The hospital did allow 24/7 access exclusively to the parents of the infants, but most of them took advantage of the concession only if their newborns were critically ill.

"I just want to see her from the window," Aaron told the nurse.

She shrugged as if trying to figure him out, and then she led him down the hall to a large open area where he could look into the room that housed at least twenty enclosed bassinettes that resembled clear plastic shipping containers with holes on the sides for attached gloves to reach in. Some of the fragile creatures, with toothpick limbs and diapers the size of handkerchiefs, were hooked up to oxygen and other devices larger than they were. Most of the infants were wailing.

The nurse assured him that despite the crying, they were all being attended to. He started to ask her which screamer was his, but another nurse summoned her with something urgent and she temporarily abandoned him, leaving him to rule out all the babies with blue blankets. Only six of them had pink blankets and two of those were dark chocolate colored. The remaining four were various shades of pale. Somehow, he doubted that either of the darker two could be his, since neither he nor Valerie had very dark skin. But it was possible. His mother had been ebony-complexioned. Squinting, he searched for any signs of familiar features, and then he remembered Valerie's telling him that Aisha had red hair. There was only one baby in the room with hair close to that color, and she was the one who wasn't screaming.

The wispy curls of hair were not bright red, more of a dark brown with reddish highlights. This baby was also one of the lucky ones not hooked up to any apparatus, although there was an oxygen line nearby. He watched her yawn and move her tiny hands. Suddenly, the baby's head turned in his direction and she looked right at him.

His heart skipped a beat. *Uh-oh. She's probably going to start screaming now.* He deliberately averted his eyes. *Wait a minute. Don't be ridiculous.* No way could that mere fledgling attach any significance to who or what she was looking at. She probably thought he was a big blob in the window. Regardless, she continued to study him contentedly and he made eye contact again.

"I'm sorry for the interruption," the nurse said upon returning. She then noticed his intense focus and followed his gaze. "Ah, you've found her. She's a real doll, that one. The most beautiful baby on the floor...and very expressive, as you can see."

Aaron managed a wry smile, assuming that the nurse said similar things to all the visiting parents.

"Are you sure you wouldn't like to go in and hold her?"

"No," he said quickly. "Not now." At least he had seen her, and there was no time left to go through the hand-washing, gown-wearing routine. The moment of truth had arrived to find out if Aisha still had a mother and he still had a wife.

Chapter 34

Aaron, Aaron. Come back. Please don't leave me here.

He floated somewhere amidst the rising mist, a dark figure in a long overcoat, walking swiftly, relentlessly away, his footsteps silent as falling snow. As the mist threatened to consume him, he turned once and looked back, his deep indigo eyes shimmering with despair and regret.

Aaron, wait! I didn't mean it!

But he turned around and continued to walk even faster.

She ran after him, her footsteps leaden, jarring, her breath puffing out in loud spurts. Hopeless, useless pursuit. He remained far ahead of her, about to vanish forever.

"Aaron!" she screamed.

"Valerie, it's okay. It's okay."

Valerie stared wildly into the face of her aunt, who was leaning over her bedside. She realized she had shouted Aaron's name, and now she felt foolish, delirious, and completely disoriented, not to mention incapacitated by various tubes and lines attached to her body.

"Everything's going to be all right," Aunt Marilyn said. "You had to have surgery again, but the bleeding has stopped for good this time and…"

"What bleeding?" She remembered she was in the hospital and that she'd had a daughter, but there was something not right about the room. It seemed to have shrunk in size, and when she turned her head to the right there was a blank wall where the outside window had been. On the left was an interior window with a view of a large command- center nursing station. She was definitely in ICU and she'd probably almost died.

"You had to have a hysterectomy," Aunt Marilyn began tentatively, as though unsure of Valerie's reaction.

"A hysterectomy?" Valerie repeated and then shook her head at the ludicrousness of the surgery. Up until the last few momentous months, she'd assumed and accepted that she'd never have children. Now, God actually had allowed her to have one. So what if she couldn't have any more. Wait a minute? Had she dreamed up the whole birth of her daughter?

"I…I don't care about any of that." If she had lost both her husband and her daughter, her own survival was pointless. "Please tell me nothing bad has happened to Aaron and Aisha."

"Aisha's fine. I can't honestly say where Aaron is right now, but I'm sure God will take care of him."

"I told him to get out," she murmured, recalling their painful exchange. "Why did I scream at him like that, when I didn't mean it? How could I?"

"Honey, don't do this. Aaron's a strong man. He'll get over it."

Valerie closed her eyes, but she could still see the burned-in-her-brain image of the man she loved walking away. Possibly even for the last time. She opened her eyes again and tried to calm down. "Jasmine…" she whispered. "Did Jasmine go home?"

"Yes. She didn't want to, and Noah had to practically drag her away. It's after midnight now. She'll be back in the morning."

As reality became even clearer, Valerie noticed her aunt's weary, strained expression, and she knew that the older woman had to be exhausted. "Aunt Marilyn, maybe you should go home now. I'll be okay…I'm in ICU and the nurses are really good here."

"You're my niece," Marilyn said, "and you've always been more like another daughter to me. There's no place else I'd even think of being. Besides, I'm not alone. Your uncle is here, too."

"Where?"

"In the waiting room. He's been in and out. They only allow one person at a time."

A nurse came in to check her temperature and blood pressure. Not wanting to converse, Valerie deliberately closed her eyes and tuned out on the conversation that ensued between her aunt and the nurse. Finally, after recording statistics on her chart, the nurse exited.

Perhaps thinking she'd fallen back to sleep, Aunt Marilyn sat down on the nearby chair and picked up her Bible to resume reading. Struggling against the heavy, grainy sensation under her eyelids, Valerie forced her eyes to remain open and she nearly gasped at the tall dark form approaching the doorway. She squeezed her eyes shut again, knowing that what she'd seen was too good to be true and therefore only an illusion. But when she opened them, the form was entering.

"Aaron," she whispered reverently, uncertainly, still not trusting her vision.

Aunt Marilyn stood abruptly, expelling a sigh of relief, albeit with some trepidation. "Thank you, Jesus. Aaron, she's been calling your name since the moment she woke up. Please don't say anything to upset her."

"I spoke to the doctor and I promise I'll be careful," Aaron said calmly, sotto-voce, as Aunt Marilyn slipped from the room.

He wasn't a mirage after all. He really was present, in the flesh. As he moved so soundlessly, cautiously, to her bedside, she lost her ability to speak. All she could do was stare dewy-eyed eyed at the father of her daughter, the complex man she loved. He looked more vulnerable than she'd ever believed possible. Traces of dark shadows underscored his eyes—concerned, shimmering eyes that were completely devoid of iciness.

"Val, if you don't want me here, just say so and I'll under…"

"No," she squeaked and then her voice strengthened. "Please don't leave. I'm sorry for what I said to you before. I love you and I didn't—"

"Stop," he whispered, leaning over her, his hand gently caressing the side of her face. "I'm the one who should apologize. I went to see…"

"Listen to me," Valerie murmured, cutting him off. She longed to just relax and bask in the sun-warmed silk sensation of his fingertips brushing against the side of her face, but she was afraid that he would vanish into thin air, without hearing what she was compelled to say. "Please…I have something important to tell you." She attempted to sit up.

"I'm listening," Aaron said, gently placing both hands on her shoulders to hold her still. "Don't try to sit up. You're going to be okay, but you have to be careful."

"I don't care about me," she stressed.

"Maybe you don't, but I do."

"Are you listening, Aaron?"

"Yes."

Tears welled up in her eyes as she reached for his hand. "You can see me and your daughter whenever and wherever you want. That can be two days from now, or two years from now. We're not going anywhere." She silenced his attempt to interrupt by squeezing his hand. "I knew exactly what I was getting into when I married you, and I haven't kept my end of the…the agreement. From day one, all I've been doing is trying to change who you are, even though I said I wouldn't and then getting angry at you for not responding the way I wanted you to." She took a deep breath and stared into his eyes. "I fell in love with you because of who you are, and at the same time I've been trying to destroy you. Not that I really could, but I've done nothing but make you miserable and hurt myself in the process."

"That's not the whole truth," Aaron said.

"Please let me finish. I don't regret Aisha. I'd never regret her. She's a gift from God, but I know this whole family, fatherhood thing isn't what you're about, so I'm letting you go. There's a saying…I'm sure you've heard it before. 'If you love someone, set them free.' Well, I love you way too much to keep you as an enemy, so go. I'll give you the divorce, because I know you've been waiting for me to finalize it." The scalding tears spilled down her cheeks. "You're free to ride off into the sunset."

369

Never once breaking eye contact, he sat on the edge of her bed. She wanted to wrap her arms around him, to feel his powerful love, his cool, effortless passion, but she didn't have the strength; perhaps it was just as well, because it wouldn't be in keeping with what she'd just told him.

"It's my turn to talk," Aaron said.

She nodded slowly, mutely, wondering if he'd at least give her a goodbye kiss. He seemed awfully slow about speaking, but then she noticed that he was reaching into his pocket and pulling something out. She drew in a ragged breath and blinked questioningly upon seeing that the small gold thing was the wedding band he'd worn only once. Holding her breath, she waited for him to hand it to her, hoping desperately that he wouldn't toss it in the wastebasket as a final affront.

He slipped it on his finger.

"First," he began, "what we have is a relationship, and not just an agreement. You're still my wife, I love you, and if you say you love me, then you can't sentence me back to solitary confinement. The only real freedom I've ever known has been when we're together." He paused for a moment to allow the words to sink in. "Obviously, I'll never completely think as you do, but being in your life has opened my eyes and made me view the world a little less cynically. And these last few hours…" He took a deep breath. "These last few hours of not knowing whether you'd live or die…you wouldn't believe what I was doing if I told you…but let's say I'm feeling a lot more receptive to the power of spirituality." His eyes shimmered. "That sunset can wait, because I'm not going anywhere without you."

Dumbstruck, Valerie searched his eyes, which truly were an inviting view into the clear, focused windows of his soul. "But," she stammered. "But what about…?"

"I've seen Aisha, and I liked what I saw." He gently smoothed her hair away from her face. "I'd be a liar and a fool to promise to be the epitome of fatherhood, but I'd like to try to be a reasonably decent one anyway."

"Do…do you really mean that?"

"Valerie, I never say things I don't mean. We can also have that belated wedding reception if you still want to."

She could no longer control her emotions and she unabashedly began to cry, all the while clinging to his hand.

"Are you okay?" Aaron asked. "Should I get the nurse?"

He sounded so anxious and concerned, that she almost laughed. "No. No. I'm crying because I'm happy. These are good tears, silly. Joyful tears."

He took out a handkerchief and gently began blotting her face. "You're sure now? You don't need the nurse?"

"Aaron, as long as you're willing to put up with me, there are a lot of things I can still teach you about the varying degrees of emotion."

"You mean women's emotions."

"Not just women, you obnoxious chauvinist…human emotions in general."

He smiled—a rakish smile that slid precariously across his handsome face, brightening it, giving him a boyish earnestness and sincerity that she always knew he possessed under his steely armor.

"There's still hope for you, Aaron Weiss, but I see I've got a lot of work ahead of me."

Aaron kissed her tenderly on the lips. "Take as long as you want, baby. Even forever."

About the Author

Kymberly Hunt resides in Rockland County. A life-long lover of music, history, and creative writing, she has been inventing stories since early childhood. Please visit her website at www.KymberlyHunt.com.

2011 Mass Market Titles

January

From This Moment
Sean Young
ISBN-13: 978-1-58571-383-7
ISBN-10: 1-58571-383-X
$6.99

Nihon Nights
Trisha/Monica Haddad
ISBN-13: 978-1-58571-382-0
ISBN-10: 1-58571-382-1
$6.99

February

The Davis Years
Nicole Green
ISBN-13: 978-1-58571-390-5
ISBN-10: 1-58571-390-2
$6.99

Allegro
Adora Bennett
ISBN-13: 978-158571-391-2
ISBN-10: 1-58571-391-0
$6.99

March

Lies in Disguise
Bernice Layton
ISBN-13: 978-1-58571-392-9
ISBN-10: 1-58571-392-9
$6.99

Steady
Ruthie Robinson
ISBN-13: 978-1-58571-393-6
ISBN-10: 1-58571-393-7
$6.99

April

The Right Maneuver
LaShell Stratton-Childers
ISBN-13: 978-1-58571-394-3
ISBN-10: 1-58571-394-5
$6.99

Riding the Corporate Ladder
Keith Walker
ISBN-13: 978-1-58571-395-0
ISBN-10: 1-58571-395-3
$6.99

May

Separate Dreams
Joan Early
ISBN-13: 978-1-58571-434-6
ISBN-10: 1-58571-434-8
$6.99

I Take This Woman
Chamein Canton
ISBN-13: 978-1-58571-435-3
ISBN-10: 1-58571-435-6
$6.99

June

Inside Out
Grayson Cole
ISBN-13: 978-1-58571-437-7
ISBN-10: 1-58571-437-2
$6.99

2011 Mass Market Titles (continued)
July

The Other Side of the
  Mountain
Janice Angelique
ISBN-13: 978-1-58571-442-1
ISBN-10: 1-58571-442-9
$6.99

Holding Her Breath
Nicole Green
ISBN-13: 978-1-58571-439-1
ISBN-10: 1-58571-439-9
$6.99

August

The Sea of Aaron
Kymberly Hunt
ISBN-13: 978-1-58571-440-7
ISBN-10: 1-58571-440-2
$6.99

The Finley Sisters' Oath of
  Romance
Keith Thomas Walker
ISBN-13: 978-1-58571-441-4
ISBN-10: 1-58571-441-0
$6.99

September

Except on Sunday
Regena Bryant
ISBN-13: 978-1-58571-443-8
ISBN-10: 1-58571-443-7
$6.99

Light's Out
Ruthie Robinson
ISBN-13: 978-1-58571-445-2
ISBN-10: 1-58571-445-3
$6.99

October

The Heart Knows
Renee Wynn
ISBN-13: 978-1-58571-444-5
ISBN-10: 1-58571-444-5
$6.99

Best Friends; Better Lovers
Celya Bowers
ISBN-13: 978-1-58571-455-1
ISBN-10: 1-58571-455-0
$6.99

November

Caress
Grayson Cole
ISBN-13: 978-1-58571-454-4
ISBN-10: 1-58571-454-2
$6.99

A Love Built to Last
L. S. Childers
ISBN-13: 978-1-58571-448-3
ISBN-10: 1-58571-448-8
$6.99

December

Fractured
Wendy Byrne
ISBN-13: 978-1-58571-449-0
ISBN-10: 1-58571-449-6
$6.99

Everything in Between
Crystal Hubbard
ISBN-13: 978-1-58571-396-7
ISBN-10: 1-58571-396-1
$6.99

Other Genesis Press, Inc. Titles

2 Good	Celya Bowers	$6.99
A Dangerous Deception	J.M. Jeffries	$8.95
A Dangerous Love	J.M. Jeffries	$8.95
A Dangerous Obsession	J.M. Jeffries	$8.95
A Drummer's Beat to Mend	Kei Swanson	$9.95
A Good Dude	Keith Walker	$6.99
A Happy Life	Charlotte Harris	$9.95
A Heart's Awakening	Veronica Parker	$9.95
A Lark on the Wing	Phyliss Hamilton	$9.95
A Love of Her Own	Cheris F. Hodges	$9.95
A Love to Cherish	Beverly Clark	$8.95
A Place Like Home	Alicia Wiggins	$6.99
A Risk of Rain	Dar Tomlinson	$8.95
A Taste of Temptation	Reneé Alexis	$9.95
A Twist of Fate	Beverly Clark	$8.95
A Voice Behind Thunder	Carrie Elizabeth Greene	$6.99
A Will to Love	Angie Daniels	$9.95
Acquisitions	Kimberley White	$8.95
Across	Carol Payne	$12.95
After the Vows	Leslie Esdaile	$10.95
(Summer Anthology)	T.T. Henderson	
	Jacqueline Thomas	
Again, My Love	Kayla Perrin	$10.95
Against the Wind	Gwynne Forster	$8.95
All I Ask	Barbara Keaton	$8.95
All I'll Ever Need	Mildred Riley	$6.99
Always You	Crystal Hubbard	$6.99
Ambrosia	T.T. Henderson	$8.95
An Unfinished Love Affair	Barbara Keaton	$8.95
And Then Came You	Dorothy Elizabeth Love	$8.95
Angel's Paradise	Janice Angelique	$9.95
Another Memory	Pamela Ridley	$6.99
Anything But Love	Celya Bowers	$6.99
At Last	Lisa G. Riley	$8.95
Best Foot Forward	Michele Sudler	$6.99
Best of Friends	Natalie Dunbar	$8.95
Best of Luck Elsewhere	Trisha Haddad	$6.99
Beyond the Rapture	Beverly Clark	$9.95
Blame It on Paradise	Crystal Hubbard	$6.99
Blaze	Barbara Keaton	$9.95

Other Genesis Press, Inc. Titles (continued)

Other Genesis Press, Inc. Titles (continued)

Do Over	Celya Bowers	$9.95
Dream Keeper	Gail McFarland	$6.99
Dream Runner	Gail McFarland	$6.99
Dreamtective	Liz Swados	$5.95
Ebony Angel	Deatri King-Bey	$9.95
Ebony Butterfly II	Delilah Dawson	$14.95
Echoes of Yesterday	Beverly Clark	$9.95
Eden's Garden	Elizabeth Rose	$8.95
Eve's Prescription	Edwina Martin Arnold	$8.95
Everlastin' Love	Gay G. Gunn	$8.95
Everlasting Moments	Dorothy Elizabeth Love	$8.95
Everything and More	Sinclair Lebeau	$8.95
Everything but Love	Natalie Dunbar	$8.95
Falling	Natalie Dunbar	$9.95
Fate	Pamela Leigh Starr	$8.95
Finding Isabella	A.J. Garrotto	$8.95
Fireflies	Joan Early	$6.99
Fixin' Tyrone	Keith Walker	$6.99
Forbidden Quest	Dar Tomlinson	$10.95
Forever Love	Wanda Y. Thomas	$8.95
Friends in Need	Joan Early	$6.99
From the Ashes	Kathleen Suzanne	$8.95
	Jeanne Sumerix	
Frost on My Window	Angela Weaver	$6.99
Gentle Yearning	Rochelle Alers	$10.95
Glory of Love	Sinclair LeBeau	$10.95
Go Gentle Into That	Malcom Boyd	$12.95
Good Night		
Goldengroove	Mary Beth Craft	$16.95
Groove, Bang, and Jive	Steve Cannon	$8.99
Hand in Glove	Andrea Jackson	$9.95
Hard to Love	Kimberley White	$9.95
Hart & Soul	Angie Daniels	$8.95
Heart of the Phoenix	A.C. Arthur	$9.95
Heartbeat	Stephanie Bedwell-Grime	$8.95
Hearts Remember	M. Loui Quezada	$8.95
Hidden Memories	Robin Allen	$10.95
Higher Ground	Leah Latimer	$19.95
Hitler, the War, and the Pope	Ronald Rychiak	$26.95
How to Kill Your Husband	Keith Walker	$6.99

Other Genesis Press, Inc. Titles (continued)

How to Write a Romance	Kathryn Falk	$18.95
I Married a Reclining Chair	Lisa M. Fuhs	$8.95
I'll Be Your Shelter	Giselle Carmichael	$8.95
I'll Paint a Sun	A.J. Garrotto	$9.95
Icie	Pamela Leigh Starr	$8.95
If I Were Your Woman	LaConnie Taylor-Jones	$6.99
Illusions	Pamela Leigh Starr	$8.95
Indigo After Dark Vol. I	Nia Dixon/Angelique	$10.95
Indigo After Dark Vol. II	Dolores Bundy/ Cole Riley	$10.95
Indigo After Dark Vol. III	Montana Blue/ Coco Morena	$10.95
Indigo After Dark Vol. IV	Cassandra Colt/	$14.95
Indigo After Dark Vol. V	Delilah Dawson	$14.95
Indiscretions	Donna Hill	$8.95
Intentional Mistakes	Michele Sudler	$9.95
Interlude	Donna Hill	$8.95
Intimate Intentions	Angie Daniels	$8.95
It's in the Rhythm	Sammie Ward	$6.99
It's Not Over Yet	J.J. Michael	$9.95
Jolie's Surrender	Edwina Martin-Arnold	$8.95
Kiss or Keep	Debra Phillips	$8.95
Lace	Giselle Carmichael	$9.95
Lady Preacher	K.T. Richey	$6.99
Last Train to Memphis	Elsa Cook	$12.95
Lasting Valor	Ken Olsen	$24.95
Let Us Prey	Hunter Lundy	$25.95
Let's Get It On	Dyanne Davis	$6.99
Lies Too Long	Pamela Ridley	$13.95
Life Is Never As It Seems	J.J. Michael	$12.95
Lighter Shade of Brown	Vicki Andrews	$8.95
Look Both Ways	Joan Early	$6.99
Looking for Lily	Africa Fine	$6.99
Love Always	Mildred E. Riley	$10.95
Love Doesn't Come Easy	Charlyne Dickerson	$8.95
Love Out of Order	Nicole Green	$6.99
Love Unveiled	Gloria Greene	$10.95
Love's Deception	Charlene Berry	$10.95
Love's Destiny	M. Loui Quezada	$8.95
Love's Secrets	Yolanda McVey	$6.99

Other Genesis Press, Inc. Titles (continued)

Mae's Promise	Melody Walcott	$8.95
Magnolia Sunset	Giselle Carmichael	$8.95
Many Shades of Gray	Dyanne Davis	$6.99
Matters of Life and Death	Lesego Malepe, Ph.D.	$15.95
Meant to Be	Jeanne Sumerix	$8.95
Midnight Clear	Leslie Esdaile	$10.95
(Anthology)	Gwynne Forster	
	Carmen Green	
	Monica Jackson	
Midnight Magic	Gwynne Forster	$8.95
Midnight Peril	Vicki Andrews	$10.95
Misconceptions	Pamela Leigh Starr	$9.95
Mixed Reality	Chamein Canton	$6.99
Moments of Clarity	Michele Cameron	$6.99
Montgomery's Children	Richard Perry	$14.95
Mr. Fix-It	Crystal Hubbard	$6.99
My Buffalo Soldier	Barbara B.K. Reeves	$8.95
Naked Soul	Gwynne Forster	$8.95
Never Say Never	Michele Cameron	$6.99
Next to Last Chance	Louisa Dixon	$24.95
No Apologies	Seressia Glass	$8.95
No Commitment Required	Seressia Glass	$8.95
No Regrets	Mildred E. Riley	$8.95
Not His Type	Chamein Canton	$6.99
Not Quite Right	Tammy Williams	$6.99
Nowhere to Run	Gay G. Gunn	$10.95
O Bed! O Breakfast!	Rob Kuehnle	$14.95
Oak Bluffs	Joan Early	$6.99
Object of His Desire	A.C. Arthur	$8.95
Office Policy	A.C. Arthur	$9.95
Once in a Blue Moon	Dorianne Cole	$9.95
One Day at a Time	Bella McFarland	$8.95
One of These Days	Michele Sudler	$9.95
Outside Chance	Louisa Dixon	$24.95
Passion	T.T. Henderson	$10.95
Passion's Blood	Cherif Fortin	$22.95
Passion's Furies	AlTonya Washington	$6.99
Passion's Journey	Wanda Y. Thomas	$8.95
Past Promises	Jahmel West	$8.95
Path of Fire	T.T. Henderson	$8.95

Other Genesis Press, Inc. Titles (continued)

Path of Thorns	Annetta P. Lee	$9.95
Peace Be Still	Colette Haywood	$12.95
Picture Perfect	Reon Carter	$8.95
Playing for Keeps	Stephanie Salinas	$8.95
Pride & Joi	Gay G. Gunn	$8.95
Promises Made	Bernice Layton	$6.99
Promises of Forever	Celya Bowers	$6.99
Promises to Keep	Alicia Wiggins	$8.95
Quiet Storm	Donna Hill	$10.95
Reckless Surrender	Rochelle Alers	$6.95
Red Polka Dot in a World Full of Plaid	Varian Johnson	$12.95
Red Sky	Renee Alexis	$6.99
Reluctant Captive	Joyce Jackson	$8.95
Rendezvous With Fate	Jeanne Sumerix	$8.95
Revelations	Cheris F. Hodges	$8.95
Reye's Gold	Ruthie Robinson	$6.99
Rivers of the Soul	Leslie Esdaile	$8.95
Rocky Mountain Romance	Kathleen Suzanne	$8.95
Rooms of the Heart	Donna Hill	$8.95
Rough on Rats and Tough on Cats	Chris Parker	$12.95
Save Me	Africa Fine	$6.99
Secret Library Vol. 1	Nina Sheridan	$18.95
Secret Library Vol. 2	Cassandra Colt	$8.95
Secret Thunder	Annetta P. Lee	$9.95
Shades of Brown	Denise Becker	$8.95
Shades of Desire	Monica White	$8.95
Shadows in the Moonlight	Jeanne Sumerix	$8.95
Show Me the Sun	Miriam Shumba	$6.99
Sin	Crystal Rhodes	$8.95
Singing a Song...	Crystal Rhodes	$6.99
Six O'Clock	Katrina Spencer	$6.99
Small Sensations	Crystal V. Rhodes	$6.99
Small Whispers	Annetta P. Lee	$6.99
So Amazing	Sinclair LeBeau	$8.95
Somebody's Someone	Sinclair LeBeau	$8.95
Someone to Love	Alicia Wiggins	$8.95
Song in the Park	Martin Brant	$15.95
Soul Eyes	Wayne L. Wilson	$12.95

Other Genesis Press, Inc. Titles (continued)

Soul to Soul	Donna Hill	$8.95
Southern Comfort	J.M. Jeffries	$8.95
Southern Fried Standards	S.R. Maddox	$6.99
Still the Storm	Sharon Robinson	$8.95
Still Waters Run Deep	Leslie Esdaile	$8.95
Still Waters...	Crystal V. Rhodes	$6.99
Stolen Jewels	Michele Sudler	$6.99
Stolen Memories	Michele Sudler	$6.99
Stories to Excite You	Anna Forrest/Divine	$14.95
Storm	Pamela Leigh Starr	$6.99
Subtle Secrets	Wanda Y. Thomas	$8.95
Suddenly You	Crystal Hubbard	$9.95
Swan	Africa Fine	$6.99
Sweet Repercussions	Kimberley White	$9.95
Sweet Sensations	Gwyneth Bolton	$9.95
Sweet Tomorrows	Kimberly White	$8.95
Taken by You	Dorothy Elizabeth Love	$9.95
Tattooed Tears	T. T. Henderson	$8.95
Tempting Faith	Crystal Hubbard	$6.99
That Which Has Horns	Miriam Shumba	$6.99
The Business of Love	Cheris F. Hodges	$6.99
The Color Line	Lizzette Grayson Carter	$9.95
The Color of Trouble	Dyanne Davis	$8.95
The Disappearance of Allison Jones	Kayla Perrin	$5.95
The Doctor's Wife	Mildred Riley	$6.99
The Fires Within	Beverly Clark	$9.95
The Foursome	Celya Bowers	$6.99
The Honey Dipper's Legacy	Myra Pannell-Allen	$14.95
The Joker's Love Tune	Sidney Rickman	$15.95
The Little Pretender	Barbara Cartland	$10.95
The Love We Had	Natalie Dunbar	$8.95
The Man Who Could Fly	Bob & Milana Beamon	$18.95
The Missing Link	Charlyne Dickerson	$8.95
The Mission	Pamela Leigh Starr	$6.99
The More Things Change	Chamein Canton	$6.99
The Perfect Frame	Beverly Clark	$9.95
The Price of Love	Sinclair LeBeau	$8.95
The Smoking Life	Ilene Barth	$29.95
The Words of the Pitcher	Kei Swanson	$8.95

Other Genesis Press, Inc. Titles (continued)

Order Form

Mail to: Genesis Press, Inc.
P.O. Box 101
Columbus, MS 39703

Name _____
Address _____
City/State _____ Zip _____
Telephone _____

Ship to (if different from above)
Name _____
Address _____
City/State _____ Zip _____
Telephone _____

Credit Card Information
Credit Card # _____ ☐Visa ☐Mastercard
Expiration Date (mm/yy) _____ ☐AmEx ☐Discover

Qty.	Author	Title	Price	Total

Use this order
form, or call
1-888-INDIGO-1

Total for books _____
Shipping and handling:
  $5 first two books,
  $1 each additional book _____
Total S & H _____
Total amount enclosed _____

Mississippi residents add 7% sales tax